J.M. CAVENDER

Blood of the Forgotten

CITY LIMITS
PUBLISHING

First published by City Limits Publishing 2021

Copyright © 2021 by City Limits Publishing

First edition

ISBN: 978-1-954403-75-8

Editing by Kimerly Macasevich
Cover design by Jelleine Joie

Dedication

This book goes to my sister, Lakyn, first and foremost. She reads all of my work as I am working on it; she sees the mess and the potential and has undying love for all of the stories in my head.

I want to mention Tiffany Easterling, you are my favorite author and a kindred spirit who never gave up on this novel.

Zack Riley, shout out to you for being one of my favorite writer friends, because you found a way to connect to this book on a personal level.

Appreciation goes to Robert Martin and City Limits Publishing. I cannot express my gratitude enough. Thank you for believing in me!

Finally, this book is for you, the reader. By just reading this novel, you make my dreams come true.

Chapter One

My muscles screamed from lack of oxygen as I pushed the girl behind a glossy pickup. The heat of the explosion seared my skin, making my face feel like a sun-dried tomato. The smell of singed hair filled my nostrils. Was that coming from me?

I hit the concrete and heat engulfed my arm. Half convinced my skin was on fire, I blinked away the rainbow-colored ringlets distorting my vision before I saw my skin shredded and oozing with blood.

Pushing my hair from my eyes, I witnessed a handful of people hurrying to our aid, while other shoppers gazed upon the scene with their cell phones in hand.

Well, geez, a little more help would be nice, but, no, no, be sure the entire world gets the opportunity to tune in as two girls are swallowed up by flames—well, *almost* swallowed up by flames.

Debris and bits of groceries lay scattered all around us. What was left of the silver sedan was still spitting fire, the sight reminding me of the bomb and its blazing red digits. Although a ringing filled my ears, the memory of the ticking reverberated in my head.

Why had I saved her? Just moments before, I'd been imagining what it would be like to kill her.

No, I wasn't, I thought. *That wasn't me.*

Most of my senses returned, alerting me of approaching individuals.

"Are you all right?" the nearest man's lips read. He was leaning over me, his uniform indicating he worked at the store.

I sat motionless, still processing the scene unraveling.

1

"An ambulance is on the way," said another man, holding a phone to his ear. Their voices were muffled as though they were speaking into a broken microphone.

An ambulance? That meant the authorities weren't far behind.

Fear washed over me, and I scrambled to my feet. My once-snug dress now hung ragged, the hem stretching past my knees.

The first man to speak tried to keep me on the ground, but after shooting him a barbaric snarl, he backed away, nearly stumbling in fright as he did so.

My hearing suddenly cleared with an explosion of noise. The shrill of sirens reached my ears before I saw the flashing lights. Taking a step back, I glanced in the direction of the girl. A group surrounded her, preventing me from seeing if she was okay. I took another step, heart drumming in my ears.

If the police got a hold of me, they would know something was wrong — I wasn't normal — and I would never see the light of day again the moment they learned of my murderous nature.

Not mine.

I needed to leave. I needed time to learn who I was before the cops decided to lock me up.

"Wait," another man said. A hand touched my bare arm, causing me to jump.

My fingers curled around the man's forearm before I was aware of my actions. A splintering vibration fluttered against my hand and I heard the undeniable sound of breaking bones. The man's arm hung limp in my grasp, angled in an odd position. I only registered his screams when others came rushing toward us.

Dropping his arm, I stepped back. "I'm sorry," I said, but I doubted anyone heard. They wouldn't believe me anyway. What girl was capable of breaking a full-grown man's arm with a single twist?

"Someone stop her!" a voice commanded. There were too many on-lookers for me to know who'd spoken.

On the farside of the supermarket was a large shadow of a hill blanketed in trees. This was clearly my one chance to escape the mob. A moment of hesitation would lead to more complications. I had enough on my plate already, thanks.

My singed hair whipped madly behind me as I ran. Where concrete once seared my feet, I soon found myself running in soft underbrush. The bushes grew thicker as I climbed higher. Twigs and sharp rocks began to cut the pads of my feet, but I pressed on.

I wanted to cry; I wanted to scream. The entire night had slipped through my fingers like sand, and still I had no answers to explain what had become of me. I had no memory of my life up until that very morning. Every time I tried to remember my past, I drew up blank. Did I live around here? Did I have a family? Was anyone missing me?

Whatever had happened to cause my memory loss, I knew it was tied to the *something* living inside of me. An alter-ego of sorts.

Involuntary tears filled my eyes, but not from emotion or pain. My body was regenerating. It had done this once before. Earlier, I'd stumbled down the rocky slope, managing to skin my knee in the process. The fleshy scar was gone within the hour.

Who was I? *What* was I? Why did I feel the urge to harm others?

To all the questions left unanswered, I at least knew one thing, and it did not ease my conscience: The reason I didn't let the girl get killed in the explosion was I wanted her myself. I saved her out of selfishness, because somewhere deep down I wanted to kill her on my own.

Chapter Two

The gas station was deserted, save for the young man behind the counter. I could see him through the tall glass windows, hunched over, eyes glued to his phone while his thumbs pecked it at an impressive speed.

Four nights had passed since the exploding vehicle, since I'd broken someone's arm. *Save one life, damage another.*

Following that night, I'd continued my habit of sneaking around town at night, but had soon become tired of living like a raccoon - stealing garbage and scurrying away into the darkness when someone came close to discovering me.

It was time for a change of routine.

The digital clock in the window glowed a four, a zero and a nine. Was it really a few hours until dawn already? Even more surprising, a beat-up SUV pulled up to the nearest gas pump. Five young men spilled out, each coming in various sizes. Four made for the sliding doors, laughing and speaking in obnoxiously loud voices, while the last hung back to fill up on gas, no doubt.

Knowing this would be my best chance to get in and out unnoticed, I slipped around the corner, entering the market after them.

"Did ya see that look in his eye, though?" one man said to his comrades.

"Damn near pissed hisself," another chortled. "I thought our Billy was fixing to do the same before we was finished."

Stealing a glance at the kid behind the register, I found him watching the male customers with disdain. The disapproving look he shot at them went unnoticed as they guffawed, throwing bags of chips at one another.

4

Harmless or not, he'd have to clean up afterwards when they left a mess of littered goods in their wake.

As I made for the back, I searched the shelves for a snack small enough to slip under my dress. There had to be something that would align with the flatness of my belly. The thought of eating something other than half eaten garbage made my mouth water. Or maybe it was just the pepperoni and cheese sticks that appealed to me.

The squealing of the sliding doors caused me to jump guiltily, but I did not turn to see who'd entered. My gut told me it was the fifth guy in the group of rambunctious men, here to join in on the food fight.

Taking a deep breath, I lifted a warm sausage biscuit from the heating rack.

"You're going to put that back."

My heart froze for a moment, until I realized the accusation had not been directed at me.

Peering around the shelves of goodies, I noticed it was not the fifth member of the gang to have entered, after all. The newcomer stood planted in front of the doors, leaving no way for anyone to get around him.

It was clear he was not acquainted with the other men. His profile alone called its protest to that. Where the other men sported untrimmed hair and beards, Mr. Baller-Shot-Caller was clean-shaven. His dark hair was short enough to pass as maintained, but long enough to be tousled where a comb wouldn't hurt in the least.

A cackle erupted from the burlier of the men. He stepped forward, towering over the newcomer. "Oh yeah? What's a little dipshit like you gonna do about it, anyway?"

That was an overstatement. Granted, Mr. Baller-Shot-Caller was not as big as the guy before him, but beneath his plaid jacket, he was evidently in better shape than any of the men. I was not about to voice my opinion, though. Last I checked, I didn't have a death wish. It was the classic 'caught in the wrong place at the wrong time,' and I badly wanted out.

"You've got one more chance," Mr. Baller said with an air of savagery. His lips thinned, but he stood at ease, hands tucked into his pockets. "Put it back."

A few guys laughed, intentionally filling their pockets with more items. Big And Tall leaned closer, smirking, and I could barely suppress a groan at his cliché words, "Why don't you make me?" He shook a bag of gummy worms in a tantalizing manner.

No other words were spoken, except for the strings of expletives uttered by the other men. Mr. Baller's movements were swift and practiced. Within seconds, Big And Tall was on his knees, blood gushing from his nose. I wasn't even sure when Mr. Baller had clocked him in the face.

Before the other guys managed to surround him, Mr. Baller smacked Big And Tall's hand, still clutching the candy, back onto the shelf.

"Any other requests?" The words weren't meant to flaunt. I could tell because Mr. Baller muttered them quietly to himself after knocking his rival out on the lower shelf.

The kid at the counter had his phone clutched to his ear, causing me to groan inwardly. Could I not do anything without having the authorities involved?

Sure, I was impressed by Mr. Baller's nerve to stand up to the four guys, even if the odds weren't in his favor. For his sake, I hoped the police got there in time before the other guys beat him to a pulp. For *my* sake, I hoped the police didn't arrive until I had the chance to hurry out of the mess. With my luck, however, the brawl was taking place at the entrance of the market. Slipping out without catching myself in the web of violence was next to impossible.

The guy standing nearest pulled a handgun from the belt of his jeans. He spat a few words that I could only guess were meant as a threat, but Mr. Baller cut him off with a swift swing of his fist. His other fist followed, striking the man in his gut. Mr. Baller then removed the gun from his grip and the clip fell to the ground. He then racked the slide-back, spitting a bullet from the chamber.

In shock, I realized he had halfway won the fight already.

The third guy brandished a knife. He charged, swinging the weapon tactlessly. In the meantime, guy number four grew a brain and jumped in next to his partner.

I watched, mesmerized, as Mr. Baller divided his attention between the two. Guy number three was down first, but that wasn't a surprise. He'd already illustrated his uselessness early on with the knife.

Guy number four, on the other hand, put up the better fight.

A car horn blasted from outside. It was difficult to see through the windows, due to the glare of the lights inside, but I knew it was a warning.

Red and blue lights twinkled in the distance. That was my cue to leave.

Mr. Baller was still battling it out with guy number four when I hurried past them. With my focus trained on not involving myself in the fight, I failed to notice the driver, a.k.a. guy number five, just outside until I smacked headfirst into him.

"Where're you going?" he huffed, peeling me off his sweaty chest. His fingers curled around my bicep.

My balance was tested as he dragged me back through the sliding doors. I felt something cold pressed against my temple.

"LEAVE 'EM ALONE OR HER BRAINS WASH THE WINDOWS."

Two thoughts crossed my mind simultaneously: *Not my brains, I'm rather fond of my brains,* and *does everyone here own a gun?*

Mr. Baller was left standing, his opponents either unconscious or moaning on the polished floor.

I waited to see what he would do.

"So kill her," he said without casting half a glance at me. His expression was almost bored and he even had the audacity to shrug.

Upon the realization that I was alone to save myself, a burning fury warmed my insides. It was like the awakening of a ferocious beast.

I remembered this feeling. It was the *other* me; the *sick* me. The first clue to reveal my corrupt behavior was when I found my face buried in the gut of a squirrel. It had been my awakening; the first memories I could recall. It was the way my teeth sliced through the animal's skin like butter — ripping its fur and tasting the warmth of its innards on my tongue. Oh, how delighted the beast had been.

For days I had tried to keep this monster tamed, but now I allowed the hot anger to flush through my body. My fingers ached and I tasted my saliva as it thickened in my mouth, hot and slimey.

Time lapsed. My legs were pumping beneath me. Everything was dark until I approached a streetlight, illuminating a quiet neighborhood.

At the hooting of an owl in the distance, I slowed to a walk.

A cloud of blood suddenly fell around me, stifling my senses. As I approached the streetlight, I found the ruby color stretching from my fingertips to my wrists. What was more, the space beneath my nails were fit to burst with a substance I did not recognize.

Skin.

I gagged.

Picking up my pace again, I cut through a yard, climbing at an incline toward a darkened treeline in the distance.

Fortune met me halfway. I came to a pond where I stopped long enough to scrub at my hands and nails. A hiss escaped me, but I clamped my teeth hard, pushing aside the fleeting thought of tasting the blood on my skin.

That wasn't normal. That was… *sick.*

What had happened? Why had I blacked out? Had I… killed someone? That man? Had I killed… everyone?

I cringed. *No.*

My feet slipped on the slick mud as I proceeded up the hill, ears prickling at any and every sound of nature. The only thing soothing my nerves was the fact that I did not have the unmistakable aftertaste of blood in my mouth. That was a good thing, right?

The ground was thick with leaves. It was late fall, by the look of it. I slowed my gait at the sound of a rustle — one different from the other sounds of nocturnal creatures.

My breath came out in white puffs, but the cold did not register. There was too much hunger and no room for any other inconvenience.

Another rustle. *Crack.*

I spun sharply. The silhouette of a man approached me, gun in hand. The barrel was trained on my head. Dilating my pupils, I sought something more in the darkness — any detail informing who I was up against.

The plaid jacket.

So I hadn't killed everyone.

"You hunt to kill," I said.

The guy stepped closer. "You'd be surprised."

"What — what happened back there?" I asked.

"You don't remember? You ripped the guy's throat out." It was too dark to gauge his facial expression, but his voice made up for what I could not see: this man loathed me. He didn't even know who I was, yet his hatred for me was clear as day.

"I—" My words failed. I blinked back tears at the realization I was indeed the monster I believed I was. "I don't remember." My voice broke at the last word. "I didn't mean to... but you weren't going to help me."

A sob slipped from my mouth, the smell of blood still lingering around me.

Mr. Baller perhaps thought me a special kind of psycho, but in all fairness, his own sanity was debatable. Who challenged a small team of men and took them out single-handedly? And then followed a murderer into the woods? Yeah, he was a special case, too.

My knees felt weak. I sank to the ground, leaves crunching beneath me as I did so. I stared at the outline of my hands, unable to believe what I was capable of.

Perhaps I deserved to die. I was a killer. Spilling blood was all I ever thought about, in truth. There was something wrong with me and I couldn't see a way I could fix myself. After what I did to that man, was there any fixing me at all?

"Hey." Mr. Baller's voice pierced the silence.

The cold finally began to resonate; a tremble passed through my limbs, wracking my bones. I peered up from my hands and saw the gun lowered at his side. There was a weighted silence before he spoke again. "I can help you."

Chapter Three

Ever since the fateful day of regaining consciousness, I was utterly empty inside; a hollowed out shell of a person, living life as if without a soul. If I was to keep on living, I'd be faced with rebuilding a personality from the ground up. Everything I knew, everything with which I was familiar boiled down to common knowledge, as well as basic activities practiced in a forgotten life. My ignorance, I realized, outweighed whatever knowledge I still possessed.

For example, I knew how much money it would cost to buy the three simple ingredients required to build a PB and J. But I didn't know my name or where to call home.

I knew what to do in order to remove the bloodstains from my dress, yet I did not know what had happened to me or how I had ended up on the side of Interstate 40, sucking on the bones of a woodland creature.

I *knew* I was dangerous, but I had no idea how or why.

This had to be some form of demonic possession. How else could I explain my haunting desire to hurt others? How else could I explain the loss of my memories?

Standing within the presence of a man, so bold as he was, who dared face my darkest secrets brought forth a wild, almost manic laugh. My hands fell to my knees and I gulped it down.

"You wanted to kill me," I said. "Now you expect me to believe you want to help? I might be insane, but I'm not stupid."

"You're not insane," he told me, holstering his weapon beneath his jacket and out of sight. "Your system is fighting toxins."

His words refused to settle.

Toxins?

In half a second, everything I knew about poisons and diseases surfaced in my mind, but all I could conclude was this man was lying.

"I am not sick." I got to my feet as I said this, swiping at my damp cheeks. "In fact, I have never felt so amazing, thank you."

From crying to laughing to sane? Even I don't believe I'm so amazing.

"You're lost." Ignoring the arrogance in his voice, I crossed my arms sternly. The man continued, "You don't remember anything about yourself. I'm willing to bet you don't even know your own name."

"And I suppose you do?"

He tilted his head. "Hayden."

I laughed. "Nice one, but that's a boy's name. Better luck next time, champ."

"It's Hutch."

"Wrong again, and you're only getting colder." Clearly he meant Hutch was *his* name, but withholding my sass was not something I was in a hurry to do.

I turned away, but Hutch advanced, gripping my arm and spinning me back around to face him. The sharp lines of his face were clearer now, though the details were still obscured by darkness. Being nearly a head shorter, I did my best to hold Hutch's glare without stepping back.

"After what you did back there, don't think I can let you walk free," he said. "You can either come with me, or I will kill you."

"What are you, some crazy cop with personal vendetta?" Just to irk him, I leaned closer, daring him to back away, but he didn't bite. He stood firm, the smell of his fabric softener filling my nose. "And why are you so concerned about my welfare all of a sudden? If I'm so *sick*, why don't you just kill me? Put me out of my misery."

Hutch's hateful expression was locked in place, eyes narrowed, but he watched my every move with caution. "Because I can use you."

"There it is, ladies and gentlemen!" I cocked my head to the side. "It's not me you care about. You're probably some sicko with a weird fetish and you

11

want me to entertain you."

"You're right," said Hutch. "I don't care about you. I would gladly kill you right now, but the truth of the matter is, I could use your help. And if you help me, I will help you in return."

"So I scratch your back and you scratch mine, right?"

In a matter of moments, I considered my options, but they all ended with Hutch shooting me in the back of the head unless I agreed to his terms. After taking down the guys at the gas station, disposing of my significantly smaller body would be a piece of cake for him. Dig a shallow hole and throw some leaves on me. No one would find me until late spring when my body began to rot.

I shivered.

The bottom line was: Hutch was my best chance of uncovering my lost life. If he remained true to his word, he could help me find my way home. At this point, that was better than nothing. If he went back on his word... I wasn't entirely powerless myself. Surely I'd put up a better fight than other guys.

"Fine," I agreed. "What do you want?"

After a moment of consideration, Hutch inclined his head as he turned away. "We shouldn't discuss it here."

"Oh, dear heavens," I groaned, before following him as he made back down the slope. "You're not going to have me rob a bank for you, I hope."

It was naïve of me, I realized, to have thought my end of the bargain would be simple.

"You are, aren't you?" I said when Hutch did not grace my previous statement with a comment. "What use to me is your help if I'm incarcerated? Unless you need me inside the county jail. But surely not the women's prison. You would need a male partner to get intel passed on to someone in the men's prison. Or do you have a lover in the women's? Is that why you need me? Hello, Hutch? Hey, what the—?"

We'd made it near the road when Hutch gripped my wrist. With a tug, he towed me around the backside of a house, motioning for me to keep quiet.

A cop car cruised by. We watched from the shadows as it rolled along, looking for signs of anything suspicious perhaps. Neither of us made a sound. Hutch's hand began to burn my wrist, constricting the blood flow. As soon as the cop was out of sight, I jerked from his hold.

"They're looking for me," I whispered, massaging the feeling back into my hand.

"Us," Hutch corrected, digging a phone from his pocket. "Follow me."

As we backtracked through the neighborhood, one more police car sailed by. While we waited for the coast to clear, Hutch pecked away on his phone, much like the kid at the gas station.

An office park sat across the highway from the gas station. Blue and red lights flashed and yellow tape circled the entrance to the market. Cars littered the scene. I hoped Hutch's was not among the chaos.

To my relief, he led us to the office park where a charcoal Audi was parked next to one of the brick buildings. As soon as it lit up, I opened the passenger door and slid into the seat next to him.

The Audi purred to life.

"It would probably be best if we skipped town," I said as Hutch eased by the busy gas station. "Pretty soon they'll have enough information to come looking for us." Especially me. Hutch hadn't killed anyone.

My stomach churned at the thought. I strayed from the memory of my victim's face, afraid it would make me sick. *It wasn't me*, I repeated quietly to myself, even though I knew I wasn't fooling anyone. Of course it had been me. I wanted nothing more than to rip the guy's arms off for holding me hostage.

"We aren't going far," Hutch said, sending my thoughts into a cloud of dust. We swayed with the twists and turns of the road that led us further from the scene. "We have business here."

"That gas station had cameras at every corner!" I said, exasperation creeping into my voice. "No doubt they will also have my fingerprints. My name and face will be all over the media!"

"The cameras are live-streamed to the owner's home," said Hutch.

The vehicle halted at a stop sign. The ticking of the blinker sounded awfully familiar. I thought about the girl I'd saved days ago at the supermarket.

"I know the guy," he went on. "I've already contacted him."

"That's convenient," I said, my tone cutting. "Oh, and by the way, withholding information on a murder case will land him a cell in prison. Are you really asking him to risk that for me?"

"I'd be more than happy to let you give yourself up." The engine revved ever so gently beneath us, the dark trees and homes whooshed by even faster. "But right now, prison is not an option for you."

"So you don't have a long-lost lover there," I mumbled. "They will still have my fingerprints. And yours."

"I have another guy on it."

"You *are* some whacked-out cop, aren't you?"

Hutch ignored me.

"How am I supposed to help if I don't know what's going on?" I propped my elbow on the window ledge, and rested my head on my knuckles. "Maybe if you would've helped me back there, I wouldn't have lost control. Was I supposed to let him kill me?"

"He wasn't going to kill you," Hutch said. His cellphone vibrated in his pocket and he reached to fish it out. "You shouldn't have done anything. I was working on a plan."

My eyebrows flew to my hairline. "You were going to save me?"

"Letting some lowlife redneck blow your head off would defeat the purpose of tracking you."

I let that sink in. "You've been tracking me? For how long?" The entire time I thought no one had a clue I existed, this guy had been tailing me?

"Four nights."

"But...why?"

"Because of the girl you saved."

His response gave me pause.

"You were there?" I asked.

Hutch didn't answer my question. Instead, he asked one of his own, stealing a glance at me before returning his eyes to the road, "Why did you save her?"

14

Taken aback by the question, I could not shake the sudden suspicion in my gut. "I… it was a knee-jerk reaction, I guess." I paused. "It was not some freak accident, you know. Someone planted a bomb in her car."

I recalled the ticking noise I'd heard while loitering near a collection of weathered buggies. My hearing was sharp, as was my sight. Seeing the blazing red digits in her trunk the moment she opened it was no trouble. Getting her far enough from the blast proved more difficult.

"I know," said Hutch, snapping me back to the present.

I stared at him, hesitating, but I couldn't hold back the accusation on my tongue. "It was you?"

The answer was clear in Hutch's reluctance to reply. His jaw tightened, eyes transfixed on the road.

"Stop the car." Nothing. "STOP THE CAR!" I yelled, reaching for the wheel. The Audi swerved violently, coming to a halt at the side of the road. Hutch had the gun in his hand just as I managed to fumble the door open. I felt the butt of it clock my kneecap, forcing me to stumble into a run. My advantage was lost. I only got a few yards away when Hutch's hand enclosed around my elbow, yanking me back with such force, I hit the ground hard.

Fighting him was futile. Every blow I tried to land on his face or rib cage was skillfully blocked. Fury burned in my chest, but I couldn't give in to it — not right now, not after what happened at the gas station.

"I will not kill for you!" I said over the sound of blood pulsing behind my ears.

With one hand, Hutch pressed both of my wrists into the soft earth above my head. His other hand steadied my writhing hips.

Pressure erupted in my forehead without warning. It grew, spreading rapidly up over the crown of my head and down to my nose, leaving me with a painful urge to sneeze. I was temporarily blinded by the pain as well as familiar scenes playing out in my memory. I groaned, but wasn't sure if the sound left my lips.

Shadows of trees surrounded me. I thrashed about on the ground, unable to breathe. My chest was painfully constricted, but my focus was on the man leaning over me.

"Please," I gasped. *"I can't—I can't..."*

His hands were hurting me. Where was James? He said he would always look after me.

"Hayden!" Hutch swore under his breath. He was no longer restraining me.

I blinked several times. Reality crashed around me as the memory faded and I found myself staring up at Hutch's troubled expression.

"I'm okay," I said reflexively when only the lingering distress of the flashback remained.

Why had I said that? He hadn't asked, and I doubted he cared.

Hutch sighed, sitting back onto the damp ground beside me. As he did so, I noticed four thin lines of scar tissue running vertically behind his ear. They swerved around his neck, just barely missing his Adam's apple. They disappeared beneath the V-neck of his shirt, leaving me to wonder how I hadn't noticed them before.

"You remembered something." It wasn't a question.

I nodded, too shaken to ask how he knew.

"How many times has this happened?"

"This is the second time," I told him after taking a deep breath. My first encounter took place the day after the incident at the supermarket. I would've believed it to be a dream, had I not experienced the pain. Luckily it hadn't lasted very long the first time. All I remembered of the memory were the woods rushing by as I ran to or from something I could not see.

A calculating expression crossed Hutch's face. I was about to ask why it mattered when he climbed to his feet.

Accepting his outstretched hand, I let Hutch pull me up.

"I am not asking you to kill the girl," he said. "I'm asking you to save her."

Chapter Four

Silence reigned.

My inner cheek was raw and bleeding. I hadn't noticed how avidly I'd been worrying it, lost in thought of recent events.

"What's happening to me?" I whispered, staring at my limp hands as they rested in my lap.

"Your body is fighting a transformation," said Hutch.

I shot him a questioning glance. "I thought I was fighting toxins. Get it right, and fast."

"I'm talking about Forgotten."

"You say that as if I'm supposed to know what that is." I said.

I caught Hutch giving me a sideways look. "It's what attacked you. You're either lucky to be alive, or a Forgotten intended to make something different out of you."

His answer only raised more questions. I was beginning to feel like a dog chasing his own tail.

"Can you tell me what it is?" I said. "These Forget-Me-Nots?"

"Some call it a disease," said Hutch. "Other's lean more toward it being a demon possession."

Knew it, I thought, fighting the urge to scream it out. Shuddering, I wiped my damp palms on the knees of my dress. "Which do you think it is?"

He was silent for a moment, as if considering my question, or so I liked to believe.

"There's a science behind it," he said. "But I haven't ruled out the demon

17

possession."

"Is that what will become of me? A Forgotten?"

Hutch's curt nod confirmed my fears.

"You really don't remember what happened at the gas station, do you?" Hutch asked.

I didn't understand why he was suddenly switching gears, but I nodded in affirmation anyway. "That's the Forgotten nature taking control," he said. "The poisoned cells found in the lateral frontal lobe of your brain went into overdrive, removing your ability to call the shots. It can come sporadically and will only last a few moments until the transformation is complete."

All right, Mr. Scientist. That's too much information for me to follow at the moment. "What happens next?" I asked.

"Let's just say, if the poisoned cells multiply, they will erase anything that is left of what makes you who you are. Once you transform, there will be no saving you."

My mind reeled, a rising panic in my chest nearly choking me. Understanding the dangers of my condition made everything the more frightening.

It was almost six in the morning when Hutch entered a parking garage, pulling the Audi into a place marked C-39. From there, I followed him through a series of doors, still digesting all he'd told me and weighing the truth of his words.

When we stepped into what I guessed to be his home, I realized just how happy I was to be inside and out of the cold.

The condo had an open floor concept with the kitchen to the left, the living room-slash-dining room to the right. Masculine as it was with the black and white themed marble and décor, I didn't peg Hutch as the type to tediously select furniture. An interior designer? Most likely.

A hallway lined with great windows ahead led to the rest of the rooms, one of which I found to be the restroom.

After arming his home security system, Hutch made for the fridge, removing a plastic container of soup. After placing it into the microwave, he left me alone long enough for the microwave to finish heating the food. I had time to sink into the nearest armchair, wondering if I'd made a wise choice to follow him back to his place.

Well, it was this or die. At least I was buying myself some time, right?

"Here." Hutch had returned with a blanket and T-shirt, dropping them on the sofa. "You can eat the food in the microwave, and crash on the couch. Do anything stupid and we go back to the original plan."

"Which was?" I took the clothes from him.

"Which was I kill you and move on with my life."

Yup. There was the reminder. Like I needed it.

Without another word, he left me alone again. A moment later, I heard a door slam and a lock click.

He didn't trust me. Shocker. If it made him feel any better, I didn't trust him either.

I hunted in my dreams, capturing a variety of prey: men, women, children, animals. My gums throbbed, teeth longing to gnaw flesh. My hands burned. A metallic taste in my mouth stirred me awake several times, only to realize my mind was playing tricks on me. I curled to my side, hoping to ease the sporadic cramps in my stomach, but to no avail. I figured eventually I would become tired enough to sleep through my discomfiture, and found this to be true — only not until the sun began to peek through the enormous windows in the hallway.

By late morning, I awoke to the front door banging shut. I sat up with a start, unable to remember where I was and why.

Hutch rearmed the security system, two nylon bags strapped around his wrist. By the looks of it, I'd been in such a deep sleep, I hadn't even heard him leave. It was a wonder he dared leave me unsupervised in the first place. But then, we both needed something from the other. He must've known I wouldn't disappear without the information I needed to get me home. Wherever home was.

Once my current living situation sunk back in, I buried my head deeper beneath a pile of throw pillows. Every now and then, Hutch bustled by, but I was reluctant to leave the warmth of the sofa.

It was the smell of sizzling ham that motivated me to sneak a look from beneath the blanket. Hutch's back faced the living room, his arms working methodically as he prepared food.

Gathering the blanket, I crossed the room to see what he was preparing. Ham and eggs? Yes, please.

Having sensed me, Hutch said, "You need to shower."

Perhaps I did not smell of a rose garden, but there was no grace in the way his words reached me.

"I'm hungry," I told him, half-annoyed by his disregard.

"You'll eat when you've cleaned up."

He knew I was staring at him. I could almost feel his abhorrence of me with every pulse of his heart as he beat the eggs.

A battle waged within. I was tempted to call him out on his insolence, but I didn't trust myself to manage doing so without sounding just as immature.

Stamping down the flame of my disapproval, I forced a small laugh. Hutch stopped what he was doing to glare at me, a silent hostility brewing in his eyes. My taunting smile remained plastered on my lips as I gave a nonchalant shrug and headed for the bathroom.

The nylon bag I'd seen him carrying earlier sat in the bathroom sink. It contained everything necessary to make myself decent. A wool dress hung on the shower door, elegant, but obviously purchased at the nearest thrift store. I fiddled with its metal belt buckle until my stomach made a not-so-subtle sound, reminding me I was half-starved.

Thirty minutes later, my damp hair was brushed to the side, appearing jet black instead of its nut-brown. My legs were shaved, and I was dressed appropriately, although I still had no shoes.

I found Hutch in the dining area. A wireless mouse in his right hand moved with irregularity on the tabletop as his eyes fixed on the screen of his laptop.

At the other end of the table was a plate covered by the non-splatter guard from the microwave. Accompanying it was a single fork and a tall glass of orange juice.

Settling into the seat, I began to eat without hesitation. I didn't exactly trust Hutch, but it was evident we needed each other for the time being, therefore the chances of him tampering with my food were slim.

"What's on the agenda today?" I asked around a mouthful of eggs.

Hutch reached into the chair to the left of him, scooping up a small handful of files. He slid them across the table and I caught them before they tumbled over the edge.

"Those include intel on Melinda and everyone in her household." Hutch was back to focusing on the screen before him, but he went on, "You need her, or one of the others, to disclose the father's whereabouts."

There was no need to ask who Melinda was. Her picture was staring right at me as soon as I opened the top file. She was the girl from the supermarket.

Melinda Allen. Daughter of Eric and Cali Allen. Seventeen years old.

Taking a swig of orange juice, I flipped over to the next file.

Michael Allen. Twenty years old, sophomore at Lipscomb University. The picture looked like it had been downloaded from a social media site. It depicted him clothed in a violet and yellow jersey, a basketball secured under one elbow. His grin was lazy, sandy hair falling in damp clumps over his forehead.

The next two files informed me of the grandparents, or else the legal guardians.

The last folder came as an unpleasant surprise. It was not a very clear picture, but there was no mistaking the boy was young. Six years old, according to the information.

"Why were you trying to kill this girl, if all you need is to know where her father is?"

The laptop closed with a thump. Hutch drummed his fingers on it, leaning back in his chair. It wasn't difficult to figure out what he was thinking.

"The less you know, the better," he said.

Score. Not surprisingly, he was reluctant to tell me anything he thought would be considered too much information.

I tried a different angle. "You're obviously not a cop, right? Do you work for someone? Kill girls and tear families apart for a living?" I dropped my fork, pushing the plate away and crossed my arms on the table. "It must pay well. How else could you afford a condo downtown?" Making him uncomfortable was an entertaining challenge. I couldn't help, but to press my luck further. "Do you specialize in killing girls, or do you kill just about anyone, depending on the pay?"

I saw a hint of a smile on Hutch's face, but it lacked mirth.

"I kill for a living," he said, his ego unperturbed, "but I am not the assassin you think I am." He cocked an eyebrow in a deriding manner.

"Oh, I see," I said. I was surprised by how calm I sounded. "You're delusional. You somehow convinced yourself it's all right to take the lives of innocent people."

With a shake of his head, Hutch released a slow breath. "Killing civilians has never been in my job description."

I watched as he studied his hand now immobile on the laptop.

"That's why you need my help?" I asked. The picture was slowly coming together. "But if your job is to kill her, isn't that expected of you? Don't get me wrong, I don't want her dead. I'm just saying that your superiors may not be ecstatic to learn you disobeyed orders."

Shifting in the chair, Hutch shook his head. "The reason I was sent to kill one of them—" he nodded to the files on the table before me, "—was to draw Eric Allen out from whatever rock he is hiding under."

"And if I get one of them to rat him out, you won't have to kill anyone," I concluded. That still left me with a serious question. Fidgeting a moment, I asked, "So if these aren't the type of people you kill, then who are?"

"People like you." We stared at each other for a long time. The face of my victim haunted my short-term memory and I searched for an excuse that proved I was not evil at heart. But truthfully, I was in denial. He killed people like me, because I was a killer. Any attempt to convince him otherwise would be nothing less than absurd.

I wet my lips. "So why bother helping me? After I do this for you… how can I be sure you won't kill me?"

He drummed a rhythm with his fingertips again. Nothing was said for a long moment and I was beginning to believe I was doomed, until, "Because you still stand a chance."

"A chance to stop the transformation?" I asked.

He nodded.

"But how?"

"If you remove the one component necessary for the transformation to progress, the toxic cell count will decrease."

There he went sounding like a scientist again. I was half-convinced he had this spiel memorized, word-for-word from some text book.

"What's the one component?" I asked.

"Blood." It was a simple word that kicked me in the gut. Logically, my brain wanted to laugh at him, but it was the memory of my dark desires that told me he wasn't lying.

"I will become one of Bram Stoker's villains?" The joke died at the emptiness in my voice, but still appeared to strike a nerve.

The feet of the chair scraped against the hardwood floor when Hutch stood. My body went rigid as he approached me.

"Your condition is not meant to amuse the world," he said. "The world doesn't even know of your existence. If they did, all hell would break loose."

"How so?" I asked.

"Innocent people would be killed out of mere suspicion. Remember the witch trials of Salem? We don't need a repeat of that." He paused. "With everything out in the open, we would be faced with a full-blown war. The longer the Forgotten think they can blend in, the easier it will be to continue to hunt them."

"You make it sound like the apocalypse," I said, pushing back from the table.

I returned my dishes to the kitchen, just to give my hands something to do while Hutch's words did cartwheels in my brain. My stomach clenched. The food I'd eaten was settling about as well as everything he had just told me.

"Say I don't have any more blackouts," I said over the sound of the flowing tap. "No blood. Will I go back to normal and get back my memories?"

Hutch had returned to his laptop. At first, I wasn't sure he'd heard me. I turned off the tap.

"Your memories will never be completely restored, but the hallucinatory palinopsia will offer certain memories if stimulated."

That was just a fancy word for flashbacks, I gathered. Seriously, where was he getting this stuff?

I was prepared to ask another question, when Hutch shut his laptop for a second time. As he donned his jacket, he beckoned me to follow.

A bad case of the nerves hit me. My hands trembled. I wasn't emotionally ready to help him. Not yet. It was like going to the pool right after gorging yourself on fine food. Everything I had been told about my condition had me thrown for a loop. How was I to convince someone I was fine when I wasn't sure I'd convinced myself just yet?

Barefoot, I stepped out of the condo after Hutch, and thus embarked on my sure journey to an uncertain destination.

Chapter Five

Our destination was a shoe store. Thankfully, Hutch had mind enough to acknowledge my ghetto appearance without having any shoes to accompany my outfit.

"It's really not that difficult to choose a pair of shoes," he grumbled as I grimaced at a selection of high heels.

"Says the one wearing Timberlands," I said in a sing-song voice.

A girl spun the corner the same time I made for the next aisle. I managed to step aside in time to avoid her and the load of shoe boxes weighing down her arms, but Hutch did not. Shoes and their respecting boxes tumbled to the floor, causing the girl to gasp in despair.

"You've got to be kidding me," she groaned. I saw her do a double-take when she looked at Hutch.

"Sorry," he said. His hands worked fast, stuffing shoes into boxes, regardless of whether they returned to the right place.

"No, don't worry," the girl said, her once annoyed expression now smoothed into a flirty smile. "I've got it."

After following me down the fifth aisle as I browsed leisurely, Hutch finally decided I was not going to strike down a fellow customer at random. It was a relief when he left me alone to sit on a cushioned bench. I wasn't fooled, though. Just because he wasn't breathing down my neck, did not mean he wasn't watching me like a hawk.

When I was finally satisfied with a pair of black flats, we made for the checkout where a young clerk loitered, clearly hoping he wouldn't have to assist us. Ignoring his greasy hair and pockmarked face, I smiled politely while Hutch reached for his wallet.

As soon as the shoes were rung up, I removed them from the box, slipping them on. I then handed the box over for the clerk to toss, while Hutch studied the card machine.

"You forgot something," said Hutch.

"What?"

"These shoes are discounted." Hutch tapped the card machine with his knuckle.

"No, they're not." The guy plucked invisible lint from his uniform, refusing to acknowledge us any more than he had to.

Hutch's impatience was almost tangible.

"Hey," he shot at the clerk. "Give me the box. You see that sticker? It means it's discounted. Just look around. Do you not see every sign in the store that says it?"

"Cut it out," I hissed. There were other ways to handle the situation, none of which included him being a jerk.

The guy called another clerk over, who happened to be the girl Hutch nearly floored. With her help, the price on the cashier screen dropped drastically. "There." She flashed the same flirty smile she had before. I swear I could cut her obvious intentions with a knife.

Hutch fumed all the way back to the parking lot. I couldn't blame him. Not entirely anyway, but I was too tired to dwell on the situation. The sun was hiding behind a blanket of clouds, yet its glow left me weary.

Distracted by sudden exhaustion, I did not sense something being off until I heard Hutch mumble an expletive.

A lean man with a defined scruff and olive skin waited for us, his sleek black Infinity parked on the passenger side of Hutch's SUV.

"McLaren," he said, removing his sunglasses. He made no attempt to hide his scrutiny of me as I shadowed Hutch.

"Josue." Hutch nodded at the man. "They keeping you on a tight leash now?"

I moved behind Hutch, out of the man's line of vision. It irked me the way he stared, his eyes crawling over my figure.

"If you're worried about me being off the hook, I can assure you I'm still just as screwed as you." He snickered. "You know what ol' Randy says. There's no one-size-fits-all when it comes to punishments."

Peeking around Hutch's shoulder, I watched Josue clean his glasses with the hem of his shirt, leaning idly against the car.

"What do you want?" Hutch said.

"You haven't checked in. Randolph was getting worried." Even I could tell the concerned look on his face was pretentious.

"I'm working on something," said Hutch.

"Your job, I hope." Josue thrust his chin in my direction. "Who's the *mamacita?*"

Hutch didn't have to look to see who he was talking about. Apparently, I was the only *mamacita* around. Other than us, the parking lot was empty. "She's one of the perks of the job."

Josue burst out laughing as if Hutch had told him an inside joke. Pushing from the car, he wiped a fake tear from his eye. "I suggest you see Randolph before you make... other arrangements."

"Randolph can wait."

"You are wrong there, McLaren." Josue gave a sideways grin. "Why don't you follow me back? I'll make sure you get there safely."

After a moment of hesitation, Hutch reached into his pocket and flipped out a switchblade. I hissed his name when Josue flashed a semi-automatic from his belt.

Looking around for witnesses, I found the parking lot still deserted apart from us. Sounds of traffic carried from the other side of the building, but unless someone looked out a window, no one would be aware of the escalating situation.

Hutch buried the blade deep into the front tire of the car. "Sure thing," he said, wrenching the knife free from the rubber. "But you might want to get that looked at first. It's a drive to Franklin from here. Wouldn't want you having any car trouble."

Josue tucked his gun back into the holster, hurling unpleasant adjectives at Hutch.

"Get in the back." This Hutch said to me. I followed him, climbing into the Audi behind the driver's seat.

It was a mistake, I realized, to underestimate the SUV, merely because it did not seem comparable to Josue's smaller, sportier car. Speed didn't matter, if the driver lacked skill.

After a brief stop by the condo, Hutch had us maneuvering steadily between traffic on I-65.

"So… Randolph, huh?" I said, forcing myself to relax. Hutch never mentioned a past involving NASCAR or Formula 1, therefore I doubted he had the driving experience. Nevertheless, this did not prevent him from gliding into tight spaces when changing lanes. "You're in a hurry to see him."

"I have to talk to him before Josue has the chance to share his uneducated guess of what's going on."

"Why would that be such a bad thing?" My eyes were squeezed shut, fingers gripping the seat. I was unable to watch Hutch cut between a tow truck and an eighteen wheeler.

"I don't have many friends in this business." There was no strain in Hutch's voice as he spoke, giving me courage to open my eyes. "After seeing you with me today, he knows I'm up to something."

"How can he know that for sure?"

"Because I was reluctant to take this job from the start."

A minivan was attempting to merge into the middle lane just as Hutch made to pass a pickup truck. The other driver's horn blared, but Hutch had already gotten us ahead.

"I'm pretty sure we have a good head start," I tried, hoping he would slow down.

It was better I kept myself distracted by talking, even if Hutch pretended I wasn't sitting next to him. "I take it Randolph is your boss — the guy that ordered the hit on Melinda's family. But what's with this Josue guy?"

"He's a sad excuse for a man," Hutch said. "A coward, among other things."

"Why's he being punished?"

Hutch pursed his lips instead of replying. It was something he liked to do.

28

Nothing I said afterwards convinced him to talk to me. Whatever. If he was going to ignore me, I would just have to find a way to distract myself from his reckless driving.

Turning to the dashboard, I tapped around in search of the radio controls. I waited for him to tell me not to mess with anything, but before he had the chance to do so, music blasted through the speakers. The windows and mirrors vibrated in response to the bass, while the artist spit lyrics too fast to follow.

"Sorry," I murmured when Hutch tapped the music off. Though I was tempted to try again, I thought it best not to, lest something I did caused our demise on the road.

As we entered the streets of the historic city, a sudden dose of familiarity washed over me. I only wished I knew why. Did I live here? Had I grown up walking these streets?

Eventually we came to an extended road, one almost hidden from the highway. The day had steadily grown grayer with incoming clouds. Bald branches arched over the broken road before us, the scene sending an eerie chill down my spine.

Hutch grew noticeably tense next to me.

I wasn't sure what I expected us to come to — a facility, maybe, with barbed fences, intimidating dogs and men bearing heavy artillery. Or even an underground bunker.

What I did not expect was for Hutch to pull into the circular drive of a colossal family home.

"Social call?" I asked. "Is there a home theater? Any house this massive is bound to have one."

As soon as we stepped into the foyer, two heavy-set men greeted Hutch, wanting to converse with him. It was a relief to know I wasn't the only one he ignored.

Even though the interior of the home was striking with its many antique pieces and high ceilings, I could not shake an uneasy feeling that crept under my skin. There was something in the atmosphere that felt tainted. The increased tension in Hutch's posture didn't make me feel any more at ease.

Through a tall window at the end of the hall I noticed a kidney-shaped pool alongside a fountain tucked away in the horseshoe shape of the house's exterior.

This place had to have a home theater.

Out of the blue, my head began to spin and my vision darkened. My chest felt constricted to the point I was unable to breathe. People were approaching, I could sense them; smell them.

Someone called Hutch's name, halting him on the spot before he had the chance to enter a set of oak double doors.

"Looking for Randolph?"

Had I not witnessed Hutch take out four guys on his own the night before, I probably would've felt threatened by the three men advancing.

I blinked several times, pushing the darkness away. Colors were sparkling vividly around me. Everything seemed sharper.

The moderately Herculean man leading the pack was the one to speak. His golden hair was tucked behind his ears, revealing the permanent lines of a frown on his face. His right hand twitched beside the nine-inch blade linked to his side.

"If I cared to tell anyone, it wouldn't be you, Stix, or your minions," said Hutch. He tried the door.

Stix stroked the scruff of his angled chin. "He ain't here. Business deal in Atlanta."

Without much regard for the other man, Hutch made to leave and I tailed him, only to have my wilting conscience cause me to run into a decorative table. In my attempt to prevent a pair of crystal candlestick holders from shattering on the ground, one busted on the edge, slicing into my wrist.

At the same time, Stix lunged, thrusting Hutch against the wall with a growl. I stumbled, unsure what to do in the midst of the chaos, until a pair of hands gripped my shoulders from behind, steadying me.

Stix held Hutch's shirt, crumpling it in his fist. He pressed his face close enough, they were almost nose-to-nose.

"Not so smart," he said, "showing your face around here. I ought to tuck my steel into your throat." Hawking, he spat into Hutch's face.

"Calm yourself, Stix," said the owner of the hands still holding my arms.

"It's all right, Red." Hutch used his sleeve to remove the spit from his cheek. Although his tone was calm, the shadow over his face was unforgiving. To Stix, he said, "You don't remember?"

"Remember what?" There was a quiver of rage in Stix's voice. "How you screwed up?"

"That I belong here."

Twisting himself free, Hutch kicked Stix behind the knee. Stix made for the fixed blade at his side, but Hutch rammed his face square into the door frame.

"Dammit, McLaren," said the third guy. He was just as brawny as his mate, his hair a darker shade of gold. He stepped back, distancing himself from the scene. At first I thought the sight of blood made him flinch as much as me, but I was proven wrong by the look of amusement on his face.

Stix groaned, staggering to his feet, his fingers groping along the wall for support. He wiped his nose, the blood leaving a thick line along his sleeve. The third guy finally stepped forward to assist him, but Stix pushed him away. "I don't need your help, Flix." He glared at Hutch. "You're making the wrong enemies, boy."

"Don't kid yourself," said Hutch. "You hated me from day one."

He motioned for the man behind me to follow. Down another hallway and into a spare bedroom, Hutch closed the door behind us.

It dawned on me then why the house was so unsettling. No matter how one scoured and disinfected the furniture, the walls, the floors, there was no masking the violence it held. Too much blood had been spilled within the walls of the mansion. I knew this, because its unmistakable odor, mingled with bleach, reeked all throughout the halls. It was fainter now, but the quality it possessed was stale enough to sicken me still.

I didn't entirely know what kind of person Hutch was, but something confirmed the suspicion that what he'd said was true: he belonged in this house stricken with grief and violence.

Chapter Six

The musky, yet sweet smell of an aged cigar emitted from the hulking man. Red glared at me with an iron intensity, tightening the knot in my stomach. Unlike Josue, he showed no sign of intrigue. This man distrusted everything about me. And why shouldn't he?

Hutch stood for a moment with his hands on his hips, jaw tightening as he pondered.

"What business deal?" he finally asked.

"It's Atlanta," Red said, still watching me. "What do you think?"

I sat on the edge of the bed in the spare room while Hutch and Red continued their conversation. My head had cleared sometime during the fight between Hutch and Stix, but I feared if I wasn't careful I could fall right back into dangerous territory. I'd almost blacked out. But why? What had triggered it?

"Muling?"

Snapping back to the present conversation, I looked at Hutch, who'd spoken.

"It's what they do best." Red's murky eyes moved away from me at last. "They were supposed to be back this morning."

"Something happen?"

"Not that we know of. Someone would've reached out if they needed backup."

"I'm surprised you weren't called to tag along."

Red chuckled, though it sounded more like a cautionary grunt. "Not since the sprain." He scuffed the carpet with his right boot. "Doc said four months. It's been six and ain't no better."

"Hate to hear it."

"Don't bother." Red waved off Hutch's attempt at sympathy. "I'm still on payroll. That's all that matters." He stabbed his chin in my direction. "Who's she?"

His question was almost threatening, as though I were a cockroach to be squashed. I crossed my arms over my chest.

"It's Hayden," I said, answering for Hutch. Answering for myself.

About a thousand snide comments died on my lips when Red gave a thick, haughty laugh.

"Not Hayden Barnes, surely?" he said to Hutch.

Both Red and I watched expectantly as Hutch's expression grew stoney. He hadn't wanted me to know.

"We should talk in private," he said after a pause.

"I don't think so." I sprang from the bed. "You might as well say what you have to say for me to hear. Whatever you know about me, I already swore I would help you."

"Like I'd take your word for it." Hutch's sarcasm was fuel to the flames.

"And I'm supposed to take *your* word for it?" I said.

"If you want to live."

I scoffed. "You're not the trustworthy type either, you know."

"Enough!" Red said. He held a hand between us to serve as a barrier.

It only dawned on me then how Hutch and I were at each other's toes, neither of us willing to back down. My face was inclined to his. Heat had risen to my cheeks, my hands were balled into fists, but this wasn't the same rage I'd felt before. I didn't feel threatened, merely cast off.

Certain we weren't prepared to have a go at each other, Red stepped back. He adjusted the pearly cattleman hat on his head, his eyes traveling over us studiously.

He couldn't have been a hair over fifty. His copper skin appeared leathery around the eyes, but he held himself like a much younger man; tall and proud. He was the leader of his own will.

"You stay here," he ordered, his gaze back on me. Then to Hutch, "We'll talk outside."

Leaving us to ourselves for the moment, Red exited the room.

Hutch was first to move away. "Lock the door. Don't let anyone in, unless it's him or me."

My limbs trembled in anger. "You realize you can't tell me what to do. You need *me* just as much as I need you. So stop pretending like I'm some pawn in your little game."

"This is not a game," Hutch said. "If you want to return home, you do as I say. Otherwise I won't hesitate to plug you with a few rounds."

"Speaking of plugging, perhaps you should remove that silver spoon from your backside and learn to behave in a civil manner," I snapped. "That's what differentiates us from buffoons."

My reflexes weren't fast enough. I shifted the moment I sensed Hutch's movements, but he caught my one arm, and then the other, dragging my body closer to his.

"This is not a game," he repeated. "The men you see here cannot be trusted. If faced with them, either they will kill you, or you them. Quite frankly, I don't need you giving me more of a mess to clean up."

My eyes prickled when Hutch released my arms with the same aggression he'd used to take hold of them.

"What if it's self-defense?" I said. "What if it's kill-or-be-killed, like you said? What choice will I have?"

"Anyone threatening you, you leave it to me." He made for the door. With the knob in hand, Hutch froze. In a more composed manner, he added, "There's no reason for us to go looking for trouble. So please, lock the door. If anyone bothers you, my room is two doors down to the right. You can wait for me there."

There wasn't a ceiling light in the spare bedroom. Two nightstands held one lamp each on either side of the oversized bed. As the afternoon darkened into evening, I came to learn one lamp was missing a bulb. The other blew the moment I switched it on.

I moped for a while, lying with my back flat on the comforter, stomach growling. It was the normal type of hunger, which I was glad to learn.

I was glad to be hungry? What was my life coming to?

The scar on my hand caused by the broken candlestick holder was healing already, just as quickly as the other wounds I'd inflicted upon myself. It was a nifty superpower. That was a plus.

When it became too dark to see, I pushed myself off the bed to try the light in the small bathroom. The glare wasn't quite bright enough to reach much of the room. It was then I decided to take matters into my own hands. Who knew when either Hutch or Red would return, or even remember I was there?

Cracking open the bedroom door, I listened for any disturbance. The hall was quiet. I slipped out, peering around the dimly lit hallway.

Two doors down to the right. It wasn't rocket science.

The room was dark. So dark, it wasn't natural. Was there even a window?

Finding a bedside lamp only cost me a bruised shin and cracked knuckle joints when I ran into an unexpected bookshelf. It was well worth it the moment the room was saturated with light. My only disappointment was learning there was but the one lamp with an extractable bulb. The desk lamp was something else entirely.

Urgh. Rich people and their fancy-shmancy lights.

An uncharacteristic clutter filled the room. It was *uncharacteristic*, because Hutch's condo was clean — immaculate. It was strange to find random items scattered about the floor, desk and shelves. Crumpled laundry waited in the swivel chair to be folded or hung. The bed was unmade. Planets and rocket ships framed the top fringe of the blueberry walls.

My stomach plummeted upon the realization that Hutch used to live here. I hadn't stumbled into the wrong room. I knew this, because his name had been etched into the wood of the nightstand. My fingers traced the rugged letters, each having been carved with such determination.

Perhaps I wasn't totally wrong about the silver spoon.

Driven by curiosity, I opened the drawer of the nightstand. I didn't know what I was looking for. A clue? Something that explained what kind of person Hutch was? Something that confirmed I could trust him?

There was nothing but USB cords and earphones tangled together at the bottom of the drawer. Thwarted, I stepped over to the bookshelf. Aside from the classics, most of the books were nonfiction, and none too interesting. After coming up empty-handed, I moved to the desk.

Buried among old acceptance letters, judging by the torn envelopes, I discovered a creased photograph in the bottom drawer.

Wiping away a layer of dust from the face of the photograph, I found a young boy sitting on the lap of, who I could only guess to be his mother. A small cake pierced with five candles perched temptingly on the table. The boy beamed into the face of the camera, whereas the woman held her head turned, her reddish-brown hair obscuring half of her face.

The writing on the back confirmed the individuals in the picture. The date had also been scribbled carelessly beneath the names.

Male voices drifted down the hall. Grabbing a shirt at random from the pile of clothes on the chair beside me, I hurried over to switch off the lamp. With the shirt, I removed the bulb, feeling the warmth of it through the fabric.

The voices grew louder. I held my breath until they passed and thought it best I returned to my room. Maybe with some luck Hutch remembered I was still human enough to starve to death.

Slipping down the hall, I was about to make it back without being seen, until —

"Hey!"

I came to an abrupt halt, dropping the bulb in fright.

"I was... just —" I stammered, turning to face Red. "I was in the dark."

Looking down helplessly at the frosted glass of the bulb, I was relieved to see it hadn't shattered on the hardwood flooring. Red grunted as I scooped it up. There was an unmistakable jingle and I knew the bulb was done for.

Back in the spare bedroom, Red placed a tray and plastic bag he'd been carrying onto the bed and disappeared, returning shortly after with two small boxes.

As I stood in the doorway watching him replace the bulb in one lamp, I realized I was still clutching Hutch's photograph beneath the random item of clothing. In the light of the hall, I scrutinized the frozen scene in the picture.

"Is he always so angry?" I asked.

The first lamp lit up and Red moved around the bed to tend to the second one.

"He's angry and for good reason," he said. "The kid's got too many ill memories here."

At twenty-one, Hutch was hardly a kid.

"He ain't nice, but at least he's fair," Red went on, testing the switch of the second lamp. Nothing happened.

"I have yet to see that side of him," I muttered, while Red made to adjust the bulb. "Why is he being ordered to kill? He only kills these... Forgotten, he said. What changed?"

Following the cord of the lamp, Red grunted, "If he didn't tell you why he's being penalized, I sure as hell won't."

"Penalized?"

Red managed to connect the end of the cord to the wall plug. The second lamp blazed to life.

"What did he do?"

"None of your business," Red huffed. I could tell he was angry for letting that little bit of information slip. "You're staying here tonight. McLaren will find you in the morning as soon as Randolph gets in."

"Hutch's condo isn't but, what... fifty minutes from here," I pointed out. "Why can't we just come back in the morning?"

"Boss Man ain't always easy to get ahold of."

That was the only explanation I was offered before he disappeared, closing the door behind him.

Dropping onto the bed, the dishes on the tray clinked from the shift of my weight. I popped a grape into my mouth, rummaging through the plastic bag.

Hutch had been back to the condo. Everything in the bag was what he'd purchased earlier that morning for me to use.

When I'd taken a few bites of the ham and cheese sandwich, I noticed the pale yellow files beneath the tray. It was the information on the Allens.

Something to read, so I didn't get bored. Because I thoroughly enjoyed reading the same sad story over and over again. Sure.

The gray V-neck I'd nicked from Hutch's room smelled relatively clean enough to serve as makeshift pajamas. I made the necessary preparations for the night, then allowed my body to sink into the bed, the covers wrapping around me like comforting arms . It was a million times better than Hutch's stiff sofa. I rolled into a burrito, sighing with pleasure.

It was a trillion times better than camping outside in the cold.

Despite having felt exhausted all day, sleep was suddenly a lifetime away. In order to seduce sleep, I perused the files Hutch had left for me, staring at the pictures of the Allens and wondering about the information the documents did *not* contain. It said nothing about Melinda's favorite class in school or if Michael had hobbies other than basketball. Neither did it include anything regarding their personalities, which would have given me something more to work with.

At some point, reading over the files had done the job I'd intended.

Soft gray light was filtering through the open window next to me when I opened my eyes. I was lying face down on the carpet, cold morning air riddling my arms with goosebumps. My fingertips burned uncontrollably accompanied by a sour taste in my mouth.

A pounding on the door shook my senses, ripping me from the invisible webs of sleep. Hutch's voice called my name, but he was distant. What? Oh. He was telling me to get ready. But that wasn't my main concern.

I stared from my hands to the open window, heart sinking.

What had I done?

Chapter Seven

Hutch never inquired after my quality of rest, and I did not volunteer the information — or lack thereof.

I was herded down the hallway, squeezed between him and Red. We eventually made it back to the great oak doors of the day before. The wretched morning got worse when I noticed Josue loitering near the door. I groaned inwardly.

"We meet again, *mamacita*," he smirked, leaning into me as I passed.

Giving a small nod, Hutch placed a hand on the small of my back, ushering me forward while Red hung back with Josue.

The study was not as impressive as the rest of the house. The curtains were drawn, no doubt to prevent a glare on the computer screen located opposite it. Consequently, the room was left to appear dim and dusty.

Books and binders lay in heaps along the shelves lining the walls. Incense burned from somewhere in the room. Following the ascending line of vapor, I found the source to be coming from a far corner.

Hutch addressed the barrel-chested individual sporting a white goatee who sat at the mammoth desk. The man, Randolph, ignored us and went on bellowing into his landline. His language was salted with swear words and he continued to feign oblivion to our entry until we stood directly across from him.

"I thought I heard someone mention you were visiting," he said, slamming the receiver into its port. Too busy with his work, he barely peered at us. "What made you break this streak of five years?"

"Four."

Hutch nudged me into a chair adjacent to the desk. I sat, though reluctantly.

"Long enough, still, you haven't heard women have been banned from this house." Randolph paused typing long enough to shoot Hutch a disapproving look. "They upset the performance of the men residing here."

"What about Natalia? Georgie and Myrtie?"

"They are exceptions. The boys know what happens if they touch the help."

Hutch crossed his arms. "When did this house become a home for thieves and murderers?"

"It only seemed right, using it for business." Randolph continued typing for a moment. "What else would I do with all this square footage, other than write it off on my taxes? You wouldn't want it up for sale, now would you?" Smirking, he finished what he was doing and met Hutch's glare head on.

"I would rather see this house bulldozed to the ground."

The grunted hiccups coming from Randolph's chest was a laugh, I realized. "You've never been the nostalgic type, have you?" The lines of laughter smoothed before he continued, "I have a loyal group here for the time being. You still have your old room, though I now question *your* loyalty."

Flicking his eyes over to me for the first time, I fought to keep my expression impassive. The man was intimidating, but I wasn't going to let him know that.

"Don't put me in line with your incompetent meatheads," Hutch said.

"Do you really think you're any different?" There was a shadow of a laugh in Randolph's eyes, though he acted as one mystified.

"Is Felix any different?"

I felt Hutch grip the back of my chair. Without meaning to, I peered over my shoulder as if to confirm his hand was there. My gaze drifted upward just as his fell, causing us to lock eyes for half a breath. We looked away at the same time, but I knew the moment I looked back at Randolph this hadn't escaped the great man's attention.

This? This, what? People accidentally meet each other's eyes all the time.

"You're my nephew, not my son." Pushing to his feet, Randolph stretched lazily, looking much like a retired WWE wrestler. He had the muscle mass, but it was the potbelly that led me to assume he no longer did the heavy lifting. That was what his henchmen were for.

"Nothing has changed," Randolph continued. "Find some other way to impress the girl."

His last words were meant as a jab at Hutch, but I took offense. I wasn't there as a means of mockery, nor did they have any right to think so little of me.

"Just so we are clear," I interrupted, "he would've been done with his job by now, if I hadn't intervened." I pushed to my feet, suddenly aware I was the only left seated. "Of course, I had no idea what was going on."

"Step outside, please," said Hutch. He didn't look at me when he said this, but it was evident who he was speaking to. "Red will take you back to your room."

"I'm not finished," I said flatly. Thrusting a finger in Randolph's direction, I added, "You may want to reconsider your original plan of luring out Eric Allen. The man left his kids after his wife died of acute pericarditis. Who's to say he will care if one of his kids is brutally murdered? You're not looking at this from the right angle."

I watched as Randolph's expression turned to something more amused. He looked like someone in the middle of a poker game, and he had a winning hand.

"What angle would you pursue, if I may ask?" He was humoring me, but I thought back to my reflections of the night before while reading the files.

"Eric's parents are not the legal guardians," I said, forcing myself to speak slowly. "Which means he must still have some legal ties to the kids. Child support, maybe, at least for the youngest child. Finding out from where he is sending the money can give us a good idea on where to begin our search for him."

Shifting my weight from one foot to the other, I wet my lips. Randolph watched me contemplatively with his arms crossed.

On my left, Hutch had been pinching the bridge of his nose with his forefinger and thumb. Pointing to the door with his other hand, he said, "Get out."

"I can do this," I told Randolph. He never broke eye contact with me; his gaze was hard.

"Out!" Hutch said again, more heated this time.

Huffing, I left. There wasn't much more I could do. I'd cast the seed of opportunity. Now I had to hope it landed someplace it could grow.

Josue was the only one in the hall. I averted my gaze from him as the door to the study clicked shut behind me.

"You've been seeing a lot of men today." The playfulness in his voice made my skin crawl. "It makes me wonder when I'll have a turn."

"I have a policy against dirty old men," I snapped.

Josue laughed. "How old do you think I am?"

"I'm debating somewhere between Yoda and Gandalf." It wasn't true, of course. The guy was middle-aged, I was sure, but I despised the way he drank in the sight of me. He looked like someone prepared to feast. All he needed to do was lick his lips to complete the picture.

No, don't do that. I shuddered.

"I've heard of them before." Josue stepped closer. "They're wise fellows, aren't they?"

"You're right." My eyes narrowed. "You're more like Jabba The Hutt."

Josue cornered me against the wall, despite my quick steps around him. Linking his fingers around my wrists, the calloused pads of his fingers chafed my skin as I attempted to free myself.

"What's so special about you, eh?" His face was mere inches from mine, breath smelling of mint tobacco. It wasn't bad, but coming from him made me want to hurl. "I've seen a number of *mamacitas* like you here, but only to serve one purpose. Are you like the others?"

I recoiled - my brain screaming *danger.* I didn't see a way I would be able to escape the man's hold, until we heard the sound of someone clearing their throat.

Red stood in the middle of the hall, his lips curling in disgust.

"If you would." He motioned to Josue's hand, still holding me captive.

Josue grinned, but he released me. "Next time I see you — " He winked, not bothering to finish his sentence. He didn't have to.

I was glad Red walked me back to the spare bedroom, but he did not beat around the bush when inquiring about what happened in the study. I didn't have anything to hide, quite literally, and so I told him, speaking carefully about the misinterpretation between Hutch and myself.

"But the way Hutch kicked me out cleared it up." My fingers released the lock of hair I'd pinched into place, allowing it to unwind into a pathetic curl.

"Why are you so determined to save the kids?" he asked.

We'd already returned to my cell-slash-bedroom. I was perched on the bed while he stood, his back set against the door. He was grinding the tail end of a toothpick between his teeth.

"You wouldn't?" I said.

"I never implied that. But considering your condition, you could have fun with the task." It was a test. I could tell by the lilt in his tone.

Taking an uneven breath, "I'm not a killer."

Red waited patiently for me to continue.

"Hutch said he would get me home if I helped him, and I refuse to do so at the expense of another's life."

That wasn't the entire truth, but it was the simplest version. It seemed to be enough for Red, in any case.

Leaving me with a promise to return with a late breakfast, I was relieved to see I could take him for his word. He delivered a steaming plate of bacon, eggs and grits not a quarter of an hour later.

After setting down the tray, he was about to leave when I stopped him at the door. "He grew up here with his uncle?"

Without asking who I was referring to, Red nodded, though not without hesitation.

"Where are his parents?" I asked.

"Father was decapitated in a car accident," he said. "Mother overdosed on opiates. His mother's sister — Boss Man's wife — hung herself about six years ago. They found her in the pool house with a note telling how sorry she was."

43

"I…didn't need so much detail." I shuddered at the additional information I had not requested. "I was saving your breath," Red said. "Your next questions were predictable."

"Okay, then next on my list is, sorry for what?"

Red sucked on his teeth. "Killing herself, I would imagine." Upon seeing the compassion on my face, he added, "Don't go feeling sorry for him. He'll only hate you more for it."

Those were all the answers I was getting. When Red left, I spent the next few hours waiting to hear from Hutch, locked in the room. I fought the urge to nap. After what I'd experienced the night before, I was determined to stay awake for as long as possible.

Lunch was delivered by a white-haired lady dressed in a light blue uniform. I guessed her to be Myrtie. She looked like a Myrtie.

I ate hungrily, and found myself bored again. Warding off sleep with a full belly was futile. I reread the files, but doing so only made my eyes sticky with fatigue. I closed my eyes, expecting to rest them for a moment, yet swirling thoughts of escape spun into dreams, and before I knew it, I was fast asleep.

It was dark outside when I awoke. I sighed with relief as soon as I realized I hadn't shifted position on the bed.

Stretching with the grace of a tailless monkey, I prepared for a shower, after which I swept my hair into a high ponytail and donned Hutch's shirt again. Our chances of leaving before morning seemed slim.

I was tucked beneath the covers again, examining the photograph of Hutch and his mother when a soft knock came to the door.

"Who's there?" I asked. The last thing I wanted was another encounter with Josue.

"Me."

His voice was rough, but quiet. I cracked open the bedroom door and found Hutch leaning heavily against the door jamb. The smell of alcohol hung thick in the air around him.

"You've been drinking," I said.

"Just some beer."

I doubted that, but okay, sailor.

"Is that my shirt?" said Hutch, pushing the door further open.

I stepped back, feeling my personal space invaded. "I needed something to sleep in."

"Hope it was clean." Hands on his hips, Hutch viewed the room unsteadily.

"Sit down?" I motioned toward the seat in the corner. I was in no mood to deal with an unconscious human bean bag chair, flopped helplessly on the floor.

Ignoring my gestures, he dropped onto the edge of the bed, hands buried within the pockets of his jeans.

"I take it didn't go too well with your uncle?" I sank down onto the bed next to him, pulling the hem of the shirt over my knees.

"Why would you assume that?" Hutch inclined his head to gaze at me with leaded eyelids. For the first time, I noticed the odd structure of his face, shadowed by his tousled hair. This oddity could've derived from the combination of his deep-set eyes and narrow nose paired with his slim lips and the hard lines of his jaw. Every exposed part of him was defined by his solidity. He was attractive in his own way, even if he didn't possess the charisma of KJ Apa.

Remembering the young Hutch in the picture, I had a hard time believing they were the same person. The younger Hutch had a rounder face, holding no sign of the seriousness I saw before me.

"Somehow, I doubt you would be drunk if everything went according to plan," I said.

With a slow chuckle, Hutch leaned back until his body claimed the foot of the bed. He covered his eyes with the heel of his hands.

"Randolph gave us a few days," he said.

"Then we get to work first thing in the morning." I paused for a moment, mind raging with questions I needed answered. I decided to ask one I was sure he would answer. "How come Randolph can't locate Eric Allen himself? He must have perfectly capable sources. How else could you know so much about the man's family?"

Hutch groaned, his fingertips moving in slow circles on his forehead.

"Allen's gone off the grid. Disappeared after he cheated Randolph out of a deal."

"Muling?" I guessed.

Yawning, he nodded. He tucked his hands beneath his head as a makeshift pillow, eyes closed.

"What does that even mean?" I waited for him to say something, or to move, but he remained motionless. The pauses between breaths lengthened.

"Hutch?" I nudged him gently with my foot.

He was out like a light.

Unbelievable.

There was no use trying to wake him. I knew for a fact Hutch was going to be useless to me for the rest of the night. He would suffer the consequences of his actions in the morning.

"Be sure to drink enough water," I mumbled, gathering a pillow into my arms.

I didn't know how I knew this, but part of me hoped it wasn't from personal experience. What would that say about my character? That I was a rebellious teen that took part in under-aged drinking? Did I want to be under that label? Because the other option was Little Miss Goody-Two-Shoes. Which was worse?

Heaving a sigh, I locked the bedroom door from the inside on my way out, giving Hutch the privacy he probably didn't deserve to rest in peace. Not after the way he woke me these past two mornings.

There wasn't a lock on Hutch's bedroom door. This did strike me as worrisome. I angled the desk chair under the doorknob and managed to convince myself it was enough to hold, should anyone decide to stop by in the dead of night. It was a swivel chair, one that did not lean into the door very well. The possibility of it holding anyone out was slim, but I would have to take my chances.

The sheets of Hutch's single bed were chill against my skin. Staring into the darkness of the room, I waited for my body to warm the mountain of blankets covering me. All the while, I wondered what it must've been like, growing up in such an extravagant house — growing up an orphan. For all I knew, I could be one, too. A rebellious-teenaged-orphan with a knack for getting herself into trouble.

I dozed, only to wake with the sun spilling across the shaggy carpet. It wasn't clear what woke me, although it *was* a little stuffy in the room. My one leg was covered by the comforter while the other I had kicked free, curled over the other. Stretching a soft groan, I rolled to my side.

That was when I noticed Hutch, sitting in the swivel chair, the back of it pressed against the door.

I sat up quickly, tossing the comforter over my exposed leg.

He had been leaning forward, his hands in his hair. He looked up at my commotion. The early light cast a dark shadow over one side of his face.

I blinked.

That was a bruise on his jawline, not a shadow. The bridge of his nose displayed a horizontal cut stained with dried blood. His lower lip was swollen.

Chapter Eight

"What happened to you?" I asked.

Clutching his knees, Hutch leaned back in the chair. "Josue and Stix intended on paying you a visit last night."

"In here?" I asked dumbly. Then it came to me. "In the spare room."

Hutch nodded.

"But I locked the door!" I stared at him for a long moment as it began to sink in.

The cuts and bruises were meant for me. What would they have done had they found me in there as planned? The thought alone made me sick to my stomach. "Why didn't they just leave? They must've realized I wasn't there."

"It was too late," said Hutch. "I saw them, and they acted impulsively."

"Shouldn't you tell Randolph about this?"

Giving a wry laugh, Hutch stood, moving to the dresser. "Because you could tell how much he cares about me." He tossed a few articles of clothing over one shoulder. "I'll walk you back to your room."

"That's it? You nearly get beaten to a pulp and we move on as if it never happened?" I said in disbelief.

Hutch exited the room, forcing me to follow. The moment I stepped into the hall, as tightness gripped my chest. A haze fell over my mind, forcing me to a halt. My breath came rapidly as darkness ascended, consciousness fading fast.

What... was happening?

"Are you okay?"

When my sight returned, I found one hand clutching my chest, the other balled into a tight enough fist, my nails bit deep into the palm of my hand. Hutch was standing by my side, eyes searching me, concerned. Or was I imagining that?

"I... I'm fine," I said. I wasn't keen on telling him this was the second time this fogginess had washed over me since being at the mansion. Nor was I willing to tell him about waking up next to the open window the morning before. It wouldn't build a great case in my defense.

Erm. Defense against what? I haven't done anything.

Yet.

My hope of us getting down the hall without running into anyone was squashed almost instantly. Near the top of the stairs stood the last person I wanted to see.

A fresh cut ran along the length of Josue's cheek. The bruise on his cheekbone tainted his flawless olive complexion. He glared at us, eyes catapulting daggers in our direction. He was accompanied by Flix, whom I saw the first day at the mansion. His shoulder length hair was pulled behind his head, a smirk visible on his face.

This was Randolph's son?

Looking more closely at him, I could see the resemblance. Bulb nose, though not unattractive. Cleft chin. Receding hairline. I looked away before I stared too long. There was no reason to provoke him. I had enough enemies here.

When we made it back to the spare room, I found it in shambles. The bloodstain on the door knob caught my attention first. The innards of a pillow fell across the bed and floor like fresh snow; one lamp was shattered on the other side of the room. The sheets had been twisted several times and left discarded on the chair. A severe crack slithered down the glass of the window.

Had I really slept through this? Hutch's room was not far down the hall.

"Geez," I mumbled.

When Hutch made to leave, I stopped him.

"You can't leave me here," I said. "What if they come back?"

It was all I could do to push the thought of Josue's infuriated expression from my mind.

"You'll be fine for now," Hutch said. "I will send for Red to keep an eye out until we leave."

Arguing wouldn't help. The dismissive look on Hutch's face told me as much. Instead, I locked the door after him and pushed the armchair in front of it. Hopefully it held up better than the swivel chair in the other room.

I straightened up what I could. As much as I disliked Randolph and his so-called employees, I knew they wouldn't be the ones clearing the mess.

There was a knock on the door just as I finished brushing my teeth. Red gave me a questioning look at the armchair I'd pushed aside to let him in. It didn't take long for the broken window and lamp to catch his eye next. "Busy night?"

"Just the usual," I said. I took a seat in the arm chair, slipping on my flats. "Hutch passed out drunk, so we switched rooms. Stix and Josue found him here instead of me."

I was proud of myself for hiding the quake in my voice.

"Same old, same old," Red muttered, gazing around at the destruction I'd been unable to mend.

"Does this kind of thing happen often?" I asked.

"Which part, exactly?"

"All of it."

Red considered this for a moment. "We never see women around here, no, so that's new. But a little scuffle is nothing out of the ordinary."

If this was the result of a little scuffle, I did not wish to know how things went down under dire circumstances.

"What about Hutch?" I prompted. "Does he have a history of DUIs or bar fights I need to know about?"

"He caused a four-car pileup a few years back," said Red, adjusting his hat to scratch his forehead with his thumb.

I stared at Red, mouth agape. He laughed outright at my reaction. "I'm joking."

"So he drinks, but doesn't drive drunk," I said. At least that was reassuring.

"Don't go jumping to conclusions." I heard the emphasis of his northern accent. "With the line of work he's in, I'd say he drinks next to never."

"So how do you explain last night?" I said.

"Maybe you should ask him to explain that."

Like that will get me anywhere, I thought. Hutch was a wall of steel. Asking him anything personal was fruitless.

"What's your story?" I asked, crossing one leg over the other.

Red's darkened look chilled me to the bone. The expression made me feel guilty for my inquiry, as though I'd overstepped a line.

"I don't—I just..." taking a breath, I said more evenly, "I'm sorry. I guess I was just hoping to find something real here." When he said nothing, I went on, "My last few days have been an absolute disaster. It's as though everyone I've met has some self-seeking goal that benefits no one, but themselves."

I provided an apologetic smile, but Red merely shrugged, absolved by my explanation.

"Welcome to humanity," he said, scuffing the ground with his injured foot as he had done the other day. "My story is no exception to the cruelty of mankind."

There was a long pause, where Red removed a faded Zippo lighter from the inside pocket of his blazer. He lit it, allowing the flame to wave for a moment. After staring at it, he snapped the lid shut, and repeated the motion.

"You don't have to tell me," I said.

"There's not much to tell." He flipped the lighter shut again. "My home was broken into while I was on the road. I was a truck driver at the time, living up north. My wife and daughter were home. They were molested and beaten to death. Detectives chalked it up to being a hate crime."

My heart sank.

"I'm so sorry," I said, but the words failed to grasp the extent of my sorrow for the man. What did one say to something so horrible.

Red went on as if he hadn't heard me. "After I lost them, I came here to find a means of living and Randolph hired me. That's all there is to it."

I winced at the harshness of his words. He stared dispassionately at the flame again before putting it out.

"Everyone here's got a self-seeking goal," he said. "It's a harsh world. Take my advice when I tell you it never hurts to find someone you can trust. There's no use going it alone."

"And you trust Hutch?" I asked.

"With my life."

***

We had almost made it downtown when Hutch hung up from his second phone call. He'd been on his cell the entire drive back, and his mood was spiraling.

"What's going on?" I asked.

"Still waiting to hear back on Michael and Melinda's current position."

Hoping Hutch's four-car pileup story was truly a myth, I gripped the armrest of the door as he tailed closely behind a Smart car. As soon as he had the opportunity, he maneuvered into the lane around it.

"There are more guys on the job?"

"I called Damian to monitor the situation in my absence."

"Yet he lost track of the Allens."

Hutch cursed, affirming my last statement.

"What exactly is our plan here?" I wanted to know. All earnestness was lost when the last word came out a squeak, due to another unexpected swerve of the SUV. Recovering slightly, I asked, "Am I to become BFFs with Melinda or something?"

"You've already gained their trust by saving her," said Hutch. "All you have to do now is get the intel we need and get out."

"It's not going to be that simple."

He ground his teeth. "I know. That's the problem."

"How much time do we have?" I asked.

"Less than a week," he said. "By noon Saturday we have to report back to Randolph."

"And if we don't?"

The phone vibrated.

"Hopefully it won't come to that."

After answering the phone, he fell silent, steering with his left hand. He merged over to the lane on the far right, taking the next exit.

"Keep me updated," he said and hung up.

"Anything?" I wondered.

"They're at the mall." He turned us around, getting back onto the interstate.

Twenty minutes later, we stepped through the entrance of a busy store.

"What's with all the kids?" I said, observing the throng of students surrounding us. "Shouldn't they be in school?"

"Thanksgiving break," said Hutch, typing a message on his phone.

"Thanksgiving?" I hadn't even thought about it. A sense of bitterness filled me as I looked back at the students, some with their families, others with friends. They had not a care in the world; no dread of what was to come.

If only my return home to my own family was as secure as their tomorrows. I longed to recall at least one happy Thanksgiving memory, surrounded by loved ones. The holiday *felt* cheerful, but I desperately wished to remember why.

Hutch pinched the sleeve of my dress, calling my attention back to him. Cocking his head, he motioned I followed him toward the front.

If I had to guess, Damian was the only guy that looked out-of-place among the women's lingerie. I followed his line of vision over his green-rimmed glasses and my stomach flopped.

Melinda was deciding between two dresses, balancing one in each hand. Her pale blonde hair was tied back in a high ponytail, exposing scabbed lines on her cheek. She pushed the surplice lace dress into the face of the person accompanying her.

Michael was taller than I'd imagined. One arm he had propped on the rack displaying cardigans, the other he used to jab at the second dress his sister held.

"They've been at it for a while."

I hadn't even heard Damian approach.

"Anything else happen since?" Hutch asked.

Damian shook his head, though he stared at me as he did so. His eyes

were as dark as his skin, and although he had a friendlier regard for me —
compared to Stix and Josue — I still felt judged.

"Ready?" Hutch asked me.

"What? No. I don't know." I spun away from the other two. Panic was
building in my chest. How was I supposed to do this? By Saturday, no less?

The weight of the danger I was in finally came crashing down. I was to get
the job done, or else, and honestly, that *or else* scared me more than anything.
My gut was telling me whatever Stix and Josue had planned on doing to me,
Randolph would top them.

Why? *Why* had I gotten myself entangled in this mess?

Sensing my distress, Hutch nodded at Damian, who immediately started
to browse through the nearest clothes line. Hutch then glanced around
before gripping my elbows.

"Listen," he said, forcing me to meet his gaze. "It's no big deal. I need you
to calm down, otherwise people will think you are about to have a seizure."

I hadn't realized my frantic breathing until he pointed it out.

"Introduce yourself," he suggested, shooting another quick look around
us. "Your name is Hayden. If they ask, you're home-schooled. You live in a
condo downtown. Keep it simple and easy to remember."

"Is any of this true?" I asked.

"That doesn't matter right now."

Meh. It was worth a shot.

"Are you sure she's going to be able to do this without raising suspicion?"
Damian asked.

Gee, thanks for the vote of confidence there, pal. It wasn't like I was
insecure enough.

Hutch ignored him. "Ready?" he asked.

This time I nodded, swallowing the lump in my throat.

I counted the steps I took toward the Allens. Melinda was clearly infuriated
with her brother and hung the dresses on the nearest rack with more force
than necessary.

My movements illustrated the awkwardness I felt as I advanced. I grabbed
a blouse at random to give my fingers something to hold on to.

"It's fine, just try it on," Michael insisted, pushing one of the dresses back into her hands.

Not half a yard from them, I halted. My palms had grown clammy; a familiar numbness spilled across the length of my scalp.

Eyes growing wide with fear, I suddenly found myself tripping over my feet to remain upright as an abrupt flashback assumed control over my vision.

Chest blooming with eagerness, I stepped out of the bedroom and made for the living room of the dimly lit double-wide. The glossy dress clung neatly to my figure, the price tag tickling the skin between my shoulder blades.

I wanted to impress him. I must have meant something to him if he took the time to get me the dress; and an expensive one at that.

Voices exploded from the living room. Concerned about the sudden change of atmosphere, I hurried through the kitchen. James had lunged at one of the young men — our hosts. I screamed his name, hoping he didn't hurt him — hoping he did not wind up hurt in the end.

Our hosts were Forgotten. I knew that much, yet I did not fear them. Why should I? They were so generous to us.

The others formed a circle, their movements noiseless and agile. One laid a hand on James. I begged and pleaded that they overlooked his rash behavior. He was still in mourning, after all.

I was gripping a pair of hands, tears trickling past my temples and into my hair.

"You're okay, just breathe," said a voice. "Mel, get help!"

"N-no!" I stammered, my vision clearing. The lights blinded me. "I'm fine. I'm okay."

Forcing myself to my feet, I realized belatedly I was still holding on to Michael.

"I — my head — migraine." My world was spinning. I ordered my fingers to release Michael's, but his solidity prevented me from forfeiting to vertigo.

"You need medical attention," he said.

"I don't have insurance," I lied, the words slipping out quick and easy. "I'm fine, really. I'm sorry."

I didn't know why I was apologizing. With trembling fingers, I finally released him to wipe the remaining tears from my eyes. My smile was forced, but I was relieved to see Michael return it.

"If you're sure." His tone offered the option of my taking him up on his suggestion to help.

"I'm sure," I said firmly.

People were watching the scene, customers and retailers alike. My face flushed, being the center of entertainment.

Why was I so good at calling attention to myself?

"Don't worry about it," Michael said, having noticed my reason for discomfiture. "Nothing interesting ever happens to these people. When a less mundane event crosses them, they try to appreciate every moment of it."

The smile he flashed me was wider this time, displaying a clean set of perfect teeth.

Was he flirting?

On the other side of him, Melinda was gaping at me. I saw the recognition strike her like a slap on the face.

She knew exactly who I was.

Chapter Nine

"My name's Hayden." I felt out of place when I said this, resisting the urge to offer my hand to Michael.

"I'm Mike," he said, then gestured to his sister. "This is Melinda, my kid sister."

The buzzing of a phone made its introduction next. Mike reached into his pocket, declining the incoming call.

"And that's Brad," he said, though more to himself.

Melinda said nothing. She continued to gape at me and I began to feel anxiety fizz in my veins. I glanced around the store, hoping to catch a glimpse of Hutch. I needed to talk to him about the flashback. I needed to ask him questions. Was James well? What happened to the Forgotten in the double-wide?

Having noticed the oddity of his sister's behavior, Mike punched Melinda gently on the shoulder.

"Don't mind her," he chuckled. "This is her first time out of the house in a week. She's readjusting to the world."

"Really?" I smiled, despite feeling weighed down by Melinda's glare.

"Yep. You heard about the faulty wiring in the car that exploded last Monday?" said Mike.

"Of course, she has." Melinda spoke up for the first time. Her face was suddenly drained of blood. The rustic scab from that night showed more clearly on her cheekbone. "She was there."

Mike suddenly looked embarrassed. "Mel... I don't think so."

"You were the one who pulled me away," she continued as if her brother had said nothing at all. "You saw the explosive in the trunk. Didn't you?"

"That's enough, Mel," said Mike. He shot me an apologetic glance.

I gulped, my stomach doing unpleasant whirls. "I saw it."

It was almost comical the way they both looked at me. Mike was in utter disbelief, whereas Melinda's expression shifted from shock to relief and finally fright.

"I didn't think I would run into you here." I was lying between my teeth and did not like how it came so naturally.

"It was you?" said Mike. As soon as I nodded, he ran a hand through his hair causing it to stick up in odd places. If anything, he looked skeptical. "How is that possible?"

The whirling of my stomach ascended to the area between my ribcage. My head still throbbed from the flashback. Despite my conversation with the Allens, all I could think about was James. The urge to talk to Hutch pressed. What if something bad had happened?

"I'm sorry, but I need to go," I told them.

Mike's touch on my forearm was light; a mere brush of my skin.

"Was it really — you were there?" His eyes narrowed inquisitively. He was torn between not wanting to believe what I said, but not wanting to believe I was crazy. "My sister's not a basket case?"

"No, she's not." I looked past him at Melinda. There was a shadow of a smile on her face, but her eyes showed signs of unease.

"You're a hero!" Mike exclaimed. "You do realize that? You saved her life!"

"No." I shook my head.

I broke a man's arm. Not to mention, I was wanted for murder. I was anything but heroic.

"I was in shock that night," I said. "I hurt someone. I didn't mean to. They were just trying to help."

My eyes brimmed with tears of shame, but I blinked them back. "Please, I don't need any trouble."

They both stared blankly at me. As I turned for a second time to go, Melinda stopped me.

"We won't tell anyone."

Draping an arm around his sister's shoulders, Mike nodded in agreement. "As far as we're concerned, you kept our family together." He gave a winning smile, one that drew girls in with a magnetic force.

"Glad I could help," I said, half-aware of the words leaving my lips.

I was stopped for a third time.

"Maybe we can talk. Hang out sometime?" Melinda suggested. She'd taken a step forward, as though eagerly wishing for me to stay.

"I'll call you." I said. It sounded like a question.

"Sure," Mike said, all too willing to help. He pulled out his cell. "What's your number? I'll text you."

"I don't have a phone," I told them, feeling more foolish than before. Receiving curious looks from the two, I quickly added, "I lost it that night."

"No problem." Mike left us to hunt down a pen and something to write on. He returned in record timing with a business card from the makeup section of the store.

"The top number is mine," he explained, pointing to the scribbles added to one side. "Melinda's is the second."

I thanked him, taking the card.

Bidding them a brief farewell, I walked out of the store and into the common area of the mall. I had no idea where Hutch had skulked off to, but there was no doubt in my mind that he would follow me out of the store.

The mall was crowded. I weaved between bodies, suffocating from the mixed smells of perfume and body odor.

Clutching the business card between my fingers in hopes of steadying my nerves, I began to wonder if Hutch noticed me leave at all.

A hand touched my waist, directing me to a corridor filled with vending machines and public restrooms.

I took a breath, my mind finding peace.

"Did something happen?" Hutch wanted to know as soon as we had a little privacy. People were still trotting by to the restrooms, but no one paid us any attention.

"My brother," I said.

"What about him?" His scrutiny of me was unsettling.

"You know. You have to," I said. "He attacked a Forgotten."

Hutch groaned at my words. I was talking about the flashback. There was no possible way he'd missed me faceplanting onto the floor.

"This is why you ditched the chance to talk to the Allens?" he fumed, fists clenched at his sides. "Both of our lives are on the line here, and you want us to squander our time talking memories? When we have nothing to present to Randolph, you're dead and I'm not far behind."

I pressed harder against the wall behind me. He'd just spoken my fear aloud.

"Tell me James is all right and we can move on," I said. It was a weak argument. My throat was tight from withholding countless emotions, but I needed him to say it. If he knew my name, he had to know something about my family. Did he have a yellow folder similar to the Allens, only with information on James stashed somewhere in the condo?

"I'm not telling you anything," Hutch said, gritting his teeth.

Rage amassed, rolling off him, and I was frightened to comprehend he was just as panicked as I was. Stepping back, he turned, thumping the nearest vending machine with the underside of his fist and leaving a dent in the plastic.

"Why don't you just leave?" I asked, still holding my position against the wall.

"What?"

"Just leave!" I said, louder this time. "Why are you allowing your uncle to force you to do something you know is wrong?"

"This is what I do," he said. "It's what I've always done."

"You don't leave, because you're afraid you aren't good enough for anything else?"

Hutch shook his head. "I don't leave, because I'm not a coward. I deal with my problems. I don't run from them."

"It looks to me like staying in the comfort of Randolph's pocket is easier than leaving him to face the world," I said. "Be a man for once and take initiative. Do what *you* want to do!"

"It's a bit late for that now," said Hutch. "Even if I wanted to leave, Randolph wouldn't let me."

"Oh, please. To think your uncle would kill you is insane."

Someone else stepped into the corridor.

"Is everything all right here?" asked a man dressed in a crisp, white security shirt and dark slacks. He stood stock-still at the mouth of the corridor, hands on his belt.

"We're fine," Hutch growled.

"Ma'am?" The man looked at me as I continued to brace myself against the wall.

Nodding, I noticed security cameras in the corners of the corridor. "I'm great." I straightened, pushing from the wall. "We were just having a discussion."

After giving me a significant look, the security guard nodded toward the vending machine. "What happened there?"

"I'm not having a good day." Hutch snarled as if to add *that's all*.

The man assessed the situation a moment longer, before, "Try not to take your rage out on the other machines, or any of the shoppers for that matter."

***

Hutch stewed all the way to the condo. I knew he was mad at me for wasting a perfect opportunity to talk to the Allens, but if he thought I would get the information upon first meeting them, he had another thing coming.

When we got back, he locked himself in his bedroom to do heaven knows what. The only time he came out was to meet a delivery guy for the takeout he'd apparently ordered. I watched silently as he reactivated the home security system, his thumb punching the buttons with ferocity.

Leaving me with a bag of food to rummage through, he locked himself in his room again.

After picking at the fried rice and orange chicken, I wandered about the condo in my attempt to keep my mind from slipping into dark corners.

The second bedroom across the hall from the master had been transformed into a weight room, complete with dumbbells and a complicated multi-purpose machine. A full-length mirror ran along the opposite wall. It was a small room, but the space had been used efficiently. After testing the weight of certain dumbbells, I got bored and decided to move on.

Once I'd made full circle around the condo (avoiding Hutch's room), agitation struck. It was as though a sphere of energy crackled within my chest, yet I was forced to remain stagnant. I wondered if I'd always grown restless when left to keep myself company.

In the coat closet, I rummaged through a stack of magazines on a shelf, all introducing the differences between tactical knives and reviewing semi-automatics accessories. What else would I expect to find? Home & Garden magazines, or Reader's Digest?

I carried one of the magazines to the sofa. Even if I didn't read many of the articles, there were still pictures to look at.

Studying a piece on OTF knives, my mind began to wander from the text to Hutch's behavior at the mall.

Quite honestly, I didn't know how much I could really trust him. Nor did I know if I would truly be able to make it out alive when all was said and done. All I knew for certain, was I had to do something about the Allen situation. It was my only hope of returning to my brother. Hutch was reluctant to tell me anything, so I would just have to do everything on my own.

***

Following the thudding bass and the metallic grinding, I pulled the throw tighter over my shoulders.

My eyes squinted in response to the bright sunlight beaming in through the windows of the hall.

Hutch was up bright and early, finishing a set of hammer curls. He dropped the weights and turned to meet me the moment I stepped through the doorway. After all, the reflection of my bundled appearance was difficult to ignore. A part of me wished I'd taken the time to brush my hair instead of coming straight from the couch.

"What is it?" he asked with a grunt as he returned the equipment to the stand.

I was slightly taken aback by the lack of revulsion in his tone. Having let him think I'd failed miserably at befriending the Allens, I was surprised he had any tolerance left of me.

He adjusted the snapback on his head.

"I need your phone," I said. "I'm going to call Melinda and see if she wants to meet."

Hutch simply stood and watched me. The neckline of his shirt was damp with sweat.

He continued to say nothing, so I thought it best to explain. "They gave me their number yesterday."

"And you're just telling me this now?"

"You never asked," I said.

I took a moment to remind myself of all I'd contemplated, lying awake on the couch, while Hutch thumped around the weight room.

This wasn't solely about getting me home. I could mope and be nasty all I wanted until Hutch told me what I needed to know about my family, but that would only endanger Melinda and her family even more. I had to accept that my time would come, and I would reunite with my own family. The Allen's situation, however, was a time-sensitive matter.

"Can I please have your phone?"

Glad Hutch did not choose to argue, I accepted the Android the moment he handed it over.

The call went straight to voicemail. Hesitating, I left a vague message, asking her to call me back.

Hutch had ended his workout session and locked himself in his room again by the time I made it to the living room with a bowl of cereal. Typical. He was definitely displaying the signs of an introverted nature.

I sunk into the soft leather of the couch, balancing the bowl of food in one hand and the remote for the TV in the other. A piece of food lodged into my throat, nearly choking me, when I caught the headline news on Channel Five.

Pictures of missing persons flashed across the screen, all victims having disappeared from the area within the last week. The last image was of a young woman, her confident laughter captured in the sparkle of her eyes.

According to the sliding text at the bottom of the screen, she'd been the only one found. An unnamed individual reported finding her body in a parking lot on his way home from the graveyard shift.

An atrocious homicide, they called it. The words spun in my head like a broken record.

No more information was offered as the authorities were still investigating the case, but deep within me, a dark laugh pulsed to life. I knew instinctively what, if not who, the *atrocious* killer was.

Chapter Ten

My heart skipped a beat at the sound of Hutch's bedroom door opening. I had just enough time to turn the channel before he rounded the corner.

He made straight for the kitchen, saying, "We're leaving soon. Get ready."

"Where are we going?" *Breathe. He doesn't suspect you. He doesn't* know.

I continued to flip through the channels as though getting further from the news channel would make my anxiety disappear.

"You need a change of clothes," Hutch said. "They'll start asking questions if they don't see you wear anything but that dress."

I didn't disagree. I welcomed the thought of getting some new clothes. The dress was warm, sure, but it exposed too much skin for the season.

It took me under ten minutes to get myself together. When I stepped out of the bathroom, looping my hair into a hair tie, a muffled voice met my ears. It was coming from the direction of Hutch's room.

Being able to amplify my hearing was definitely a perk of my condition. In no way was it normal that I should be able to hear Hutch clearly through the sturdy structure of the walls. It was like when I'd heard Mike and Melinda discussing the two items of clothing at the mall. They'd been too far for any else to hear, but picking out their voices and focusing on their conversation had come naturally.

"...about upping the dosage of one of my prescriptions." The sound of his voice rolled like ripples in water as I focused on holding his baritone. Pause. "The last one." There was another pause where Hutch cleared his throat.

My muscles twitched. I was poised, ready to glide back to the living room before he caught me eavesdropping. "It's not helping the way it's supposed to."

Willing my hearing to sharpen further, I tried to make out the speaker on the line, but all I could grasp was the high-pitched hum of a female voice, perhaps a nurse or receptionist.

"I don't have time for that," said Hutch. "Just forget about it."

When Hutch returned to the living room, I was perched on the sofa, pretending to be absorbed in a quirky game show.

"Let's go," he said. He barely gave me a passing glance as he made for the front door.

The traffic in Green Hills was impossible. Cars cut others off as they made daring swerves on the road. Hutch was no exception. The pads of my feet just about punched the floorboard every time he braked last minute.

"Can you stop that?" he said, nodding at my feet.

"Your driving is trash," I said through gritted teeth.

"I get us where we need to go. My driving's fine."

"Yeah, well, it only takes one accident to determine who's right here," I said.

We made it back to the mall at last. Nothing made me happier than to get my feet on solid ground.

The building was nearly exploding with shoppers, the cell phone charging stations were swarming with lazy bodies all claiming whatever sofa space they could. This was what our society had come to: everyone ignoring the others around them to focus instead on people on their screens.

"Only get what you need," said Hutch. "Get a jacket. Whatever will keep you warm."

My eyes widened when he relinquished his matte black credit card into my custody.

"Are you seriously giving me this?" I asked.

"It's the business card." There was a hint of a smirk in his voice. "Don't take long."

"You're not coming with?" I ran my fingers along the edges of the heavy plastic.

"I'll be close by," he said and pulled out his phone.

In a daze, I took a few steps. More shoppers passed me, some shooting passive aggressive words in my direction for my slow pace.

I didn't know where to start. Looking back, Hutch was staring at the screen of his phone. He was reading something, a text.

A grin spread across my face. Turning back, my steps now bore purpose as I entered the nearest store.

***

Almost a dozen shops and a pumpkin spiced latte later, my fingers cramped under the weight of the bags I carried.

Bubbling with excitement, I glanced around in search of Hutch. As I leisurely sipped my latte, I took in the early decorations for Christmas. It was barely Thanksgiving, people really couldn't wait three more days?

Garland, fake snow and colorful ornaments hung from anywhere and everywhere, each accompanied by twinkling lights. The scent of gingerbread and molasses lingered in the atmosphere. A winter wonderland had been built with an oversized sled as the centerpiece. Giant candy canes enclosed the area like a fence, but there wasn't a Santa or any of his elves in sight.

Reaching the upper level, Tiffany's came into view, and I realized I had made a full circle around the mall. I stopped to peer behind me, but there was no sign of Hutch.

Time to backtrack.

Bodies swerved around me as I made back for the escalator. Heat began to rise in my chest. I felt my face turn blotchy, due to my efforts of avoiding everyone walking in the opposite direction. My hands trembled and uneasiness settled over me, though I wasn't sure why until the edges of my vision became daubed by a dark fog.

No, I thought desperately. *Not now, not ever.*

Focusing on a sign up ahead, I willed my vision to clear.

"Watch it!"

My focus was broken. A frizzy-haired woman glared at me, rubbing her shoulder.

"*No*," I muttered in fear for what was coming.

The constriction in my chest broke loose, spreading freely into my arms and legs. My muscles contracted. The fog in my mind poured over me, overwhelming my senses.

It felt as though only a second had passed. Coming to, I found myself sitting with my back against the guardrail. I was back at Tiffany's, my bags piled in my lap and on the floor beside me. The sound of incoherent chattering resurfaced from the engulfing blackness and it took me a moment to realize I was chewing something flat with sharp edges. My mouth felt swollen and tasted of blood.

I spat the flat object into the palm of my hand. A string of saliva mixed with blood followed. I stared for a moment before comprehending it was a torn sliver of the lid of my latte, now masticated and wet.

Sure enough, I found my empty cup on the ground next to my hip. Bite marks decorated the rim; the lid was inside, shredded.

Before I had time to contemplate the matter, I heard a sharp voice call Hutch's name.

Scrambling to my feet, I gathered my shopping bags and was about to step around a cluster of socializing young adults when Hutch and I located one another.

He was still a few yards away when I opened my mouth to say something, but the severe look on his face hushed me immediately. He jerked his head to the right, eyes holding mine with significance.

A man I recognized was pursuing him, his muscles bulging through the sleeves of his leather jacket.

Nodding in comprehension to Hutch's muted gestures, I stepped around the corner of Tiffany's toward the mall's exit, stopping short of the sliding doors. I then slid behind a tall plant, and peered back at the scene.

The man called Hutch's name once more before he finally turned to meet him.

Straining my ears as I had earlier that morning, I tuned out the buzz of conversation surrounding us.

"Felix," Hutch said.

"I haven't been able to talk to you since Sam's funeral," the man smirked.

"You weren't at the funeral."

"Right." Felix gave a toothy grin while brushing a strand of tawny hair behind his ear. "I was at your mom's funeral. Once you see one, you've seen 'em all, am I right?"

"Did you say that about your own mother's funeral?"

Burn.

Felix barked a laugh, one that sent chills down my spine. "Touché."

"I see how it has scarred you for life," said Hutch with an air of sarcasm.

"Life goes on," Felix shrugged. He buried his hands in the pockets of his jacket. "You would know. You've had more practice with this coping thing."

"Is this all you came to talk about?" Hutch snapped. "I'm too busy to stop and chat about coping skills."

"I ain't gonna lie, you never struck me as a coward," Felix said suddenly, taking a step closer to Hutch, his rugged jaw inclined probingly. "After all you've been through you must have some sick desire to exhaust your anger. Why's this job so hard for you?"

"No two people are alike," Hutch said.

"Is that something Samuel taught you?" Felix asked with a chuckle.

"It means I'm not as sick as you," Hutch spat. He was clenching his right fist, as if ready to take up a defensive position at any given moment. "I actually have morals I live by."

A *tut-tut* came from the other man. He was still grinning. "I heard you cooked up some pathetic plan. You do realize what will happen when you fail. You'll go back to your little hole and I deal with the vixen you hired."

Hutch gave a dark smirk. "She would sooner shred your entrails."

I flinched, not wishing to picture such a morbid scene.

"At least I will die happy knowing you are back where you belong," he leaned in to add in an audible whisper, "even if I can no longer hear you cry for your dead mother."

They were fighting words. Felix wanted to get a rise out of Hutch and he wanted it public.

Whether Hutch would've acted upon the challenge or not, I never found out. As soon as the final words left Felix's lips, the faint sound of a shriek met my ears. Very soon, alarm bells resounded across the mall, followed by flashing lights. An automated voice instructed everyone to evacuate immediately.

Panic-stricken bodies began to rush for the doors behind me. A blur of colors streaked before my eyes, and I was thrown off balance by an elbow nudging me into the wall. My grip on the shopping bags grew slack as I landed on the solid tiles of the ground. Before I knew it, someone was yanking at the bags in my one hand, but I curled my fingers tighter around the handles. If they ripped, so be it, but I could not believe in such haste to safety, someone would dare take advantage of me.

It was an average-looking guy with a beige vest and a black beanie. I kicked my heel, aiming for his shin, but missed. A mangled cry escaped me in my struggle.

My senses alerted me of Hutch's nearness before I saw him. An elbow flashed, and the man backed away, clutching his nose. In his stupor, he took no heed to the fleeing crowd and was soon immersed by the raging current.

Hutch offered a hand and I took it, clambering to my feet. We made it outside in time to see police cars skidding to a halt.

"Don't stop," Hutch mumbled.

When we made it to the car, I fixed my ears on the chatter of others. Maybe someone knew what was going on.

"Hayden, get in," Hutch said.

I nodded, but waited a moment longer, disregarding the unimportant information I was catching.

Then I heard it: a breathless voice, hurrying to catch up with its companions. "The cops are questioning the person who found the body."

Chapter Eleven

There was no telling if Hutch knew what happened at the mall, but he was constantly on his phone. One might think a news app would have notified him of recent events. I did not dare turn on the television either way. I didn't think I would be able to fake my surprise at learning the news of a body being found at the mall.

My gut clenched at the thought; fingers trembled. I rummaged through the shopping bags a third time, pulling out a green blouse.

Clanking and thumping came from the kitchen, followed by the flow of the tap. Hutch was making some kind of protein beverage for himself from what I could tell. When he left the kitchen, he clutched a shaker bottle in one hand, and thumbed through his phone with the other.

My fingers grew cold and numb. As soon as he found out what happened, he would likely hold me accountable. What were the odds? Me, deadly and unpredictable, in the same facility when a dead body surfaces?

Bile rose in my throat. I needed to do *something* otherwise my anxiety was going to spill from the inside out.

"That was crazy what happened at the mall," I said, tossing a pair of navy blue yoga pants onto the coffee table. My attempt at nonchalance felt weak, but I soon realized how little it mattered when Hutch was engrossed in something else. "I didn't see any smoke or fire. Wonder what the evacuation was all about."

I couldn't tell if Hutch heard me and chose to ignore what I said, or if he had zoned me out entirely. I hoped he was just ignoring me. If anything, I wanted it on the record that I had no idea the reason for chaos.

Okay. New tactic. "Was Samuel your father?"

This got his attention. Hutch looked up from his phone. "He was my mentor."

"You had a mentor?"

"For what I do," he explained.

That made sense. "Who trained *him*?"

Hutch offered a shrug. "He was already on Randolph's payroll when my—when I moved in."

"What happened to him?" I asked.

"He was killed," he said. The hardness of his expression made my stomach queasy.

Felix had mentioned the man's funeral.

"Forgotten?" I was well aware I was on the verge of agitating him with my promptings, but was determined to press as far as I could before he shut me down.

He nodded.

So the hunted got the hunter.

"Melinda left a voice message." Hutch tactfully changed the subject. "She wants to meet at a juice bar tomorrow afternoon."

I couldn't quite tell if I was relieved or nervous by this. Maybe I was a little bit of both. Melinda wanted to meet, which meant she would ask questions. Perhaps Mike would be there also. They'd want the most from my perspective on the matter they could get. Someone had tried to kill her. Who wouldn't want to follow a lead?

And I was working for the attempted murderer.

***

Wispy clouds hung over rooftops. Rain pounded the windshield of the Audi as we made it back to the Green Hills area. The juice bar was across the parking lot from the mall. When Hutch noted how the mess appeared to have cleared from the havoc of the day before, the knot in my stomach tightened.

Hutch stayed in the car as I hurried through the rain to the shop. Under the shelter of the roof, I could already make out Melinda's pale blonde hair through the windows. She had it pulled into a high ponytail again. Having noticed me, she waved, a warm smile accompanying her welcome.

"Hope you don't mind, I already ordered for myself," she said, gesturing to the tall plastic cup filled with a green beverage on the table. Next to it was her phone, the screen lit up and displaying a scenic view of the ocean.

"No worries," I smiled, glad to find she was alone.

Ordering a berry drink, I handed the cashier the dollar bills Hutch had earlier provided. Wringing my hands, I calmed my nerves, trusting a fitting opportunity to talk about her parents would present itself in due course.

"I hate to say it, but I can't stay long," Melinda admitted with a sheepish grin as soon as I took the seat across from her. "I think the patrol car may have followed me here."

My eyes widened at Melinda's words. She caught my uneasy expression, adding in a hurry, "Ever since the incident, they've been stationed outside our house."

"I thought they blamed the explosion on faulty wiring."

Melinda's gaze carried weight. There was a glint of urgency in her eyes. "I know you aren't keen on talking about that night, but—" she danced the straw in her drink, "did you happen to see anyone lurking near my car? Did you see anyone suspicious?"

I shook my head slowly. "I didn't." And it was the truth. Although I knew Hutch was guilty of preparing the explosive, I had not seen him place it in her car.

The bell mounted above the door jingled. Sounds of passing cars flowed into the shop until the door fell shut again. Hutch stepped in, shrugging the rain from his sleeves.

Why had I thought he would idly sit and wait for me in the car? Of course he would want to keep a close eye on me, and I couldn't blame him. Not a single day had dawned without conflict of some sort. Not since the day I met him. Perhaps it was for the best that I never mentioned my recurring dreams of late-night hunting.

I shuddered upon remembering my latest dream, for this time the victim's terrified face was more vivid than any of my prior nightmares. What made it worse was I clearly remembered ripping into the man's chest, my nails bursting with torn skin. It had been one of the missing persons from the news.

"I just don't understand," Melinda went on, a distraction from my dark thoughts. "Everyone refuses to believe me when I tell them someone has it out for me. You'd think the firemen would've found proof of some sort."

"And if it was all a freak accident, why are cops watching your house — or following you for that matter?" I asked, keeping tabs on Hutch from the corner of my eye. He was examining the sliced fruit through the glass and questioning the girl who worked there. She obligingly gave him a sample of the mango, her smile widening as she giggled. I knew it was a forced laugh, because Hutch didn't tell jokes.

"That's just it, isn't it? Nothing adds up." It was evident Melinda was a nervous wreck. The cops refused to believe she'd seen the explosive in her vehicle, and neither could her brother take her seriously. As far as she knew, there was still someone who wanted her dead and she was to face the matter alone. I was impressed by how well she kept herself from a mental breakdown.

"I'm at such a loss," Melinda sighed, exposing the first signs of her undoing. Without her friendly smile she didn't look seventeen. She was aged, one who ate little and slept even less. "No one will listen to me and you're the only one who could testify as witness to the bomb."

Finding an opening, I asked, "What do your parents think?"

"Grandparents. And they're no help." She tapped her phone, lighting the screen. "They keep telling me to leave it to the cops, but not even they have been much help. They're either covering up the truth, goodness knows why, or they absolutely suck at their jobs."

"Where are your parents?" I asked lightly. Upon receiving a strange look from Melinda, I feared I had pressed too hard too soon.

"My mom passed away and Dad up and left afterwards."

74

"I hate to hear it," I told her, sympathy etched in my face. I was surprised how much I truly meant it.

"Yeah, Mom got sick. As soon as she passed, Dad told us his job was relocating him. He said he didn't want to drag us from our home and friends, and thought it best we stayed with our grandparents."

"But you don't believe him," I said slowly, hearing the doubt in her voice.

"I don't think he could bear to stay here without Mom." Using her sleeve, she wiped at the smudges on her phone. "Sometimes the memories of the good old days suffocate me, too."

"Does he ever come to visit?" Despite my tentativeness, I still received a wary glance from Melinda, her coral eyes untrusting.

She gave me an insecure smile. "What's with all the questions about my family?"

I could tell she was growing suspicious of me, and I couldn't blame her. Someone had tried to blow her up over a week ago. She would be awfully foolish to be so trusting.

Fumbling, I made something up. "My family is the dysfunctional type, so I know all too well what it's like to be disappointed."

"Dysfunctional how?" Melinda asked, putting me on the spot. She leaned in, dropping her chin into the palm of her hand.

I gnawed my lower lip. "Divorced parents. My brother and I tried to get them back together once."

Wrinkling her nose, a look of compassion crossed her face. "How did that go?"

"Not too well," I said.

Melinda checked her phone again and sighed. "I'm sorry I can't stay longer. When I told you to meet me here, I'd completely forgotten about tonight's service."

"Service?" My brow puckered in bewilderment.

"Yeah." She took another sip of her juice. "Thanksgiving service." When I still showed no sign of understanding, she added, "We attend the church just down the road from here."

"Right."

Melinda watched me intently. "Would you like to join us?"

"Thanks, but I wouldn't want to impose on a family event." I cursed myself the moment the words left my lips. I shouldn't have been so quick to decline.

Shrugging, Melinda finished her drink, tossing it into the trash behind her. "You wouldn't be imposing, but it really isn't anything mind boggling. We don't stay longer than six o'clock. Meemee has medications and my little brother, Max, can't behave that long." She smirked, standing as her keys clinking in her hand. "Have you got any plans for tomorrow?"

"Tomorrow?" I repeated dumbly.

"Thanksgiving."

"Oh, yeah. No, actually. Like I said. Dysfunctional family."

"You should join us." Before I had time to either accept or decline her invitation, she continued, "I'll go ahead and text you our address. We eat around five, so feel free to come by. It's the least we can do for you."

"Sure." I smiled.

"Bring your brother if you want."

We exchanged our goodbyes and the jingling bell above the door announced her departure.

Hutch was seated in the opposite corner of the shop. With my drink in hand, I sat in the booth across from him.

"Anything?" he asked.

"Nothing from her yet," I said, "but I have a plan."

Hutch put his phone away, giving me his full attention.

"They will be out of the house until six tonight." I ran my damp palms up and down the legs of my jeans. I was nervous. "If we make it past the patrol car, we can snoop around their house for something on this Eric Allen."

Chapter Twelve

"It's the perfect opportunity!" I burst out as soon as Hutch slammed the door behind me. Setting what was left of the juice on the dining room table, I turned to watch him arm the security system, as he never failed to do. "We can't just sit around and keep waiting for chances to talk to them. It could take days to find anything out. And we only have three left."

The reality of my words hit home. Hutch stopped on his way to the kitchen. Scratching a spot on his forehead with his thumb, he braced the corner wall with his other hand.

"Aren't you burning to do something?" I pressed.

"There's too much to consider," Hutch finally said. I was relieved he hadn't shut me down with another firm *no*.

"Sure." I nodded. "We can come up with a thorough plan."

"Not only is there a patrol watching the house, but we have to take into account that the Allens are likely to have a home security system."

I nodded again, slower this time.

"And then we must decide if we are to stage it as a simple break-in."

"Can't we just slip in and out?" I asked, feeling naïve.

"Sure, if Melinda provided you with a spare key."

I did not appreciate Hutch's sarcasm, yet I was reluctant to admit how I had failed to grasp the obstacles in our way.

Shooting him a withering look, I crossed my arms. "Can't you pick their locks or something?"

"Unfortunately my skills are limited to assassinating the Forgotten," he said dryly. "The art of picking locks was somehow lost in my training."

Releasing a sound of irrefutable annoyance, I dropped into one of the chairs, my sure hopes of finding clues on Eric Allen's whereabouts disintegrating. Without Hutch on board, there was nothing left to consider. I had no idea how to skip past a patrol car, locked doors and a home security all on my own.

Neither of us moved for a full minute, nor did we utter a word to shatter the fragile silence between us. I was wondering how I could possibly get Mike to talk about his father when Hutch finally spoke up.

"I can make a call and get the information we need."

I looked up from the floor, hope caught in my chest.

Hutch was already dialing a number. He pressed the phone to his ear. "We'll see how feasible this plan of yours really is."

***

This *ingenious* plan of mine proved more and more daunting when I reiterated the main points quietly to myself. As Hutch put the Audi into park two blocks from the house, my nerves kicked into high gear, bringing tremors to my limbs.

At half past four, the sun had already begun its descent, leaving us to scamper through shadows of back yards until we made it to the Allens' home.

The house had a blocky structure. Maintained as it was, I noticed it to be much smaller compared to its neighboring homes. This was one of those richy-rich neighborhoods, after all. Every lawn was kept in pristine condition; every luxury vehicle parked in driveways was merely another way to attest hefty pockets. As impressive as these homes and cars were, there was something modest about our target residence.

Peering around the front, Hutch spied the cruiser sitting out front as expected. There were two officers. From where I stood, I could see the driver was reading from a tablet, the glow illuminating his dark features. Next to him, the other officer had his seat reclined, eyes shut.

Turning back to face me, Hutch motioned for us to move to the carport at the back of the house. We played a mime game, waving pre-discussed signals, our voices mute.

As soon as we came to a basement window located half a foot from the ground, Hutch removed the backpack from my shoulders. Somehow the plastic latch on the right arm had managed to wound itself into my braid. I gasped sharply as Hutch unknowingly attempted to tear a good chunk of hair from my head. Quickly catching sight of the issue, he gingerly unwound my dark strands from the plastic, but the damage had already been done. The messy braid I'd struggled with earlier that morning was now downright chaotic. Loose strands hung in front of my face, forcing me to tuck them behind my ears.

Whatever. I'd have to make do for now.

I accepted the lavender gloves he passed to me, and reclaimed the bag after he retrieved the crowbar.

Hutch signaled for me to keep watch while he worked. I prayed the information he'd attained an hour or so before was accurate and the windows were not armed.

Inching around the side of the house, the muscles of my torso tightened involuntarily. I half-anticipated a deafening screech of the alarm to rack the passive neighborhood into distress. Instead, I was met with another inconvenience: scrutinizing the cop car parked near the end of the driveway, I discovered only one officer in the vehicle.

Snoozing cop was no longer snoozing.

Heart pounding in my ears, my gaze darted around the slope of the front lawn. I stepped closer to the corner for a better view. That was then I noticed the officer disappearing around the opposite side of the house.

He would have *to make rounds this very moment.*

Just before I managed to skirt the corner back to Hutch, I heard a loud thump. It sounded like a sledgehammer pulverizing a wooden frame. The scouting officer must've heard it too.

As I returned to the scene, Hutch glanced up, studying the horrified expression on my face.

All muted hand gestures he'd shown me previous to our excursion vanished from my memory in a wild panic. Dumbly, I propelled a sequence of movements, desperate to bring to his attention the advancing police officer. Any moment now, he could reach us from the other side of the house. My anxious breathing grew rapid. Sweat beaded my forehead, despite the cool autumn air. Hutch reached out, gripping my shoulders in an attempt to calm my frantic behavior. We were crouched before the window — now successfully open. Silently, I pleaded with my eyes that he understood my intentions.

In the brief moment of stillness, my brain decided to gear back into motion. I lifted my quivering hand, offering the appropriate signal, and forcing calm bouts of breaths through my nose.

An audible cough in the distance startled us. Without further hesitation, Hutch urged me through the window.

My body responded before my mind had time to react. As soon as my feet slammed onto a counter top inside, I made room for Hutch, who slipped in effortlessly behind me. The sound of scuffling feet on brick grew closer. The officer was on the back patio. All he had to do was descend the few steps down to the carport in order to get a clear view of the window.

Once Hutch made it inside, I tugged at the panel with little result. I could tell the window was rarely used, if ever at all, by the way it refused to slide into place.

The officer was almost in range now. He walked slowly, as though he were a sightseeing tourist in a foreign land. Clenching my jaw in despair, I could only hope his attention was stolen by the large hill and trees consuming the backyard.

The warmth of a body hugged me to the wall, sending a surprised jolt through me. It was an odd angle, from the counter to the window, but with Hutch's hands next to mine, the panel fell reluctantly back into the frame.

Gathering our wits, we skipped from the counter and out of what I noted to be a bathroom. Hutch made it out first, whipping around the corner of the doorway and halting just on the other side, his back pressed against the wall. I stopped, too, only to peer back at the two windows in the room. We'd entered the one on the left; the cop's shiny black shoes appeared in the one on the right.

Those can't be comfortable to run in.

As soon as he made it down the brick steps, he became visible up to the hip.

"Hayden," Hutch whispered. The sound was cautionary.

The palm of my hand blindly nudged his torso, silencing him. If the cop detected the blistered paint and shredded wood from where the crowbar was forced into the ledge, we were done for. This adventure would be as good as over and all that awaited us would be a prison cell. Perhaps worse, considering Randolph's wrath. I didn't know the man well, but my instincts told me he was the type that enjoyed the sufferings of others.

The officer disappeared in the blind spot between windows. I waited with halted breath to see him reappear.

"Hayden," Hutch said a second time, only now his voice was strained. His fingers curled around my outstretched hand, still pressing his chest.

"What?" I shot him a quick glance, but caught something off in his expression. He'd lost all his usual intensity. His eyes were squinted, making him appear vulnerable. I couldn't place what had instigated the change in him until he covered the lower half of his face with his free hand.

"Don't do it," I said quietly. I could tell his urge to sneeze was growing into something uncontainable.

Desperately glimpsing back at the window, the officer had finally made his appearance. To my dismay, however, he wasn't moving. He stood stock still, feet facing the driveway.

"Can't you just...shake it off?" I whispered.

Hutch shook his head.

"Why not?" A little dust couldn't be torturing him this much.

Eyes red and unblinking, he stared dead ahead of him. "There's a cat somewhere."

"A *cat?*"

Hutch was incapable of providing a cohesive answer. His breathing grew shallow. His eyes darted to meet mine, as if apologizing in advance for the destruction he was about to rain upon us.

Gritting my teeth, I refused to let ourselves get caught, because of Hutch's unexpected allergies. Hastily, I seized the tail of his shirt, wrenching it over his nose. The pale skin of his abdomen was suddenly exposed in the dimly lit room, but there was no time to dwell upon his athletic build.

The officer was still standing just beyond the window. I had no idea what he was doing. Pushing my hearing as far as my senses allowed, I could just make out the rasp of a lighter. He was struggling to ignite it, for he stroked it several times until the flame caught.

A gentle breeze carried a grey cloud of smoke across the carport. The officer pocketed the lighter and walked on.

My lungs filled with air. Adrenaline pumped through me like a wild drum.

"You okay?" I asked Hutch the moment the coast was clear.

He coughed in response.

Amplifying all of my senses, I searched for sounds or smells that could serve as a caution to our task at hand.

There was, in fact, a cat somewhere. Now that I was no longer under the risk of getting caught, I was able to determine its distinct odor and even its proximity.

Other than the cat, the premises of the house were undisturbed.

"What's the time?" I asked.

Hutch showed me his watch. Ten to five. We still had at least fifty minutes before it was time to sneak back through the window.

The room in which we stood proved to be a family room. An L shaped sofa took up the far corner. Bookshelves lined the opposite wall next to a mounted television. My guess was the owners had the basement renovated to suit grandchildren, who happened to move in without forewarning.

A single flight of steps to our left led up to the main floor. It was wide enough to accommodate a stair lift on the wall.

Hutch climbed the steps carefully, his shirttail still held over his nose like a mask. I followed him up until we made it to the den.

Bingo.

The room served as part office, part den. Across the room was a brick fireplace, crowded by two leather armchairs. A curio cabinet displaying assorted porcelain ornaments stood against the wall between the door to the kitchen and an archway to the hall. Large windows and a sliding door leading to the patio took up the wall on the other side.

I located the cat immediately. It was lying in a patch of sunlight on the rug. Upon our entrance, it looked up at us lazily before resuming its relaxed position once more.

Hutch grumbled something impolite about the cat, but I ignored him, my attention focused solely on the computer desk pushed up to the wall nearest us. It was drowning in paperwork. There were well-worn legal pads covered in scribbles, half-opened envelopes, medical bills, utility bills, and who knew what else. It was practically a gold mine.

The silence was broken when Hutch sneezed, the sound muffled by his shirt, but loud enough to disturb the cat. Annoyed, the feline climbed to its feet and skulked away.

"Bless you," I said, still gazing at the mess of papers. There was no reason to worry about anyone hearing us now. "I need your phone."

"Why?" Hutch's voice was hoarse. He sneezed again, grunting immediately afterwards.

"Because I need to update my Twitter feed," I retorted, annoyed he was stopping to question me at such a critical time.

Grimacing, Hutch didn't argue. "You look through those," he motioned to the mail. "I'll search the rooms. Presumably where that ball of death is not present."

Left to myself, I sank into the leather computer chair and began sorting through the papers. Using Hutch's phone, I took snapshots of any return addresses that seemed to be possible leads. I kept my ears alert for any sounds of approaching vehicles or footsteps. Hutch sneezed upstairs a few more times, but other than that, all was quiet.

Not twenty minutes had gone by when I heard a fifth car in the streets approach the house. I paused in my work, expecting it to drive by as all the others had, but this one grew closer. It came to a stop, the engine shutting off. Doors opened and closed while voices filled the empty void of silence.

Darting to my feet, Hutch met me in the doorway of the hall.

"They're coming through the basement," he said.

My heart sank in my chest. The basement was our only way out without setting off an alarm.

Chapter Thirteen

A triple-noted melody resonated throughout the house, signaling an open door.

"Come on." Hutch took wide strides to the kitchen. It was outdated with wooden cupboards that had seen a great many years. A counter at the far side came up short, leaving a four-by-twelve space open behind it. Cat toys and a litter box besieged the area. A pair of bi-fold doors stained a chestnut brown stood open on the right, exposing a small place fit to contain the stackable washer and dryer. My eyes darted to the side door next to it. An exit.

Hutch's gloved hand swatted mine from the handle. "Are you insane?" he hissed, his other palm placed firmly against the door to ensure it remained shut. "Do you *want* to alert them?"

The argument of two female voices drifted up from the family room.

"They've already deactivated the alarm," I whispered back.

"The system is set to alert the homeowners of any opened doors." He zipped the crowbar into the bag still strapped to my shoulders, and took the phone from my possession. Nodding to the window beside the door, "We'll have to go through there."

It should not have come as a surprise when the window got stuck half a foot from the ledge.

Forced to give up first, Hutch pulled away to cover up a sneeze. With all my efforts thrown into driving the window further open, I ignored the cat pressing its body against my ankles.

85

The hum of the stair lift brought the voices closer. My fingers were near bleeding, but I couldn't give up.

"Get out of here," Hutch shooed at the cat. "Hayden, we've got to move."

"I've almost got it," I lied, breathless.

The cat hissed at Hutch, who swore under his breath in return. He wrapped an arm around my crouched form, hoisting me to my feet.

I was close to asking where he thought we could possibly hide in such little time. Melinda and her grandmother were about to appear at the top of the steps.

Hutch slid the backpack from my shoulders, and kicked it behind the counter out of immediate sight.

"It's humiliating, Meemee," Melinda said, her heels thumping onto the polished floors of the den. "Why can't we just drop the whole thing in public? People already think I'm desperate for attention."

"Stop that, Melly, you're overreacting," replied a fragile voice. "Everyone cares about you. Of course they want to see how you are doing."

Sandwiched between Hutch and the stacked washer dryer, we took turns breathing, our chests having limited space to expand. Hutch writhed restlessly while the feline watched us with mock curiosity.

"They want in on the drama," Melinda corrected her grandmother. "Everyone's heard the rumors about me diving after that cop's gun."

"But it isn't true."

"Of course, it isn't. I'm guilty of telling my piece and nothing more. The only reason everyone decided to make a big deal about it, is because I happened to be talking loud enough for everyone to hear. But what else can you do when someone won't listen?"

Tension matured within Hutch, urgent and threatening to break loose. I crumpled the front of his shirt within my hands. He needed temporary distraction from his turmoil, and this was my best attempt to attract his attention.

Meemee sighed, the sound traveling weakly from the den. "They should know better. You don't have an aggressive bone in your body."

"And I also don't have time to keep talking about this." The thumps grew fainter as Melinda called out, "I'll help you up as soon as I get everything together."

"I'm in no rush," Meemee said, more to herself. An indistinct ticking roamed into the kitchen. "Ollie, what are you looking at?"

The cat did not break his gaze as he continued to stare at us.

Cupboards opened and closed, followed by the boisterous noise from the ice dispenser. Hutch groaned, his voice concealed by the clanking ice. My wide eyes held Hutch's watery gaze for a moment. I pressed a finger to my lips, while his contorted into a grimace. Barring his teeth, he lowered his head, and buried his face into the nape of my neck.

A sick feeling fluttered in my chest.

"Come here, Ollie," Meemee beckoned with a crinkling sound of plastic. "I have something for you."

Ollie rewarded the elderly woman with a moment's consideration, but instead of taking her up on the offer, he lifted a paw and began to clean his face.

"What's the matter with you?" The ticking stopped on the other side of the bi-fold door.

A wheelchair could not make it down the single step to the cat's area. We were momentarily safe.

The warmth of Hutch's skin held me locked me in a half-dazed state. His throat was mere inches away, close enough I could taste his aroma on my lips. His blood raced just beyond the aged scar tissue on his skin, pulsing rapidly by the erratic thumping of his heart. He was incredibly vulnerable; it left me spellbound with raking desires. I pressed my lips into a solid line, fighting my fading consciousness. Heat gathered in the tips of my fingers. It was a wonder they did not burn holes into his shirt.

"I'll come get you, but you can't tell Melly," Meemee said quietly.

Her bones cracked as she unfolded herself from the chair. I gripped Hutch's shirt tighter, wishing we could become small enough to disappear altogether.

Hutch did not respond to my actions. His breath barely touched my neck, informing me he was scarcely breathing.

Melinda's footfalls saved us.

"What are you doing?" she demanded.

Meemee groaned like a child caught doing something inappropriate. "Ollie's acting strange. I was just trying to see if he's all right."

"I'll get him," Melinda told her. "You know you shouldn't be getting out of the chair. Remember what happened last year? Arthritis isn't a laughing matter."

As Meemee grumbled something incomprehensible, I dropped my hand to Hutch's waistline. He was temporarily weakened, which resigned him from the situation. If anything could be done to prevent us from being detected, I would have to find a way to pull it off.

Melinda continued to scold her grandmother. In the meantime, my gloved hand slipped into the front pocket of Hutch's jeans. There between our hard-pressed thighs, my fingertip brushed along the smooth plastic of the cell phone. Thankfully, the rubber grip of the gloves made it easier to retrieve.

"Wait a second." Melinda fell silent in response to her obnoxious ringtone. "Meemee, I have to take this. Don't worry about Ollie right now."

I disconnected the call before Melinda had time to answer, and checked to be sure Hutch's phone was on silent.

Melinda wheeled her grandmother away. As soon as I heard the electric hum of the second stair lift, I pushed us back into the open. Hutch kicked one of the miniature mouse toys, sending it flying into the den. Ollie, stimulated by the game, skipped after it.

After a great deal of joint effort, we managed to slide the window open just enough to heave ourselves through.

Only the miles separating us from the Allens' home could calm the frenzied thrum of our hearts. #

"Is that all of them?"

I skimmed through the images on the phone one last time. "That's all of them," I confirmed bitterly. "So, what do we have?" My untidy scrawl on the notepad was nothing short of depressing. I cleared my throat. "Three private practices, one law firm, and the rest were junk. To sum up: a big fat *nothing*."

The painful realization buried me like an avalanche. Everything had been done in vain. Evading the cop, nearly getting caught by Melinda and her grandmother, and Hutch's allergies — after all of this, we were back to square one.

Following the return to the condo, Hutch had searched every room for the medication to reverse his allergic reaction. Once he found it, the medicine had eventually knocked him out for the rest of the night.

"Not so fast," Hutch murmured, stroking his jawline thoughtfully with the pad of his thumb.

Waiting patiently for him to verbalize his thoughts, my eyes wandered across his face as though I were trying to glimpse into his mind.

It was evident a full night's rest had served him well. His skin was no longer splotchy, eyes were clear and lit with awareness. Although he did not possess the unforgettably good looks as Mike Allen, it was his iron intensity that somehow made him...

Focus.

Hutch switched tabs back to the law firm's website. The words *Cornerstone Alliance* were highlighted in bold above a silhouetted logo. With another click of the mouse, he enlarged the logo image of a heap of stones cracking beneath the strike of a gavel.

"Kinda corny," I noted, gnawing on the pen's clicker. "They should take the web designer to court for that."

Paying no heed to my lame attempt at a joke, Hutch reached for his coffee. Grumbling, he set the mug back down, having realized he'd already drained it. "I saw this in Mike's room. It was on one of his sweatshirts."

It took a moment for me to place his words. "Are you sure?"

When Hutch nodded, I dropped the pen onto the table next to the remains of my breakfast. "A sweatshirt? Since when do law firms put their logos on sweatshirts? It's not like they're musicians or something."

"For advertising purposes," said Hutch, raking a hand through his hair.

"Do you think Mike is an intern there?"

Hutch shook his head. "We'd have a record of it."

"He could've gotten it at a convention or something," I tried, but Hutch clearly wasn't convinced.

"There has to be more to this." Glancing at me, he said, "Allen is tied to this firm somehow. Otherwise Mike wouldn't keep some random hoodie lying around, let alone wear it."

"How can you be sure? He's a guy. Why would he care about what he's wearing, so long as it fits?"

"Because of the crowd he calls his friends. He's a jock, Hayden."

"And jocks have a dress code?"

"If they attend Lipscomb University they do." Hutch retrieved his phone and began typing out a message. "We have to figure out what Eric's connection is to this firm. If I can get Damian to access their files, we could possibly get a hit on his location, or at least a current residence."

"Easier said than done," I scoffed. "I'm no hacker, but this is a law firm. They keep confidential information on lockdown."

"We'll leave the hacking to the qualified hackers," Hutch said. "In the meantime, you can use this information as a reference when talking to Allen's kids."

"About that." I hesitated. "Yesterday I mentioned having a brother to Melinda, and she invited him to their Thanksgiving dinner."

Hutch frowned.

"You could play the role and tag along tonight," I suggested, feeling foolish for bringing it up. "The two of us would have a better chance at making progress."

"I don't think that's a good idea," he replied slowly.

Heat flushed my cheeks. I couldn't tell if his rejection made me feel inferior or simply angry. "Are you too good for the job?" I said, unable to suppress my indignation. Before he had time to respond, I snapped, "This is *your* job; *your* punishment. But I'll just do the dirty work for you. After all, I'm the Forgotten. Hopefully I don't end up slaughtering every last Allen tonight."

My eyes brimmed in embarrassment as I suddenly understood the true reason for my resentment. I wasn't angry with Hutch as much as I despised what I'd become. I was ashamed of the battle I faced each day as I refrained from doing unspeakable things. I hated that I could not trust myself and that I was lost without Hutch.

Chewing my inner cheek until I tasted blood on my tongue, I dared a glance at him, knowing full well there was no hiding the glimmer of tears in my eyes.

Hutch regarded me, his silent rage simmering. I bit back my apology, too proud to yield to his anger.

"I didn't think it a good idea," he began steadily, "because of the cat. But I appreciate your honest opinion of me. I didn't realize I was the diabolical tyrant." His words mocked sincerity, slapping me in the face.

I probably deserved that.

Hutch grabbed his cup for a refill, leaving me alone at the table.

Amidst my disgrace of bursting with wrongful accusations, I noticed Hutch's phone light up. Thinking it could be Melinda responding to an earlier text, I unlocked the screen and read the message.

My stomach plummeted.

"Hutch." I handed him the phone, the message seared into my memory.

Wanna know what happened to ur parents?
 Try murdered.
 Guess who's next.
 HTG

Chapter Fourteen

"*HTG*?" I said out loud. "Who's that? And what sort of morbid joke is this?"

"It's not a joke," Hutch said. With his blank expression, I could not tell how the message truly affected him. "He's trying to unnerve me."

"Who is?" I stared at the anonymous number over Hutch's shoulder.

"Stix."

"Stix? Why would he sign as *HTG*?"

Hutch shook his head impatiently. "Happy Thanksgiving."

Remembering Stix's untamed hatred toward Hutch, I could comprehend his revolting desire to vex Hutch somehow. He and Josue had, in fact, tried to harm me during our brief stay at Randolph's mansion, in hopes of getting at him. Only their plan backfired.

"But why send this text?" I asked, the moment the question bubbled in my mind.

"He blames me for his brother's death." The blank expression remained intact.

"Was he a Forgotten?"

"No."

"Did you kill him?"

Hutch hesitated. "No."

"Then what happened? What makes him think you're to blame?" I watched him closely.

Apprehension flashed across his face for a moment, until his expression hardened. "How did you get into the phone?" he asked.

"What do you mean?" I was taken aback by the sudden change of topic. "I unlocked it when I saw a text."

"Are you going to read all of my messages now?" He tucked the phone into the safety of his pocket. "I changed the code last night. How did you get in?"

I stared at him in disbelief. His accusatory tone was insulting. "I'm not blind," I snarled. "I see you get on that thing a million times. It's not hard to memorize the code." Just to annoy him, I added, "You're also pretty obsessive about arming the security system. I'm not sure who you're trying to keep out."

Hutch's eyes narrowed, posture stiffening. I was satisfied to see he understood my insinuation: he wasn't the only one who knew that code, as well.

"Did you ever think I might be trying to keep *you* inside?" he growled. Biting my lip, I realized it hadn't crossed my mind at all.

Even Hutch knew the scope of my unpredictable behaviors; of course he wouldn't leave me unsupervised. But I refused to let him know he'd struck a nerve. I mustered as much hatred as I could into my withering glare.

Without offering another word at my expense, Hutch collected his laptop and left, shutting himself in his bedroom. In response, I planted myself on the sofa, arm crossed like a defiant child.

As soon as my anger deflated, I was left with nothing but concern. A fear I'd pushed aside all week resurfaced at long last. Though I wanted to deny having anything to do with the murders and disappearances I'd seen on the news, I couldn't help but wonder if instead of falling asleep each night, I really blacked out. My dreams had grown incredibly realistic of late. Was I slowly becoming the monster I fought so hard against?

Strains of Hutch's muffled voice penetrated through the walls, slicing into my dark musings.

"You don't know where he is?" After a moment, Hutch cursed under his breath. "All the more reason to hate me." Drawers thumped inside the bedroom as I approached the door. "I already talked to Damian about it. He'll see what he can do. Could you at least ask about the message for me?" There was a grunt. "Yeah, I know what I was told." I leaned closer to the door, longing to hear the other side of the conversation. "Forget it, Red."

When Hutch headed for the weight room, I was clearing our mess from breakfast. He didn't waste a single glance in my direction, and I gave him no reason to do so.

***

The course of the day was easily measured by the fading of light as afternoon shadows extended across the floor. When my thoughts began to suffocate me, I huddled on the sofa, skipping through channels.

After failing to entertain myself with movies and television shows, I thought it time I stopped avoiding Hutch altogether.

Treading lightly to the weight room, I found him sitting on the floor, clad in sweats and a light hoodie, his back against the wall. He was watching a video on his phone, absently combing the end of a screwdriver through his hair. A black toolbox lay open beside him.

I cleared my throat. Hutch's head snapped up, catching my reflection in the mirror.

"I'm trying to fix the machine," he muttered, motioning to the multipurpose piece of equipment in the corner. It had a loose wire, causing the entire left side to sag.

Hutch tossed the screwdriver back into the box with the other tools. My heart wavered in my chest, my brain yelling at me to return to the melodramatic show I'd been watching.

"I'm sorry about earlier," I said. There was no use prolonging the conversation by beating around the bush.

"Which part?" Hutch climbed to his feet, examining the weights and broken wire of the machine.

Sighing nervously, I sought the shaggy carpet for a boost of valor. "You're not a diabolical tyrant. I shouldn't have jumped to conclusions when you said it wouldn't be a good idea to join for dinner tonight." I wrung my hands, wishing for nothing more than to dart from the room.

Hutch leveled himself, pausing for a moment before facing me. He rested his shoulder against the inner door frame, and I was awarded his undivided attention.

I kind of preferred it when he pretended I was nothing more than wall art.

"I hate apologies," I laughed. It was an awkward laugh, and I cringed at the forced sound of it. "Not that I would remember. But I like to think I did the right thing — even if it made me feel weak and exposed." I couldn't believe I was still talking. I willed myself to shut up, but the humiliated part of me needed to repair the damage.

"It would suck to find out I'm a narcissistic person." I tried to say this casually, but the unexpected reality of my words stung like salt in the wound. I remembered the smug feeling in my flashback when I'd tried on the dress — right before the fight broke out.

My throat tightened. Hutch still said nothing, giving my gloomy thoughts the chance to reel out of control.

"But what if I am?" I blurted out. "What if everything that happened to me is my fault somehow? What if I'm nothing more than a worthless diva?"

Hutch's silence was overbearing by now. I had to purse my lips in order to keep from embarrassing myself further. The tip of my foot tapped an inconsistent rhythm as I waited for him to say something. Just when I was about to give up and leave, he said, "So?"

"So?" That was all he had to say? My life was in shambles and all he had to offer was that one syllable?

"So what if you were narcissistic?" He shrugged. "Wouldn't this be your opportunity to change?"

I considered this, surveying him thoughtfully. Although his stance was relaxed, his eyes betrayed his strive for nonchalance. They read my expression, exploring the frame of my face and everything within. He skimmed past my lips before blinking, his gaze faltering.

When Josue let his eyes wander across me, I always felt the desperate need to wash myself. He left me feeling gross and violated.

This was different. Hutch's analysis of me made me self-aware. I could hear my heart thumping in my chest, and... familiar sensations stirred to life.

The warning of another flashback tingled in my brain.

My knees turned fluid when the pain struck. The room vanished into a series of flickers.

A distorted scene played out among the intruding juts of emotions.

"You're not going back there," the boy said. It was Scottie Dunkin from senior year. The flashes of memories bombarding the scene reminded me of our growing relationship, one that went beyond friendship. *"It's not safe. And you've already got so much going for you. Just think about your scholarship! And think about Jo, and...and your other friends. Think about us! Spending time with these crooks will only crush your future."*

"Just because you don't like them doesn't mean they're crooks." I didn't want to have this conversation on my front lawn. The risk of Mom or James overhearing us was too great.

"No one trusts them!"

"Only because no one cares to get to know them!"

"You don't think anyone has tried?" Scottie shook his head.

He took a step forward, and I took a responsive step away as though we were two magnets with our twin poles facing each other.

"They don't let anyone near them," he said.

"I guess that makes me special," I spat.

I didn't have to listen to Scottie's ignorant opinion on the matter, so I took my leave.

"If you go back there," Scottie called after me, "we can't be together anymore." His voice broke on the last word.

"An ultimatum?" I gave a patronizing laugh. "I didn't think you had it in you, Scottie."

Without another word, I crossed the lawn back to the house, his voice chasing me through the dimming light outside.

"Hayden."

My eyes fluttered open, the world doing laps around me. I settled on Hutch's sepia irises until I was stable enough to comprehend we had moved from the door. He was kneeling before me, hands cupping my elbows to keep me from falling from the bench.

"Are you back?" he asked. A shadow of a smile twitched at the corners of his lips.

His reaction did not make sense until I registered the ache in my fingers. Bashfully, I unclenched my hands from his steady shoulders, muttering an apology.

"What did you remember?" All earnestness returned to his face when he asked this.

Replaying what I'd seen in the flashback, I recalled old feelings I'd experienced for Scottie Dunkin. It began with a friendly awareness, ultimately leading to attraction. My fascination for him didn't last very long. I'd grown to resent him as soon as I began to sense his control over me. He despised my new group of acquaintances.

My strained attempt to remember anything after that day was futile. I kept coming up blank. Did Scottie really leave me?

"What happened?" Hutch asked, disrupting my train of thought.

"I'm not even sure," I said. "I think I could use a Tylenol, though. What time is it?"

When Hutch told me, I staged a groan, claiming I had to get ready for dinner. He made no attempt to stop me.

The flashback filled me with shame and remorse. Scottie's broken voice followed me into the bathroom, haunting my selfish decision to abandon him. And for what? A group of people I longed to call my friends? A group of people I could not even remember? My mind took me back to a previous flashback, and with a shudder I realized Scottie and I hadn't been arguing about a group of ordinary people, after all. Scottie wasn't trying to control me or tell me what to do. He was only trying to protect me from the handful of Forgotten living in the cramped double-wide. He knew something wasn't right with them.

A loud rap sounded on the bathroom door just as I was touching up the mascara on my lashes. Fog still clung to the edges of the mirror from my shower, but I had wiped most of it away in my busyness to make myself decent for Thanksgiving with the Allens.

"Come in," I called, examining my work with care.

The door swung open, revealing Hutch in the doorway. His hair was combed to the side, which was the first shock. I hadn't thought it possible, being so accustomed to its unkempt state. The second surprise was his ensemble. The dark khakis harmonized well with the midnight blue of his fleece sweater. The material tugged across his shoulders, emphasizing his toned chest. I even caught a waft of aftershave in the air between us.

"It's time to go," he said, looking at his watch for effect.

"You're dressed nicely," I noted, adding, "for someone who's spending the evening in the car."

"You made a point earlier," he said, even if reluctantly. I turned from the mirror to peer at him. "Someone's got to make sure you don't go off on a killing spree."

Shooting him a scornful look, I pushed passed him out of the bathroom to gather my coat and shoes.

Although I refused to talk to him after his inconsiderately harsh words, I was still relieved he had changed his mind about coming to the dinner. Not only would he pose helpful in our time-crunch to save this family, but he would also keep them safe, should I black out again.

Chapter Fifteen

I t was unusually warm for the middle of fall. The late afternoon sun painted the streets with an orange hue. Although the A/C hummed inconspicuously in the Audi, my new trench coat prevented me from experiencing its coolness.

Heat crept up my neck and by the time we were headed down West End, my stomach was churning from the overwhelming warmth.

"What are you going to do about the cat?" I asked, removing the coat and tossing it to the back seat. Cool air danced along the exposed skin of my shoulders, the relieving effect almost immediate. Sickness still plagued my stomach, but I guessed it to have more to do with skipping lunch.

Adjusting the moss-colored blouse around my front, I hoped the retailer at the mall hadn't been lying when she said it complimented my eyes. That would mean I was gullible when flattered. Not an admirable trait.

"I took something for it," Hutch said curtly as he weaved his way through light traffic.

"Didn't that something knock you out last night?" I picked a bit of lint from my leggings.

"No."

"I recall you sleeping the afternoon away." Hutch ignored me. "If you fall asleep on the job, it won't help your reputation."

It was meant as a joke, but Hutch did not so much as crack a smile. Perhaps his nerves were as shot as mine. The growing severity of the situation weighed on us both. We had less than forty-eight hours to find out where

Eric Allen was residing.

"Have you heard back from Damian yet?"

"No."

"Not even an update? Was he able to access the firm's records?"

"I don't know."

"You don't know, or you don't want to tell me?"

Hutch's irritable grunt led me to assume it was the former.

We passed a statue of a horse and its foal upon entering the general neighborhood. From there it did not take us long to reach our destination. A different cruiser sat near the driveway. Hutch parked behind it and we both clambered out of the vehicle.

"Keep your head down," he murmured.

Right. I was still wanted for murder. The vision of blood caked on my hands and torn flesh burrowed beneath my fingernails flashed before my eyes. My stomach rolled again.

Fighting to keep a neutral expression in place, I followed Hutch up the driveway. I waited for the cops to spring from the car and call me to a halt, reading my rights as they knocked handcuffs around my wrists.

No such thing happened as we crossed the lawn.

I released the breath I hadn't realized I'd been holding as we made it to the front door and Hutch pressed the doorbell. We listened to it reverberate throughout the foyer, a steady rhythm of chimes. Moments passed before I sensed anyone approach.

An unfamiliar individual with a buzz cut answered the door. He was dressed casually in a burgundy shirt and pale jeans. His eyes jumped from Hutch, fixing on me next.

"Well, who are you?" he said, not so politely.

Hutch and I exchanged bemused glances. "Melinda invited us for dinner." My statement sounded more like a question.

Materializing at the sound of her name, Melinda whipped around the corner, her appearance bedraggled. "Brad, have you seen Max?" she asked, pushing strands of loose hair behind her ear. She straightened, having noticed us at the door. "Hayden! I'm so glad you could make it. We're just about to sit down for dinner." Her gaze shifted to Hutch.

"Melinda, this is my brother," I said quickly. "Erm, James."

"Pleased to meet you," Hutch said, his eyes locked on Brad.

"You are most welcome," Melinda beamed. "Brad, could you grab an extra plate for the table? Come on in. I'm just rounding up the wild turkey."

Presuming she was referring to the young boy peeking around the corner, I inclined my head in his direction. "That little beast?"

Melinda spun on her heels, catching sight of Max. The boy shrieked with delight and darted into the next room. Melinda stalked off, calling after him.

"You didn't have to change my name," said Hutch as soon as we were left to ourselves.

"I'm sorry I panicked," I snapped, following Melinda's footsteps.

By the time we made it to the dining room, everyone was already present. The elderly Mr. Allen was seated at the head of the table, his wife in her wheelchair beside him. Mike, I noticed, occupied the other end of the table. Next to him sat Brad and then little Max.

"Pops, Meemee, this is Hayden and her brother, James," Melinda announced. "Hayden is the one I told you about."

Needing no further explanation, Mr. Allen stood, extending a hand in our direction. I shook it first while his icy blue eyes studied me. His glare was piercing; I could've sworn he saw right through our deceit before we had the chance to open our mouths.

Meemee pivoted as far as she could in her chair. She beckoned me over, and I was prepared to shake her hand in greeting also, but was surprised by her strength when she pulled me into an awkward hug.

"You don't know the good you have done for this family." Her fragile voice splintered as she spoke the words into my ear. "May the Lord bless you and your family sevenfold."

With a polite smile, I straightened, unsure of how to respond. I was grateful when Mike saved me from the situation.

"Have a seat," he insisted, holding out a chair for me. It was conveniently the empty chair beside him, across from Brad.

Everyone returned to their places, Hutch taking the seat on my other side. There was not a single square inch of the table that remained unused. Aromatic dishes lined the center of the table in a clumsy order. I couldn't remember another time my mouth watered for food. I could already taste the moistness of the honey-glazed ham on my tongue. The steaming bacon-wrapped asparagus, sweet potato casserole, and buttery cornbread brought a rumble out of my stomach.

"Hayden," Mike chortled, offering his outstretched hand to me. Before I had time to perceive what was going on, Hutch kicked my chair, taking my other hand in his. That was when I saw everyone else doing the same, hands resting on the linen tablecloth.

"Pops, would you like to say grace?" Mike asked, his fingers now tenderly wrapped around my own. The difference between his gentleness and Hutch's solidity was night and day. The only similarity I found was the dampness of both palms — or maybe my own hands were sweating. It was difficult to say.

Mr. Allen closed his eyes as he led us into prayer, his voice raspy.

Glancing at the bowed heads around the table, I soon found Mike watching me, mouth twisted into a crooked grin. My cheeks flushed at being caught staring. I lowered my face in my attempt to listen to Mr. Allen's words.

"In Your holy nam—"

A crashing interrupted James. We both glanced up to find the stumbling shadow of our mother as she made her way to the table.

"There's nothing here for you," James told her.

"James," I said just above a whisper.

"No." He shook his head. "She can sit down with us when she's sober."

"We're all grieving," I said beseechingly. "Emily was almost a sister to me and a daughter to—"

"I said no." James stood. "If you want to eat with her, go ahead. But I'm not looking to add to my grief."

A second kick to my chair brought me back to the present. My eyes were bleary from the startling flashback.

Two in one day. Urgh. That was going to hurt worse in the morning.

I peeked over at Hutch to find him watching me with concern. I shrugged to let him know I was all right.

"Amen."

Hands scooped and groped at food without hesitation. I tried to keep up with passing along the dishes that came my way. All was a flurry of motions until we each settled on our loaded plates.

Mr. Allen cleared his throat, calling attention to himself. "Melinda told us about your noble deed," he said, directing his words to me. "We thank you for your quick actions. There's no telling where we would be without having Melly around." He touched Melinda's hand briefly and smiled at his granddaughter. Then his stern expression returned. "If I may ask," he went on, biting into the cornbread, "how did you know the car was going to explode?"

"Pops," Mike said sharply before I had time to respond. "We're not talking about this right now."

"I second that," Melinda agreed after downing her tea. "It's Thanksgiving. Let's just be thankful things turned out the way they did."

Mr. Allen's upper lip twitched with displeasure. I was suddenly beginning to feel his suspicions of Hutch and me spring to life.

"Very true," he said casually. "Tell me about yourself. What do you two do? Where do you live? I think we would all like to know a bit about our heroine and her family." He added the last bit in response to Mike's severe look.

Something told me Mr. Allen's misgivings were a greater deal than he was letting on.

"It's all right," said Hutch, catching Mike's glare aimed at his grandfather. "We live downtown."

"Downtown?" Mr. Allen was obviously glad Hutch was humoring him. And so was I for that matter. I did not like being under his penetrating scrutiny. "That's impressive. You have to be making a good buck to get a place there."

"Our father secured himself a good job." Hutch dipped his fork into the mashed potatoes on his plate. His coolness certainly had me fooled.

"Is that so? What does he do?"

"He's a lawyer for CA."

This caught Mr. Allen off guard. "CA? Cornerstone Alliance?"

"The one and only. You've heard of it?"

Mr. Allen nodded. "What's your father's name?"

"Caleb Wyer."

I had to check myself to be sure my own surprise was not visible. Hutch had obviously done his homework.

Sitting back in his seat, the elderly man regarded Hutch with fascination. I could only hope he did not look into the information further to find this Caleb didn't really have children with our names. "Are you following in his footsteps, son?"

"Unfortunately, law does not interest me the way it does my father," said Hutch. "Though he wishes otherwise."

"Of course," Mr. Allen sipped his drink. "All parents want the best for their children, but sometimes it will be done on different terms. What is it you are pursuing?"

"Sports."

A scoff distracted everyone from the ongoing conversation. Brad was reclined in his chair, staring at Hutch with an apathetic smirk. "It's not really pursuing when daddy funds your success."

"Not every parent decides to spend money rather than time when it comes to their children." Hutch's expression had changed from pleasant to sour within mere seconds. The hard look in his eyes made it clear who he was referring to.

Mike snorted into his casserole.

Thrusting his elbows onto the table, Brad leaned forward, pointing his fork at Hutch. "Just because you dress like an old psychotherapist who's about to croak doesn't mean you know anything about me," he snarled.

I bit back a laugh, because he had no idea how right he was. Every time Hutch opened his mouth, he sounded older for a guy his age. It was hard to believe he was barely much older than me.

My hand dropped to Hutch's knee under the table. With a gentle squeeze, I tried to remind him of our purpose for being there.

"Brad, come one, man," Mike interfered. He was still smirking.

Hutch cleared his throat, his rage walloping through his pulse. I wasn't sure if it was my hyperactive senses, but I could feel he was on the verge of going off the deep end.

"My apologies," he managed to say. "My talent for deduction is not as adept as my father's."

I rolled my eyes. There he went again, sounding like an old man.

"You'd be surprised," Mike laughed, punching his friend in the arm.

"Yeah!" Max piped in for the first time, thumping Brad's other arm enthusiastically. "You'd be surprised!"

"You don't even know what you're talking about." Brad tickled the little boy until his foot kicked Melinda in the side.

"I think that's enough for now," she called over the boy's shrieks of laughter.

The rest of the meal proceeded in agitation disguised as amusement. Max took the floor, boasting about his performance during service the evening before. At some point, Mike caught my attention, pointing out the soundless string of glares going around the table. Had the situation been less dire, I would've been entertained watching Mr. Allen glare at Melinda for sneaking shy glances at Hutch, who in turn proceeded in a silent battle of scowls with Brad for the role of the alpha male. Only Max and Meemee appeared oblivious to the underlying drama at the dinner table.

Mike cocked an eyebrow in my direction as if to confirm the awkwardness of family gatherings. I gave a small shrug in response. Due to my buried memories, I couldn't agree wholeheartedly, even though my most recent flashback had offered a taste of such events.

I found I was now eagerly waiting for dinner to be over. Having been wrapped up in my worries about tackling the darkness nestled within me, I hadn't stopped to consider Hutch and his ego posing a threat to our task at hand. A storm was surely brewing between him and Mike's friend. I hoped Hutch realized acting on impulse could very well put everyone's future in jeopardy.

Chapter Sixteen

"Don't trust them?"

Mike's voice was muffled and distant, but his words rang clear as day in my ears. I drummed my fingers against the ladder leading to the attic, impatiently waiting for the two men to appear with the boxed-up Christmas tree. Although it was evident my help was little needed, I still took Mike up on the request to assist him and his grandfather with the tree. We would've been done had Mr. Allen not chosen this moment to share his concerns with his eldest grandson.

"Does Meemee know about your paranoia?" Mike wanted to know. "Geez, that's why Mel can't get over the accident. You've been filling her head with lies."

"Your father agrees with my concerns," Mr. Allen said stoutly. My ears pricked at the reference to Eric Allen.

"And you think just because he agrees it makes more sense?" Mike laughed in disbelief. "I learned not to trust his judgement years ago. Hayden *saved* Mel's life. You'd have to be an idiot to think she had anything to do with what happened. Don't you think the cops would've called her in for questioning if it was at all a possibility?"

"Not if they couldn't find her." The insinuation behind Mr. Allen's words was unmistakable. He knew I was hiding something.

"You are out of your mind," Mike said between clenched teeth.

As much as I appreciated him sticking up for me, even I had to admit Mr. Allen was right to worry about his family.

The argument continued, and by then I'd heard enough. Mike was supposed to be taking me on a tour of the house while Hutch helped Melinda in the kitchen with the dishes. This tree-deal was Mr. Allen's excuse to warn his grandson about how untrustworthy Hutch and I were.

Sounds of giggling drifted up the stairs. Peering over the top step, I spotted Brad and Max making their way up.

A groan escaped me. With no wish to share Brad's company after his insufferable behavior at the dinner table, I slipped behind the ladder and turned the corner. I hoped Mike wouldn't be too sore with me for leaving my post.

In search of the bathroom to serve as a good reason for deserting him and his grandfather, I slipped through the nearest door. The moment I closed it behind me, I knew it wasn't the room I was looking for.

A lamp in the corner illuminated two unmade beds. Next to one was a handsome guitar along with a rumpled stack of loose leaf pages. The guitar was a cherry red, bearing not a speck of dust on its surface; a sure sign of frequent use.

Absently strumming three strings, I scooped up the pages with my other hand. They were chords and tabs for songs, all heavily scribbled by Mike, himself, I guessed. The lyrics were somber. My eyes narrowed as I scanned the others. Although I knew nothing about reading music, each song expressed melancholy at its finest.

The sound of the door startled me. Clutching the papers to my chest, I whirled around.

"Find anything interesting?" A lopsided grin etched into Mike's attractive features. I smiled in return, shrugging. His jubilant expression dropped a fraction. "I noticed you'd disappeared."

My face flushed, and I hated myself for it. "I was just... I had to find the bathroom." I winced at the ring of dishonesty in my voice.

To my surprise, Mike stepped closer. He looked as guilty as I felt. "So, it had nothing to do with you witnessing my grandfather's unhinged state of mind?" he suggested.

I shrugged again. "Only a little." When Mike sighed, I added, "He means well."

"I'm just sorry he has to be a moron about it." Motioning to the papers, he changed the subject. "Do you play?"

I laughed out loud. "That's a joke. You're asking someone who is clinically tone-deaf."

"I don't believe that."

Yeah, well you haven't heard me sing along to Christmas songs, I resisted the urge to say aloud. "What's all this about?" I inquired, thrusting the songs into his face.

"What's what about it? You're not into the genre?"

"More like I'm not into depression." I pointed to the first song. "Sounds like a nasty break up."

"Everyone relates in their own way," said Mike. He stared at his own scribbles across the page.

I watched as his eyes skimmed the words.

"How do you relate?" I prodded gently. The last thing I needed was for him to become suspicious of my snooping around his personal life.

Scratching the back of his head, he gave a nervous laugh. "Ah. Well, I started practicing this piece around the time my mom's health declined."

I opened my mouth to say something, but shut it abruptly. Waves of guilt hit me with rapid force. Learning his meaning of the words nearly broke my heart.

"Melinda told me about her."

"This is Brad's favorite." He held out one of the pages from the bottom of the stack. I wasn't ignorant to the fact he didn't want to dwell on the topic.

"Please don't tell me you serenade him." I laughed.

"He's our bassist and vocalist."

"I didn't realize you were in a band." My face radiated with admiration. "Is it serious?"

"You mean, have we made it out of the basement?" Mike seemed pleased to hear me giggle. "We've played at the Hardrock a few times."

I moved around him, having spotted the computer chair at the other end of the room. In it sat a small pile of clothes, reminding me of the sweatshirt

Hutch had found. If I located it, perhaps our conversation could lead to something fruitful. "What's it like having throngs of girls dying to meet you."

"You'd have to talk to Brad about that," Mike told me sheepishly.

"Brad's obnoxious." I looked up from the chair, regretting my words in haste. "I'm sorry, I didn't—"

Mike waved my apology away with his hand. "I don't know what his deal was at dinner. He can be a douche wad, but he usually saves it for people he's well-acquainted with."

"Why isn't he spending Thanksgiving with his family?" I asked, eying the articles of clothing in the chair again.

"His parents are on a cruise. The rest of his family lives up in Indiana."

"Well, then. I find it very considerate of you to invite him over." There was no sign of the sweatshirt Hutch had mentioned. I did my best to hide my disappointment. That meant I would have to find another way to bring up Eric's ties to the law firm.

"He knows he is always welcome here," Mike said.

Having been so lost in thought, I hadn't noticed him approaching from behind. When I turned to meet his gaze, my backside pressed against the lip of the desk to keep a casual distance between us.

"You know that you are always welcome here, too," he added.

One more step and Mike closed the space between us. My fingers gripped the edge of the table, but I did not break eye contact with him.

"And my brother?" My attempt to sound lighthearted failed at the unsteadiness of my breath.

Mike chuckled. "And, of course, your brother." The pad of his thumb brushed aside a loose strand of hair from my face. I held my breath, but he misinterpreted the sharp intake of air for something else. His eyes fluttered shut and he leaned in, head tilting.

Grounding my teeth, there was no stopping my focus from straying to the sound of his pounding heart. Morbid thoughts flashed across my mind, each fed by dark desires. My fingers dug into the underside of the desk, gathering small wood shavings beneath my nails.

If I did not breathe I was going to pass out; yet inhaling the tender scent of his flesh would only lead me to dangerous territories. I could not black out right now.

The bedroom door burst open, and the room suddenly felt overly-crowded.

Hutch observed the scene with an inscrutable expression on his face. Melinda stood next to him, little Max on her hip. The boy grimaced, moaning in disgust.

"We have to go," said Hutch, still glancing between Mike and me. I was just glad Mike had the mind to step back.

"Something wrong?" I asked, clearing my throat.

"Dad wants to see us." There was concern in the shape of Hutch's eyes. I could not fathom what had gone down while helping Melinda in the kitchen. Hopefully he did not blow our cover.

Within minutes, we were in the Audi, speeding along the curves of the road. We'd exchanged brief goodbyes with the Allens and Brad, who had been content with calling his farewell from the living room.

Streetlights lit the blacktop. Although it had grown dark, the temperature was still abnormally warm for the season. I rolled the window down, allowing the wind to carry away every last bit of sick craving that had held me hostage in the room with Mike.

"What's going on?" I asked, letting the window back up. "Did you find out about Eric?"

Whatever Hutch had learned worried him. I could tell by the way he set his jaw and held his shoulders. "I need to see Damian."

"This couldn't wait until later?"

"I need him to figure out where the texts are coming from." He pulled out his phone, dropping it into one of the cup holders between us.

Curiously, I reached out and grabbed it. "I thought we agreed it was Stix who sent the text." After unlocking the phone, I realized two more messages had been sent throughout the day, each one more cryptic than the last. The first read *2 scared 2 play?* The most recent one had been sent barely twenty minutes ago. *Time's running out.*

I stole a glimpse at Hutch. "Is he going to hurt someone?" I finally asked.

"That's what I need to see Damian about." He swore under his breath.

At the risk of upsetting Hutch further, I did not question how Damian could possibly know what was going on.

It did not take long for Hutch to pull up to a row of condominiums. His breathing faltered for a moment and I knew why. There was something wrong with the building before us. I could not pinpoint what made it seem so out of place until I compared it to the neighboring buildings.

This was the only condo without a single light glowing in the windows.

"Maybe he's not home," I tried. "Why don't you call him?"

"He's not picking up," Hutch told me. "I've tried him, I've tried Red. I even called Randolph to see if he knows anything, but no one's answering."

"What if he's with family? It *is* Thanksgiving."

Reaching behind my seat, Hutch retrieved a hard case with large letters spelling the word GLOCK on the top. Within was his semi-automatic along with its few attachments. Immediately, he began to assemble the parts quickly and proficiently.

"That's his car next to us," he told me, nodding at the red Prius to our right. "He hasn't gone anywhere."

"What are you doing?" I asked, as he secured a suppressor to the end of the barrel. "You're going to get yourself killed with that."

"Don't worry about me." He peered up, expression as solemn as the songs in Mike's room. "You stay here. I'll be back in a minute."

"That's a lie," I grumbled, but he'd already slammed the door shut after him, the gun half hidden in the shadows.

I watched with anticipation as he approached the doorstep. He was hesitating.

Straining my eyes, I could just make out the reason for his apprehension: there was nothing but a dark, gaping hole in the place of the door.

"I wouldn't go in if I were you," I whispered to the unhearing Hutch.

After a beat, Hutch disappeared into the darkness.

Once more, I trained my eyes on the doorway, wishing with all my might that I could see what was happening.

The phone vibrated on the console next to me. I jumped, snatching it up at once. A new message lit up the screen, causing my heart to sink.

U couldve saved him.

Chapter Seventeen

The smell of rot smothered like a tidal wave as soon as I stepped out of the Audi. Steeling myself, I pushed aside the dreadful reality of the situation. If I let myself think too much about it, I would lose my nerve to follow Hutch. I had to warn him.

As I grew closer to the veranda, I could almost taste the scent of blood draped across the air. It hung around me, warm and dewy, like the humidity of a long summer day in the south. My gut roared from a hunger that could not be satisfied. Vertigo ripped at my mind, bringing a totter to my steps. I lurched for the doorframe, desperate for something to help steady the spiraling world.

"Hutch." My whisper was hoarse, and went unanswered. I swallowed hard at the gathering saliva in my mouth. Either I was going to black out at the smell of blood, or be sick by it. A vision of Damian concealed behind a rack of women's lingerie at the mall alighted my short-term memory. Just picturing the possible state he was now in brought a tremble to my limbs. *"Hutch!"*

Through the darkness, I could make out the lumpy shape of a couch and an armchair just beyond the door. I fumbled with the phone until I located the flashlight app.

Despite the overwhelming odor of death, the living room appeared undisturbed.

Passing the staircase to the left, I found a light switch at the entrance to the kitchen. My hand reached for it, but froze at the sound of a slamming door. It came from the upper landing. Footsteps pounded on the floor above. Hutch must have found something.

Something shot out of the darkness of the kitchen, ensnaring my outstretched arm by the wrist. I opened my mouth to scream, but all I managed was a muffled sob. A palm pressed firmly against my lips. With everything happening so rapidly, it took me a moment to gather my bearings.

Hutch did not release his hold on me. One arm he looped around my front, the other hand kept me silent. I wondered fleetingly where he'd stashed his gun.

"Be quiet," he breathed, the side of his face pressed against my cheek.

Removing Hutch's hand from my mouth, I turned slowly.

Constriction. Fog. Anxiety.

Hunger.

I was sure he couldn't see my face, but for once I wished he could. He needed to know I was on the verge of breaking, my focus slipping. I couldn't fight the darkness this time.

The footsteps grew steadily closer, thumping down the steps.

Mumbling something in the dark, I clutched Hutch's shoulder as I leaned against the side of his arm. It was my last attempt at a warning.

The darkness swallowed my mind, forcing the scene before me to become warped and distant, as though I was watching it from someone else's eyes.

Hutch growled, trying to push my hand away, but I clung to him. A wicked smile splayed across my face at the satisfaction of feeling my nails dig into his skin, tearing through layers of clothing.

Without warning, my back slammed into the refrigerator, the handle burying into my spine. Snarling, I straightened, but Hutch had already disappeared — gone after the third in our party. What he didn't realize, was we were now alone in the condo. There was no need to strain my senses to confirm this, as they had locked into their highest level of competence. I gritted my teeth, smirking at the bursting energy pouring through my veins.

It was just him and me, and this time I was the hunter.

***

My lungs deflated in shock as awareness crashed into me like a freight train. Tears dampened my temples in response to the agony setting my body aflame. I ached all over, but the blistering pain in my forearm overshadowed all. I tried to move, but the weight straddling my hips was insistent on not budging. A hand clamped firmly on my chin made it clear that screaming was futile.

I opened my eyes and blinked several times against the pressing darkness. My focus finally settled on Hutch, hovering above me with a tapering blade tucked between his teeth. Blood dripped from the tip.

"What happened?" I asked the moment Hutch withdrew his hand from my face.

Convinced I had returned to my right mind, he stood, wiping the blade on his sleeve. "Pain stimulates the brain," he said, his voice detached. "I didn't have a choice."

There was no need to ask what he was talking about. The fire in my forearm spoke for itself. Hugging it to my abdomen, I felt wetness seep into the light material of my blouse.

"I attacked you," I said, the memory of my hand ripping into his sweater foggy in my mind. Standing up from the carpeted steps, I felt a twinge in my ribcage. My left knee was bruised, as though I'd landed hard on it.

"Did I hurt you?" I hated that the question sounded as intimate as it did. More so, I worried he'd have reason to kill me if I posed as a serious threat to him.

"No." He wavered. "Let's get to the car."

In the glow of a streetlight, I noticed a black stain on the torn shoulder of Hutch's fleece sweater, and suddenly remembered the stickiness of his blood on my fingertips.

Horrified, I glimpsed at my hand. Sure enough, there were signs of the damage I'd caused beneath the whites of my nails.

"You said I didn't hurt you," I blurted out as he opened the back of the Audi.

"Flesh wound," he said, almost jeeringly.

Reaching into the back, Hutch opened a first aid kit, and tossed a roll of gauze at me. "Wrap your arm."

I peered down at the slit on my forearm. It glistened with blood, but the bleeding had mostly stopped.

"What are you doing?" I asked, watching him remove his sweater and roll up the sleeves of his checkered button-down.

"Taking precautionary measures," he replied.

The method Hutch used to collect items from the med kit was done with certitude, a task completed many times before. After a rubber tourniquet was secured around his bicep, he disinfected the tender skin of his inner elbow.

"What's that?" I nodded at the injection he readied for use. I'd completely forgotten about assessing my own wound.

Hutch did not respond until he'd successfully administered the fusion. "It's anti-venom."

"For what?" I recoiled at the thought. "Did I... I didn't bite you?" Hutch's earlier explanation of being exposed to toxins whirled in my mind.

"Discharge of Forgotten venom is not limited to a bite," he informed me, releasing the tourniquet. "You're confusing your condition with folklore again."

I looked at my nails again, comprehension dawning on me. "So, if you hadn't given yourself that injection, you would've ended up in the same predicament as me? Because I scratched you?"

"Venom in the bloodstream is fatal. It won't turn you," Hutch said. He locked up the back of the Audi.

"Then the other day when you said I was *exposed to toxins*, what did you mean?"

"We'll talk about this later." Hutch opened the passenger door, and waited for me to get in. "I need you to stay here while I deal with this."

Swallowing the argument that rose to my lips, I did as Hutch told me. My questions could wait. Damian could not.

***

It was half past ten when we made it back downtown. Hutch had been adamant about staying while Randolph's cleaning crew, disguised as a moving company, removed evidence of the carnage upstairs and repaired the front door.

Although I did not know Damian, it felt wrong that he should've died at the expense of Stix's vile games. All to avenge his brother's death.

"So, what now?" I wondered as soon as we stepped over the threshold of the condo. It had been a long evening, but the nightmare of it all still hung over us like a dark shroud.

Hutch stuffed his frayed sweater into the garbage can, ignoring the fact that his shirt was in a similar, if not worse, condition. "We'll try to get some rest tonight," he said, still sounding detached as he had at Damian's. "In the morning we'll work out a plan on talking to the Allens."

This wasn't what I'd meant by my question, but his statement reminded me of my thoughts while waiting on the cleaning crew to complete their job.

"You were going to tell me how someone can become a Forgotten," I said.

Hutch had disappeared into the kitchen closet for a moment, reappearing with a half case of water. He began restocking the refrigerator, pretending not to have heard me.

"How does it happen?" I pressed, leaning my hips against the counter.

"I don't want to talk about this right now." He sighed, pausing in his work long enough to tell me this.

Frustration bubbled beneath my calm surface. "I understand it's been a difficult past few hours for you, and I'm sorry. Truly, I am. But I feel like I, too, am about to receive some devastating news… about my family. I'm just trying to prepare for it."

"What are you talking about?" Impatient. Angry.

"My *brother*, Hutch," I shot at him. "We were together when everything went down. I don't remember what happened. I don't know how we got separated, or if…" My voice trailed off, unable to state my fears of losing the one person left who genuinely cared about me.

Pulling myself together, I continued, "I have been contemplating the options, since you're neglecting to tell me anything specific. What if he was exposed to becoming a Forgotten, just like me? I need to know how it can happen. I need you to tell me."

"No." He didn't even bother to look at me when he said this. Instead, he made for the garbage can a second time to toss the plastic.

Whipping around the counter, I came up behind him, insults rising to my lips at his insensitive behavior. Without thinking, I laid my hand on his injured shoulder. My intention was to turn him around so we could discuss the matter face to face, though I regretted my actions at once. Hutch responded instinctively to my touch. I watched the flash of movements, but I was too shocked to fight when he curled his fingers around my neck. Gyrating, he pinned me against the closet door with a harsh thrust. My bones screamed in protest to the violent jerk, all still aching from the last time I'd blacked out.

"I'm sorry," I managed between gasps. My hands encircled his wrist gently; imploringly. The look of irrefutable loathing set deep within his expression somehow hurt more than the constriction of my windpipe. Tears blurred my vision, but I kept them in check.

Hutch's grip slackened on my throat. After searching his face long enough, I saw something alter in his gaze before he turned away and retreated to his room.

When alone, I sank slowly to the floor and wept unabashedly. I cried for Damian, and perhaps my own lost family. I cried for the Allens, as well as myself. I even cried for Hutch.

Chapter Eighteen

Athunderstorm moved in some time after midnight. I listened to the rain patter on the stone of the balcony while staring at the active television screen. The meteorologist said more thunderstorms were to be expected over the weekend, and urged all Black Friday shoppers to be extra careful on the roads.

I knew the warm weather was brewing something nasty in its wake.

Blinking the dryness from my eyes, I clung to the throw blanket enveloping me. Occasionally a flash of lightning lit up the room, followed by a deep rumble of thunder. I couldn't tell if I was calmed by the storm, or bothered by it. The frantic rain and claps of thunder stirred chaos in the world outside of the condo. It was a chaos I could relate to, seeing as something similar flourished within me.

There was no use trying to sleep. My mind was plagued with concerns regarding the events of the day. Who else could say they spent their Thanksgiving deceiving a decent family, witnessing a murder scene and getting strangled?

Heaving a sigh, I rolled to my back. In the bluish light of the television, I could make out the thin cut on my arm. It didn't look fresh anymore, but it didn't look healed, either. My fingers traced along the jagged scab, and I wondered why Hutch had restrained himself from simply getting rid of me. I was unpredictable. I was a threat. He had Randolph's cleaning crew summoned. What was one more body to dispose of?

The logical answer was he still needed me to save his own skin, and he was going to make sure we both succeeded or died trying. As honorable as it sounded, it did little to improve my thoughts on the matter. I didn't have anything to do with Randolph's business, so why should my performance affect my future?

A triple flash of lightning impaled the darkness. Mere seconds passed before thunder rolled, traveling from an eerily high clap to a deep boom. The windows shook in their frames. I held my breath until it passed, firmly deciding I did not like storms.

I was breathing normally again when a nearby *thump* sat me bolt upright on the sofa. Hutch stopped moving the moment he realized I was awake. As creepy as his skulking was, I wondered how I hadn't heard him leave his room. Perhaps he'd chosen the moment the thunder sounded, throwing off my senses.

We watched each other for a moment, measuring one another. I gave in first, too tired for a confrontation — too tired to decipher his strange actions. With a shrug, I turned to my side, drawing the blanket over me again as I lay down.

Hutch's unhurried footsteps proceeded until he was right at my head. I didn't move, not even when he sat down in the armchair adjacent to the sofa. The flickering commercials made his skin appear paler than usual as he scrutinized the rug.

"What are you doing?" I asked.

"Couldn't sleep."

"And you thought watching me would inspire you?"

For a moment, Hutch did not move, nor did he make any attempt to respond. I studied him, trying to understand the purpose of his visit.

"I'm sorry about what happened earlier," he said at last. "I had no intention of hurting you."

"I can hardly blame you for wanting to get even after I attacked you," I said after a pause. I knew if I accepted his apology, I would be admitting to the fact that he had, in fact, hurt me, and showing signs of weakness to him was the last thing on my mind.

Despite my flippancy, Hutch's despondent expression began to tug at my humanity. The last thing he needed was someone else who barely tolerated him.

"I'm sorry about Damian," I whispered. My eyes followed his movements as he shifted uneasily. "I was trying to warn you," I went on. "That's why I followed you inside. Stix had sent another message."

"I know," Hutch said, rubbing his eyes. "I saw it after I got off the phone with Randolph."

"What did he say about the whole thing?"

"He's not the least bit concerned."

"But one of his men was killed!" I exclaimed. I couldn't believe a man could be so cold and heartless. "One of his guys killed another. Doesn't that warrant a penalty of some sort?"

"Randolph would only worry himself over his guys going AWOL or an outsider putting a hit out on one of them," Hutch said. "He could care less about rivalries between the employees."

"Then why are you being punished for Stix's brother's death?"

"Randolph doesn't have a lot of rules," he said. "Don't abandon your crew is one of them." He stood, heading for the kitchen, and flipping on the lights. I knew him enough to know he wasn't going to say anything further on the topic.

Another round of thunder shook the windows as I kicked the blanket to the edge of the sofa and followed him. Perching myself on a bar stool, I watched Hutch busy himself with setting up the blender.

"Something weird happened at Damian's," I said, but then regretted my words. How was I supposed to tell him I'd been briefly overcome by the want to kill him?

Redirecting, I said, "I felt stronger. It was like my senses were in overdrive or something. Then I blacked out."

"Forgotten have maximized senses and capabilities," he said, sounding all professor-y again. "They aren't supernaturally strong. They just have greater access to senses and muscle contraction. I assume since you were about to have an episode, you were able to gain this access." He paused on his way back from the pantry with a bowl of fruit in his hands, but shook his head as if deciding against saying something.

"What's going to happen with Damian's family?" I asked. "Will they be notified about what happened?"

"Damian didn't have family," he said. "No one working for Randolph has family ties, unless they are all on payroll."

"Just like Red," I realized. "He said he moved here after he lost his family."

Hutch nodded, slicing a banana into thin cylinder shapes. "Randolph first hired him on the legitimate side of the business."

"And that would be?" I crossed my arms over the counter as a chill swept across my skin. The continuous pounding of the rain tempted me to return to the sofa for the throw blanket.

"Security service."

"More specifically?"

Hutch reached into the fridge next for the yogurt. "He sends his ruffians to protect celebrities, politicians and anyone who can afford his services."

"If the security service is the legitimate side of his business," I said, "then muling must be the illegitimate side."

Hutch paused, and then nodded.

"What *is* muling?" I asked.

I gave Hutch a second to contemplate the answer, although my patience was wearing thin. Finally, he said, "Randolph has a special crew that smuggles contraband from one organization to another."

"You mean like drugs?"

"Drugs. Guns. Venom." After adding the final ingredients to the blender, he worked the lid on carefully, saying, "And now the fool is trying to cut costs by storing some of the shipments in his basement. All because he doesn't want to mess with traphouses anymore."

I could tell these words weren't necessarily meant for me to hear, but I listened with intrigue, nonetheless.

"I didn't realize venom was considered contraband," I said.

Our conversation was put on hold as the blender drowned all noise, including the thunder. Hutch glared at the appliance, his posture taunt with restlessness. From where I sat, I could clearly see the scars curving from behind his ear. For one irrational moment I wanted to comfort him somehow; a friendly smile or a touch of the hand. Immediately, I purged the feeling, blaming the fleeting moment of sympathy on my lack of sleep.

"Forgotten venom," he said as the blender slowed to a stop. "It has extraordinary value on the black market."

"How can you get Forgotten venom in the first place?" I wondered, picturing a twisted scene of a Forgotten selling their venom in vials for bars of gold.

"Certain crews hunt and capture them." Hutch retrieved two tall glasses from another cupboard and filled them with the thick, rosy blend. "The Forgotten have to be kept alive until the venom is extracted."

"Are they all killed after the extraction?" I asked. "Why not use them as venom banks?"

"Trust me. That would be the case, if it were possible."

I accepted one of the glasses he offered, rolling it between my hands pensively before taking a sip. A rush of strawberry and peanut butter flavors erupted on my tongue at once. I took a second, longer swig of the beverage.

"Is Randolph in on it, too?" I asked, wiping my upper lip clean with the back of my hand.

With a shake of his head, Hutch stared into his own beverage. "He wants to be. I can only presume it's the topic of his undisclosed meetings with his bookkeeper. All he cares about is how he can keep the money flowing into his pockets."

"Do you think he plans on including you in the future?"

"Most definitely." He sounded unhappy about this. "As of right now, I am the only one on his team trained to handle Forgotten."

"He could have more guys trained."

"Sure," Hutch agreed, "but that will be time consuming and costly."

"Maybe that's why he let go of his traphouses." I shrugged. "He's trying to put that money to use elsewhere."

Hutch contemplated this, drinking slowly.

Hopping from the bar stool, I circled the counter, and propped my now empty cup into the sink. "What does it matter what Randolph does with his home, anyway?" I asked. "I thought you hated that place."

"I do." Hutch said stiffly.

"Any particular reason?" Besides being an orphan and not getting along with whatever family he had left. I pressed my waist against the counter opposite him. We stood facing each other in silence for what seemed an eternity, listening to the splattering rain outside.

Just when I thought Hutch was about to respond, he shook his head, reaching past me to leave his glass in the sink.

Disappointed at the realization that he was not going to supply an answer to my question, I made to touch him encouragingly on the arm as he pulled back. I recoiled, however, remembering what happened the last time I made contact with him.

My sudden shift of movement did not go unnoticed. Hutch's eyes flickered to my pained expression, and his frown deepened.

Embarrassed by my revealing actions, I braided my arms across my chest, as though doing so would prevent me from feeling as foolish as I did. "If you can't share anything about my life, can't you tell me something about yours?" I ventured.

It was interesting to watch the silent dilemma play out on Hutch's face. With gritted teeth, he drummed a fist lightly on the counter, the vibration pulsating through me where my hip met the granite.

I wished to be privy to his thoughts for once.

Hutch turned away with a small sigh, pinching the bridge of his nose with his thumb and forefinger. He looked like he was suffering from a migraine. "I'm not a monster," he said to the microwave.

In my bewilderment, I bit back the responses that sprung to my lips. Hutch inhaled and continued, "Randolph is the ruthless one. Not me." He looked away, training his gaze on me. "When you took me by surprise earlier," he paused, and I could feel the flare of the bruises from when his fingers clamped around my throat. "I saw your face. You were prepared for the worst." He stiffened. "I wore that same expression for nine years. If I did not meet Randolph's expectations in school, in training, or if I said something he didn't particularly want to hear, that was the face he saw."

"He beat you?" I whispered, horrified.

"And left me in the hole afterwards."

Felix had mentioned the hole when provoking him at the mall a few days prior. I hadn't actually comprehended the gravity of the taunt at the time.

"When I realized what I was doing to you," Hutch said quietly, "I found I was no different from the man who made my every day and night unbearable. That's not who I want to compare with. I don't want to be the man I loathe."

"You're not," I said, still hugging myself.

Hutch chuckled. As bleak as the sound was, his trifling smile stirred something inside me. I feared if I did not restrain myself, I might try to reach out to him again.

"You wanted to know why I hate the mansion," he said. "That's it in a nutshell."

Chapter Nineteen

Morning shadows adorned the walls of the condo, stretching across the floor in lazy shapes.

I rubbed sleep from my eyes, noting the smell of fresh coffee reaching me from the kitchen.

"You're awake." Hutch resumed his place in the armchair, setting his mug on the coffee table.

"Did you sleep at all?" I asked with a yawn, recalling the hours we'd spent lounging before the television. While Hutch was too troubled to be bothered by rest, I had my own struggles sleeping, due to the raging storm.

"I finished the documentary." He stole a glance at my disheveled appearance.

Struck by self-consciousness, I slowly worked the bun from the top of my head, letting my hair fall over my shoulders. In my attempt to bring some order to it, I said, "I see you found something else to watch."

"Just a couple of cold cases."

I studied Hutch as he sipped his coffee. After the events of the night before, he seemed different in the morning light. The lines of grief on his face were now replaced by determination, his square shoulders radiating a new-found strength. He bore the look of one with a plan.

"Anything interesting happen while I was asleep?" I asked.

"Melinda texted," Hutch said.

I perked up. "What did she say?"

"She apologized for her brother's behavior." Hutch turned off the television. "She also invited you to the movies."

Hopping from the couch, I began to gather clothes from one of the shopping bags. "Did she say when?"

"I told her noon."

Glancing at the clock on the wall I saw we had two and a half hours. "This is going to be a good day," I proclaimed with my clothes slung over one arm. "I just know it." I flashed Hutch a confident smile before retreating to the bathroom.

***

Parking was no simple task. With shoppers bound and determined to take advantage of the great deals Black Friday offered, the drive to the mall alone was more hectic than usual.

I could feel tension rising in Hutch as we weaved through the masses, headed straight for the movie theater .

"So what's the plan?" I asked, hoping to divert his attention from the guy who rammed past him on our walk to the theater's entrance.

"Plan?"

"Are you going to be tagging along with me and Melinda?" I stepped around a family of five. Two of the three children were shrieking about some toy their parents hadn't gotten them.

"I'll be close by," Hutch said. "Only Melinda won't know I'm there."

He held the door for me, and I stepped into the chilly lobby, running my hands up and down my arms for warmth. "It might be warm outside," I said, glancing around for Melinda, "but that doesn't mean they have to freeze us out."

When Hutch didn't respond, I looked back, only to find I was alone. "Didn't realize we were starting so soon," I mumbled.

I stood foolishly for a while, pretending to read the movie times on the screens above the concession counter, but I couldn't help but feel awkward and out of place.

"Parking was a disaster."

Starting at the voice, I looked around to find Mike grinning at me.

"Mike," I said in surprise.

"That would be me." He winked, the action complimenting his features.

"I didn't expect you to join us." I clutched the small handbag I'd picked up on my shopping endeavor. Hutch had grumbled about it, but it proved useful, carrying the wad of cash he'd given me for the afternoon.

Mike's grin turned sheepish. "I have a confession to make." I furrowed my brows questioningly, and he continued, "I may have used Mel's phone to text you this morning."

My mouth fell open. I couldn't help but laugh in disbelief. "You catfished me?"

"I wouldn't put it that way," he objected.

"Why didn't you just text me yourself?"

Mike hesitated. "I didn't think you would respond. Not after Mel so kindly informed me how strongly I came on to you yesterday. I wanted to be sure I'd have the chance to prove that I'm not really like that."

Biting back a smile, I asked, "Why, what are you normally like?"

"I don't know." He buried his hands in his pockets. "I guess I like to get to know a young woman before I try to kiss her."

"Fair enough." I nudged him playfully with my shoulder. "The movies, huh?" Glancing around at the gathering crowd, I guessed an anticipated movie was about to begin.

"I figured it would be fun," Mike said, seeming to relax a little now that he knew I wasn't going to make a scene for his deviousness.

"Well, I don't know about you," I said, "but I plan on drenching my popcorn in butter."

***

"You really didn't like it?" Mike asked again.

Scooping a spoonful of sprinkles, I replied, "It's not necessarily that I didn't like it. There were just too many explosions."

Mike laughed, dipping his own plastic spoon into his frozen yogurt. "I can't say I've ever heard anyone complain about there being *too many explosions.*"

We turned the corner, approaching the fountain on the ground floor. Instead of holding water, it was filled with poinsettias and giant candy canes.

"I'm just saying," I said, "take the train station, for instance. It was blown up for no reason!"

"The bad guys thought the hero was taking refuge there," Mike pointed out. "They were convinced they *had* to blow it up."

"Still, it's ridiculous." I took another mouthful of the butter pecan flavored frozen yogurt.

"All right," Mike said, stopping in his tracks. I stopped too. "How about next time I take you to see some rom-com? Would that make things better?"

Before I had the chance to respond, his pocket began to buzz. "Hold that thought," he said. "Brad's been trying to reach me since we left the movies."

While he talked with Brad, I peered around at the nearby shops, pretending not to notice the rising heat in his voice. What could Brad want that infuriated him?

"I'm sorry," he said, sliding the phone back into his pocket.

"You have to go," I said, and he nodded. "Do you really have to?"

Mike grinned widely, pleased at the longing in my voice. What he didn't realize was his friend was trashing my plans to get closer to him before I started asking more serious questions about his father.

"You're not having a good time, are you?" he teased.

"You got me." I gave my best imitation of a flirtatious grin, earning another sheepish grin from Mike.

"Tell you what," he said, touching my arm. "This guy I know is hosting a party tonight just down the block from where we live. You're more than welcome to come."

I considered it for a moment before agreeing. Mike's smile reached from ear to ear. "Great! I'll text you the address."

"From your phone this time, right?" I laughed.

"Promise." He pressed my free hand gently, his warmth seeping through the numbing cold of my fingers from holding the cup of frozen yogurt. I met his gaze, and for a moment was sure he was about to lean in. But he didn't.

"Thanks for the dessert," I said.

"Any time."

I watched him walk away, disappearing into the shifting crowd. A warmth washed over me from behind, and I could smell Hutch's fabric softener.

"I'm going to get the information," I told him, without bothering to turn around. "I'm going to find out where Eric Allen is tonight."

***

The thrumming bass could be heard a street away from the actual location of the party. It was a wonder no one in the neighborhood had called it in for disruption of the peace.

Hutch pulled up to the house, but he did not put the Audi in park.

"What's wrong?" I asked, sensing his hesitance.

"I need you to hold down the fort for a little while," he said.

"You're not coming?" I glared at him.

"I have to meet Red. It shouldn't take long," he added quickly at the unforgiving look on my face.

"Hutch, I know you're socially awkward," I said, "but you can't leave me here with a bunch of strangers. What if... something happens?"

"I won't be long," he promised. I heard the urgency in his voice, and had no choice but to give in.

"Don't forget about me," I said.

"You're too much trouble for anyone to forget about."

He barely waited for the passenger door to close behind me before speeding off.

Tugging nervously at my clothes, I felt exposed in my plaid skirt and flimsy top, standing alone at the end of the driveway. My loneliness was short-lived, however.

"I haven't seen you around." The guy who spoke was tall with a red solo cup in one hand and a cigarette in the other.

"I was just heading inside," I told him, teetering away.

"You don't want to hang out and talk?"

The music was much louder inside the house. Bodies swayed to the rhythm, the bass throbbing through my veins. I threaded my way through the foyer, keeping an eye out for Mike. He'd said eight-thirty, and according to the grandfather clock in the living room, it was nearing nine.

Someone shrieked directly behind me, and I soon felt a chilly substance bubble down my back.

"Sorry!" a girl called over the music, but the level of her sincerity showed in her lack of interest to mend her slip of the hand.

"I forgot to put perfume on anyway," I shouted back, earning a puzzled look from the girl.

I shook my head and moved on. She was obviously too tipsy to get my sarcasm.

Thankfully the bathroom was empty. It was still too early for those who couldn't hold their drinks. I didn't waste any time. After rinsing the smell of beer from my neck and back, I stepped back out, only to catch a familiar face in the crowd. He saw me too.

Biting back a groan, Brad made a beeline for me. Maybe he would know where Mike was lurking.

"Funny, I didn't think I'd have the pleasure of seeing you again," he smirked.

"I'd be even more delighted if I knew where Mike was," I told him.

"Mike? Yeah, he's running a little late." Brad offered his solo cup, but I turned it down. "Ran into some problems at home. He'll be here, though."

"What kind of problems?" I asked, feeling a twinge of concern. Was Meemee all right? Surely her health hadn't declined since last night.

"I'm not at liberty to say." Brad smirked again. I would've loved to give him a reason to tuck that tantalizing grin away. Remembering Hutch's absence, however, I took a deep breath, calming my irritation.

"Can you tell me when he'll be here?" I asked between gritted teeth.

"There's no guaranteeing when he'll make it," said Brad. "But in the meantime, I would be more than happy to introduce you to a few fine ladies and gentlemen here."

"That's okay—" I began. The rest of my sentence disintegrated the moment

Brad snagged my hand. Before I knew it, he was towing me to the nearest clique.

I didn't even bother to memorize the names. A few guys asked me basic questions about where I lived and went to school. Wracking my brains, I tried to remember everything Hutch had told me to say.

When Brad got bored of the group, he led me on to another, and then another. I was asked the same questions too many times to count. At one point, someone thrust a solo cup in my hand.

We'd somehow made it back to the foyer. One of the guys I'd been introduced to earlier was trying without much success to engage me in his conversation.

Glancing at the front door for the millionth time, I finally saw Mike wrestle past a couple locked at the lips.

My face lit up and I waved. Although Mike waved back, the look on his face told me something was very wrong.

Chapter Twenty

"Mike!" I reached for his hand, a smile touching my lips. I was so relieved to see a friendly face, I could've hugged him. Despite my relief, there was no dismissing the anxious look in his eyes. "Is everything all right?" I asked.

A roar sounded from the kitchen, the volume of it putting the music to shame.

Mike inclined his head, gesturing I followed him away from the animated game of beer pong. We made it to the hallway, the walls lined with oil paintings where family photos would've been expected.

Just like every other corner of the house, this section was swarming with guests. The music was still pounding along the floorboards, but now the challenge remained hearing one another over the idle chatter of others.

"Brad told me you ran into some problems," I said, leaning in so he could hear me.

"I tried to call you," he replied, "but I kept going straight to voicemail."

"I don't have my phone on me." I shrugged apologetically. The phone was with Hutch, and for all I knew, he'd probably been rejecting Mike's call each time. "Is it anything serious?"

Mike opened his mouth but shut it on second thought.

"No one is hurt, I hope," I pressed, annoyed by his reluctance to open up to me. He was as bad as Hutch.

"Everyone's fine." He lingered near the opening to the living room, his shoulder slumped against the doorway.

Growing impatient, I stepped closer, brushing my lips to his ear to softly say, "You can talk to me." My gaze locked with his and I could almost feel him crumble under my scrutiny.

"Yo, Brad!" someone called over the music. Peering around, I noticed it to be one of the guys who had mercilessly bombarded me with questions earlier, but I couldn't remember his name. He cast a roguish grin in my direction. "Better keep an eye on your girl. Our man, Michael, is showing some competition!"

The music went silent, marking the end of the song.

Brad appeared in the crowd. A lazy smile alighted his face, the area around him shrouded in a cloud of smoke. "Naw, man," he said for everyone to hear. "I'm not worried about him. Michael told me about his vow of abstinence way back when."

Next to me, Mike's lips contorted into a weak smile, though it appeared to be more for my benefit than anyone else's. His eyes were downcast, expression lost. I wondered what issues he was facing at home to leave him so withdrawn.

Acting on impulse, I took his hand and began to steer him through the living room to the backdoor. There we were bound to be granted more privacy for our conversation.

"I think you might want to reconsider that," Chris cackled. "Looks like she's ready to let him out of the friend-zone tonight."

"Show him a good time, baby doll!" some girl yelled while others laughed.

I peered back around at Mike, expecting him to say something, but he had already resigned himself to the situation.

Overwhelmed by unnecessary comments called out by others, I halted, seeking Brad once more. This was his friend they were talking about. Was he not going to step up and tell everyone to mind their own business?

As soon as I spotted him, Brad tipped his cup in our direction as if toasting to Mike's unwarranted limelight. The amusement in his expression made it clear he was leaving his friend to fend for himself.

Releasing a small sigh, Mike turned to leave, but my hand snatched his wrist. If everyone was desperate for something to gawk at, I was going to give it to them.

I didn't give myself a chance to think about what I was doing. Gripping the front of his shirt, I pulled him in. When my lips found his, I felt his surprise in the unsureness of his kiss. He quickly recovered from his shock, his hands running down my hips as he pulled me closer.

The crowd subsided to catcalls and wolf-whistles.

Mike's breath was hot. He deepened the kiss, seeming to forget where we were.

I didn't forget, though. I couldn't. Not when his pulse suddenly seemed to pound in my head, louder than the music. He was surging with blood, warm and enticing. My gums ached, and I knew if I didn't pull away, Mike would soon be in grave danger.

***

Stars twinkled in the spaces between the clouds. The moon presented itself every now and then when dark clouds rolled out of the way.

"If I knew how you felt, I wouldn't have held back earlier," Mike teased. He was laying on his back, gazing into the sky.

Adjusting my skirt to avoid sitting on the shingles of the roof, I chortled. "Funny." I stole another glance at his face. He seemed rather smug, which was a complete one-eighty to his mood before.

I tried to relax as I looked back into the face of the night sky. The air had grown rather chill over the last two hours since I'd arrived. And still there was no sign of Hutch. What was taking him so long?

As I continued to stare at the sky, I felt a familiar shadow settle over my mind. My vision tapered away as a full moon flickered in my returning memory.

I gave into the flashback, fighting to see past the migraine accompanying it.

"Keep moving," James yelled, urging me onward. *"I can handle this!"*

"But there are two of them!" I argued. Breathless desperation filled my voice. *"You can't hold them off on your own!"*

135

"I said GO!"

I hesitated, my body trembling with fright; tired from running.

"GO!" James yelled again.

Just then, I saw them. In the pale light of the moon, their forms could be seen sprinting between the trees, as smooth as liquid metal.

I could talk to them. They would listen to me. They had to.

James reached out a hand, shoving my shoulder with incredible force. His actions did nothing, but trip me over the nearest tree root.

My back hit the cold earth, the full moon watching us between bare branches. I gazed at it, hoping, praying that if the moon could see us, surely He could too.

"You know what I mean?" Mike's voice broke through the memory.

Chills rippled down my spine when my vision cleared, and I was staring at the glistening shingles once more.

Mike inclined his head to see if I was listening.

"What I want to know," I said slowly, "is why you won't tell me what's going on. What has you so torn up?"

Grunting, Mike sat. He fell silent for a time, cracking his knuckles.

"So, after my mom died, my dad ditched us," he said. "And to be honest, I don't think I can ever forgive him for doing that."

"Maybe your father had good reason for doing what he did," I offered, knowing full well Eric had chosen to mess with the wrong people. Perhaps that was why he left his family — to keep them from suffering the backlash of his mistakes. For all the good it did, Randolph still managed to locate the Allen residence. "Have you spoken to him about this?"

Mike scoffed. "The man's full of excuses. I'm not susceptible to his brainwashing and he knows it. He can buy Max and Mel all the gifts in the world, but me? I just walked out on him."

I shot a bemused look at him, not sure if I'd misheard. "You mean, you normally just walk out on him?"

"Well, no," Mike said. "I've never actually walked out, but I had somewhere to be tonight, obviously. He shows up out of nowhere and expects everyone to celebrate his return. I just can't wait for him to get back on a plane and leave us alone again."

Upon realizing my mouth hanging open in shock, I snapped it shut. I was utterly lost on the fact that Eric had unexpectedly resurfaced. Hutch and I finally had something to show for our work. I was going home. I was going to find my brother.

"Is that James?" Mike's words startled me from my thoughts.

"What?" I followed the direction he pointed, eyes scanning the dispersed guests in the front yard.

My gaze fell almost immediately on Hutch. "Oh, yeah," I said. "He's my ride."

"He doesn't look happy," Mike observed.

"Maybe he heard about what you and his little sister's been up to." I punched him lightly on the shoulder, smirking.

Mike didn't laugh.

The party raged on below. Instead of guests trickling out, the house was even more packed than before. I slithered between the bodies, only noticing Mike's absence when I made it to the front door.

Glancing around for him, a hand gripped my wrist with a bone-crushing force.

"That *hurts*," I said, looking around at Hutch.

He ignored me, yanking me outside and to the end of the driveway where the Audi was parked.

"What's your problem?" I demanded.

Hutch never responded. We got into the vehicle and he sped us off at a dangerous speed. In the glow of the dashboard, his furious expression appeared downright murderous.

"What happened, Hutch? Did you talk to Red?"

He didn't even bother to acknowledge the fact that I was talking. I leaned over the middle console, determined he noticed me. "Did he tell you anything about Stix?" I tried.

I didn't see where the blade came from, but I felt the cool of it against my throat. Hutch glimpsed at me, bracing the weapon under my chin. "Back off," he spat, face twisted in disgust.

It finally sunk in. Hutch wasn't just mad; he was mad at *me*. I couldn't possibly imagine what I'd done to make him so upset — not until I remembered my morbid dreams of bloodshed and death. I sank back into the leather seat, mind racing.

So it *was* me. I was responsible for the deaths and disappearances. I killed an innocent person at the mall when I'd blacked out.

There was no saving me; I really was a monster. And Hutch had somehow confirmed this during our time spent apart.

Neither of us said a word. I didn't know what Hutch planned on doing with me, but I had to tell him about Eric Allen's whereabouts before it was too late. Even if doing so didn't benefit me, it would save the rest of the Allen family from Randolph's wrath.

"I thought they were just *dreams*," I blurted out the moment Hutch stepped over the threshold behind me.

The door slammed shut, but I did not hear the beeps of the keypad as I usually did when Hutch armed the system. Instead, he caught up with me in the dining area, his fingers curling around my bicep.

Instinctively, I pulled from his grip, but Hutch slammed my back against the windows facing the balcony. He then thrust his forearm against my neck, blocking my windpipe.

"Who are you working for?" he growled.

"What?" I asked between gasps.

Hutch pressed more fiercely, the tip of his blade biting into the skin just below my collar bone. His glare hardened.

Whatever this new theory he had concocted, he was not giving me a chance to speak, and I realized I had to do something before he decided to ram the dagger into my heart.

Pivoting, I pushed the hand holding the blade away from me. The tip snagged my skin, drawing a jagged line to the curve of my shoulder. I gritted my teeth against the pain, twisting under Hutch's arm and kicking out a leg in hopes of tripping him. I needed all the time I could get to come up with a plan.

Hutch's reflexes were flawless. My attempt to unbalance him didn't faze him in the least. He threw the dagger into the wooden floor, the handle pointing skyward, wavering from side to side.

As he approached, I stumbled over my words, unable to say anything coherent enough to resolve the situation. "Hutch — I don't — You have to listen—"

He launched at me, arms outstretched. I pushed off his hold as much as I could, hands swatting his as I skipped sideways out of reach. With a miscalculated step, I collided into the wall, bashing my head hard enough to rattle me. In my stupor, I saw Hutch close the space between us. I threw out my hands to push him off, but he skillfully deterred my arms in a clean motion, locking me in a bear hug.

Grunting at the force of the embrace and still slightly dazed from smashing my head into the wall, my eyes fell on the knife stuck in the floor.

Neither of us really intended to cause irreversible damage on the other. If Hutch wanted me dead, he would've been done with me already. He was trying to detain me, while I was making every effort to evade him.

There was hope, yet.

Working my left hand up between his arm and torso, I managed to free it enough to reach his shoulder. Hutch did not heal as fast as I did. I was counting on the scars I'd inflicted the night before to be sore.

The moment I pressed hard on his shoulder and heard him draw in an unsteady breath, I dropped my dead weight to the ground.

Hutch hadn't expected this.

Rolling on the floor, I pushed off the opposite wall, my bare feet providing force enough to launch me into the bathroom. Once inside, I kicked the door shut in Hutch's face, pressing the lock to secure my safety for the moment.

Chapter Twenty-One

The door rattled under the force of Hutch's blow.

"Stop!" I yelled, standing shakily to my feet. "We can discuss this without killing each other." I flattened my hand on the door and took a breath. "What did Red tell you to make you think I have something to do with Stix's games?"

"You knew from the start it wasn't Stix, didn't you?" Hutch challenged, his rage seeping through the barrier between us.

I found myself gaping. *If it isn't Stix, then who...?*

"Hutch." My hand fell to the handle. I needed him to trust me, and talking through a door would only make me appear guilty. "I'll come out, just... promise you won't go full-on assassin on me."

"Depends on how you answer my questions," Hutch spat.

"Promise me."

He didn't say anything for a moment, until, "Fine."

Chewing my inner cheek, I pulled open the door. Hutch lifted his eyes, dropping his hands from the doorframe. He straightened his posture, his expression as fierce as the storm from the night before.

"If Stix wasn't the one sending you the text messages," I said, "then who was it?"

"That's what I'd like to know," Hutch retorted. The look he gave me suggested he was convinced I was involved in the conspiracy against him.

"Hutch," I said, shaking my head. "I have nothing to do with any of this. I had nothing to do with Damian. I thought... I thought you were accusing

140

me of the recent disappearances that are all over the news."

Hutch hesitated, pursing his lips into a frown. "Have you anything to do with them?"

Wetting my lips, I said, "I really don't know." I studied the floor between us, wringing my hands. "I've been having dreams. They started the first night I stayed here. Then we spent the night at Randolph's and…" I swallowed the lump in my throat. "I woke up on the floor. The window was open and I… I didn't feel right." Tears pricked my eyes in response to the shame I felt, but I went on. "I blacked out at the mall a few days ago. Just before someone pulled the fire alarm."

Hutch was perhaps the last person with whom I needed to share all this. He was the only person I could trust, however, and the burdens of my fears had become simply too much to bear alone.

The forming tears spilled down my face when Hutch left my side. I watched him rip the dagger from the floor.

He was going to kill me. How had I expected him to react, after admitting to something so terrible?

Slowly, I slid into a sitting position on the floor.

It was too late. I'd done all the damage I could. After all the lives I'd unwillingly taken, killing me was conceivably the best thing to do at this point. This was where our alliance came to an end.

"Stand up," Hutch said, his voice quiet.

My legs were weakened by fear; I couldn't move. I saw my fate in his eyes.

"Is it going to hurt?" I whispered.

Without responding, he wound his fingers beneath my elbow, hoisting me to my feet.

I began to tremble uncontrollably. The scar on my shoulder throbbed as if sensing the proximity of the blade.

Hutch lowered the dagger to the pad of his thumb, and I watched in bemusement as he sliced into his skin. Ruby drops protruded from the cut, bringing an involuntary stutter to the rhythm of my heart. I held my breath. Did he want me to blackout — to attack him again? Curiosity prevented me from stepping from the wall.

"Hold still," he said, stashing away the blade.

With his injured hand, he pushed my hair behind my shoulder. His fingertips rested just below my earlobe, the warmth sending a jolt of electricity through my bones. I parted my lips, taking miniature bouts of air through my mouth.

Averting my gaze from the blood trickling down Hutch's thumb, I focused instead on the look of concentration in the hard lines of his face.

The moment his thumb touched my lower lip, a hiss escaped me. I bared my teeth, resisting the pulsing darkness at the edge of my vision; resisting the burning desire to taste his blood.

My sanity hung on the aching pain in my shoulder. I circled my thoughts around the flesh wound, eyes searching the ceiling above.

"Breathe, Hayden," Hutch murmured.

"I can't." I pressed my fists against the wall behind me.

He cupped my face with his other hand, studying me still. I stole a sideways glimpse at his expression and was startled by the gentleness in his eyes.

His other thumb tugged at the corner of my lips. He ran it along the backside of my teeth, just below my inflamed gums. The intrusion was disturbing, but when I moved to pull away, he held me steady.

The saltiness of his skin saturated my taste buds, making me sick with an inexpressible hunger.

"It's not you," he finally said, removing the bead of blood from my lip and retreating to the middle of the hall.

"What?" I was dumbfounded. "How do you know?"

"Considering all of the deaths reported, you would be dripping with venom, had you been the culprit," he told me. "You've got nowhere near enough."

"But…" I touched my mouth, "they hurt. My gums burn every time I'm near blood, as do my hands." I displayed my palms for effect, even if nothing could be seen with the naked eye.

"Which would explain why you woke up next to an open window," Hutch pointed out. "The temperature tends to drop at night."

There was a suggestion of a *duh* somewhere in his words. I ignored his derisive comment. "So why does it burn?"

"It's a Forgotten's natural response when drawn to feed," he explained. "They produce venom the same way a famished dog drools at the smell of food."

"If I have no venom, why does it feel like I do?"

"I never said you don't have any," Hutch corrected. "What you have is likely harmless, but you're still in the transformation stage. With the Forgotten part of you struggling to function, I can only guess it would cause you some discomfort."

"You can only guess?" I repeated. "You mean, you don't know?"

Hutch shrugged. "We don't see many who resist the transformation."

My arms circled around my middle as I allowed the truth to sink in. "So, I'm not the one behind the murders," I contemplated aloud, then added bitterly, "although I wouldn't go as far as to say I'm not a murderer."

At the wary glance Hutch cast in my direction, I reminded him of the man I'd fatally wounded at the gas station the night we met.

With a shake of his head, Hutch said, "He was still breathing when I went after you. You tore into his flesh but didn't cause enough damage to kill him on the spot. The medics would've been able to save him."

I bit my lip, encouraged by his words. Despite the awful dreams and temptations, was there still a chance everything would be all right?

Hutch sighed, heading toward the kitchen.

"I was so sure Stix was behind it all," he muttered.

I followed him. "How can you be sure he's not? I mean, he's been trying to sabotage your plan of locating Eric from the beginning. For all we know, Josue could still be helping him."

"Josue's dead," Hutch said flatly, stopping me in my tracks.

"He's... dead?" I said. "How?"

"The day after the stunt they tried to pull on you," he said, "word got out Josue was taking advantage of Natalia. Apparently, messing with the housekeepers is one thing Randolph absolutely does not tolerate."

"Enough to kill someone?" I asked, baffled.

"Considering Josue was already being penalized for something else, I can imagine Randolph grew tired of dealing with him." Hutch rounded the corner into the kitchen. "Red informed me of this a few days ago, which only convinced me of Stix's involvement in the matter."

"But how do you know he isn't involved?"

"Randolph had him thoroughly questioned this morning, after learning of Damian's death."

"I thought he didn't care about Damian," I said.

"Turns out he cared enough to temporarily disable Stix's left hand during the interrogation," he said.

I shuddered. "And what made you think I had anything to do with all of this?" I asked.

"I'm not blind to what's been going on," he told me, holding his thumb under the flowing tap. He shut it off and reached for a box of band-aides in the cupboard above the microwave. "There's another Forgotten lurking nearby, reeking havoc all around us. I doubt it's a coincidence."

My brow furrowed. "Are you sure it's a Forgotten?"

Nodding, Hutch trashed the paper from the band-aide. "I do more than just watch the news."

He did not elaborate on this, but remembering what he'd told me about having connections among the authorities, I was led to believe he had access to more information than most. That would certainly explain why he was on his phone all the time. Perhaps he was receiving updates from his contact regarding the crisis in the area.

Hutch drummed his fist on the counter top — a habit of his, I realized, when he grew thoughtful. "Forgotten have a tendency of being aware of one other," he said, eyes gazing into the distance. I could almost hear the wheels turning in his mind.

"You're saying there are two Forgotten terrorizing the city?" I asked, horrified.

Hutch shook his head. "You said you felt different before you blacked out last night. I assumed it was from the exposure to blood, but what if it also had to do with a Forgotten being in that condo? Forgotten are hyper-aware of each other — mostly for hunting purposes. With you not being a

CHAPTER TWENTY-ONE

Forgotten entirely, crossing one last night could've caused you to blackout."

"A Forgotten killed Damian," I concluded, speaking slowly as it all came together.

"The same Forgotten responsible for the chaos in town," Hutch nodded.

"And you think this Forgotten is working with whoever sent you those texts?" I asked.

Staring pensively at the floor, Hutch did not say anything for a long time. "Randolph has Forgotten work for him all the time."

"You kill them, don't you?" I said. "After Randolph's done with them?" It made sense. Why would Randolph pay a Forgotten to do his dirty work when he had Hutch to dispose of them? If the man was callous enough to harm a child, sentencing monsters to death was nothing.

Hutch nodded again. His eyes found mine and my heart sank.

"Is he going to have me killed, too?" I asked quietly.

He chose his next words carefully. "You're not technically a Forgotten," he replied. "But considering our current situation, there's no telling what Randolph plans to do with us tomorrow when we show up empty handed."

"Tomorrow…" I echoed, remembering the party — remembering Mike. "Eric's home."

Hutch started.

"Mike told me," I continued, hurriedly. "His father showed up tonight out of the blue. I wanted to tell you, but… we got sidetracked."

Within a matter of seconds, Hutch had his phone at his ear.

"This is good news, right?" I said, unable to read his expression.

"The best news we've gotten all week."

Chapter Twenty-Two

I took my time in the bathroom, scrubbing away the lingering smell of alcohol. The scar on my shoulder stung, but I ignored it, concentrating instead on other matters, such as applying scented lotion to my skin and brushing knots from my wet hair.

By the time I finally donned my cotton pajama pants and matching orange and yellow top, I stepped out into the hallway.

At that same moment, Hutch exited his bedroom. He was dressed in a fresh T-shirt, revealing more of his arms than was usual. My eyes fell immediately on the white lines criss-crossing along the curve of his biceps. Hutch regarded me for a moment, as if daring me to remark on the unsightliness of the scars. When I did not, he breezed by, making for the kitchen.

He was scooping coffee grounds as I stepped out onto the balcony. The chill air brought gooseflesh to my arms. I leaned over the railing, drinking in the city lights. Even at the late hour a country tune drifted up from the streets below.

Welcome to the South.

My thoughts returned to my last flashback and the Forgotten pursuing my brother and me. Was that the moment my life drastically changed? Had those been my last human moments?

I'm not a monster.

The balcony door opened, inviting the smell of fresh-brewed coffee outside.

"I didn't know if you wanted any," Hutch said.

Peering over my shoulder, I saw him set an extra mug on the iron table.

"Is this a thing now?" I chortled. "You make me a beverage when feeling apologetic for manhandling me?"

Hutch didn't respond, only making my joke feel like a jab at his thoughtfulness.

We stood side-by-side for long minutes, me contemplating the depths of my past-self while Hutch sipped his coffee leisurely.

I couldn't shake the last image of the flashback from my mind. The silver light of the moon had somehow been comforting and haunting at the same time. It reminded me of the prayer clinging to my lips, one filled with hopeless desperation.

"Do you believe in God?" I asked without preamble, my eyes held by the glow of life in the city below.

It didn't seem Hutch registered my question. Which wasn't a bad thing. It was more of a rhetorical musing.

"I do."

My eyebrows puckered in disbelief. "You do?"

Hutch sipped from his cup again. "Why does that surprise you?"

"Your life revolves around hunting Forgotten."

"And?"

I faced him. "How can you believe in God when you witness so much wrong in the world?"

"Because I don't believe evil can exist without good." The answer was too simple to satisfy me, and Hutch could tell. "My aunt and I used to go to church. Before that, my mother took me. Every Sunday."

It sounded to me like the keeping of his faith was something he did in remembrance of his family. When I mentioned this, however, Hutch shook his head.

"I'm not the optimistic type," he pointed out. "I don't believe in fairy tales with happy endings, and I don't believe there is a heaven just because I hope that's where loved ones lost end up." He inclined his head to better hold my gaze. "After Aunt Erin died, I decided the universe hadn't randomly spit us out. I was fifteen, and I'd already seen my fair share of harsh times, training with Samuel." He paused. "I don't know everything, but what I deciphered from this life is if evil exists, then there must be some balance of good, too."

Good doesn't have to mean God. I refrained from saying the words out loud. Who was I to challenge his beliefs? I didn't even know what I believed in.

"Do you still go to church?" I asked, genuinely interested. I could not picture Hutch in a pew, singing hymns to the great volume and timbre of an old-fashioned organ.

"Not since Erin's funeral," he said with a shake of his head. He clutched the railing with his free hand.

"Why did you stop going?"

Hutch fell silent for a moment, his expression calculating. "Church is not meant for the passive. I stopped going, because I got tired of seeing blank faces during every Sunday service. Attendance won't earn you a life of wealth and happiness. It's not about showing up on time. It's about taking action."

"Like you," I said.

"No." Hutch shook his head. "I'm not a good example."

"Why not?"

Hutch stared at the changing traffic lights at the nearest intersection. He took another sip of his drink before he replied, "I don't believe it matters how much good you alone do."

"You just contradicted yourself," I said, pushing my back to the railing. "You said more people need to take action. And now you're saying it doesn't matter what anyone does."

Hutch chuckled, his half smile infectious. "What I mean is, what's the point of doing good if someone does it solely for themselves?"

"I don't know, Karma?" I muttered. The conversation was about to go over my head.

"Sure." Hutch rested his elbows on the railing now, rolling the cup between his fingers. "If you claim the cosmic universe has a say in your life. That it created you and wants what's best for you."

"I still don't get your point." I crossed my arms against a rising breeze, fighting a shiver.

"My point is I would've given up what I do long ago if it weren't for what I believe in." He gave a weak shrug. "But that doesn't make me a good example for a man of faith."

I wet my lips, uncomfortable by the depth of the discussion. To redirect the conversation, I asked, "Do you hunt and kill Forgotten on Randolph's orders alone, or do you do some freelance hunting of your own?"

"I get the order from Randolph most of the time," he said. "There were only a handful of times I sought out a rogue Forgotten on my own."

"What's the ratio of the male and female Forgotten you've encountered?" I asked quizzically, toeing the railing.

"I don't encounter many females," he said. "Only two — three, if I count you."

"There aren't many female Forgotten?" This surprised me.

"It's not that." Hutch stretched his arms behind his head, shoulders flexing. The cold was getting to him, too. "Randolph doesn't care to invest in them."

"Except for the two," I said.

"Not even them," Hutch turned toward me. "The first one I came across on my own while working a job in New Mexico. The other was a classified case Randolph handed me. My understanding was he had some outside reason for wanting to eliminate her. Not even I was granted more information than was necessary for the job."

"You've been to New Mexico?" I abandoned the railing and approached the table. The cup of coffee Hutch left for me had cooled somewhat, but I took a sip from it anyway. The bitterness made me cringe. A little cream and sugar would've improved the taste.

"There, and a few other places," Hutch said. He joined me at the table.

I curled into one of the chairs, while Hutch sat across from me. We stared into the night, listening to the muffled sounds of whatever traffic remained.

"What did Eric Allen do to target himself?" I asked, propping my chin on my knee.

"He did not pay Randolph for his services," he said. "He fell off the map. Took his goods and ran. All Randolph was left with was Allen's alias. It took him over a year to track down any legit information on the man."

"And now Randolph knows where to find him," I said slowly, thinking of the rest of the Allen family. "He's just going to collect payment, right?"

"That payment's long overdue," Hutch said. "Randolph's out for blood now. He can't let others think they can just pull one over on him and get away with it."

"But," I gnawed my lip, "he's only going after Eric. Not his family."

"Depends on who Randolph sends to do the job."

"What do you mean?" My heart was thumping unpleasantly in my chest now.

"If he sends a Forgotten, which is likely, there won't be a chance of any witnesses."

I sprang from the chair.

"When?" I nearly shouted, my thoughts halting on the memory of Max's laughter. "When will Randolph call in the order?"

Hutch studied me, almost as if he were bewildered by my actions. "He would've called it in already," he said. "He's not going to chance Allen disappearing again."

My breath came heavily. The aftertaste of the coffee in my mouth sickened my stomach. I ran my hands through my hair, unable to digest the fact that I had helped sentence an entire family to death.

"How can you let this happen?" I whispered. Looking Hutch square in the face, I went on, "How can you preach about all the good you try to do and then leave the fate of innocent lives to a man you despise?"

"I didn't have a choice," Hutch said darkly. He placed his mug on the table, a little too forcefully.

"Of course you had a choice!" I said, louder this time. "You're just a coward. As long as you don't have to hurt anyone, you're just dandy, aren't you? Who cares if it's your fault this family is murdered? Who cares if you lead anyone to the butcher block, so long as you aren't the one actually doing the butchering?"

"Yeah, well, it wouldn't be the first time someone died because of me!" Hutch roared. He stood suddenly, his thigh ramming the table with such force, it upset both mugs. Coffee dripped through the gaps of the iron table to the stone floor. "Just take Stix's brother, Leo. I let a handful of Forgotten tear into him on my last job. So, I guess you're right. I am a coward. I'm a coward for not trying to save him. I'm a coward for running to save my own neck."

I studied Hutch, eyes wide. "That's what happened?"

Hutch glared straight ahead of him.

"How were you expected to take on a handful of Forgotten on your own?" I asked quietly.

"I wasn't," he said, still avoiding me. "I was only escorting Leo. His job was to rough someone up for Randolph, but he'd been tipped off there might be a Forgotten present." He finally lifted his eyes to mine. "It was a trap. Only Josue and I got out alive."

"Josue was there too?" I asked.

"He was waiting in the car in case anything went south," he explained. "But he ditched us when he realized the potential danger he was in."

"And he was being punished, too," I concluded. "But then why did Stix forgive him? Josue could've been held responsible for his brother's death."

Hutch shook his head. "They were close. Josue would've come up with some excuse, putting all the blame on me."

I chafed my arms nervously. "Randolph didn't believe it was a trap?"

"He refused to take my word for it," Hutch said. "And with Leo's death appearing a desertion, he couldn't let it pass without reprimanding those involved."

"What was Josue's punishment?" I asked only to have Hutch shrug in response.

"He was benched," he said. "Suspended pay."

Focusing on the puddle of coffee on the floor, time began to press on me. The Allens were in danger. I had to do something.

"Let me get something for that," I said, motioning to the mess as I turned back to the condo.

Hutch nodded, pulling his chair further from the table to make the area accessible.

My heart pounded with such force, I was amazed it hadn't shattered into a million pieces. I tried to hide my apprehension, but feared the choice I'd made was clearly written on my face.

Stepping back inside, I took a deep breath. The balcony door shut and locked smoothly beneath my trembling hands, while Hutch remained outside. He'd only get in my way. I needed to get to the Allens' without wasting any more precious moments.

Chapter Twenty-Three

The keys were splayed on the kitchen counter. I scooped them up, ignoring the rattling handle of the balcony door. Hutch would have to understand this was for the best. I couldn't have him try and stop me.

I reached for the wooden knife set next to the keys.

"HAYDEN!" Hutch bellowed.

I gulped, anxiety threatening to make me sick. With a cook knife in one hand and the keys in the other, I approached the door. Hutch was seething, his breath fogging up the glass.

"I have to help them," I said, hoping he could hear me through the barrier. "Only Eric is to blame for what he did. His family has nothing to do with this."

"Interfering will only get you killed," he barked, his voice muffled.

"Then I'll die making sure they get to safety," I argued.

"Open the door!"

"I'm really sorry," I said, but I doubted he believed me.

When he called after me again, I did not turn back.

The route to the Allens' was mostly retraced from memory. It took longer to get there compared to when Hutch drove us, mainly because I got turned around at one of the four-way stops in the neighborhood.

A knot formed in my stomach when I pulled to a stop. I parked the Audi next to a thick cluster of trees and bushes, knowing the house was adjacent to the road on the other side. The trees would make decent cover for escape should I need it.

I wasn't sure what I expected to do, or how I expected to rescue the family. All I could hope was Randolph's thug hadn't beaten me to the house. I needed time to warn them. Surely Eric would understand and herd his family to safety. But if I was too late? What if Randolph's guy was already there?

That's why I brought the knife, I thought, forcing myself to exit the vehicle.

Having no pockets, I tucked the keys beneath the floor mat. The last thing I needed was to lose them and give Hutch another reason to kill me after all of this.

The bared trees gave less opportunity for concealment than I would've liked. I stayed as close to the shadows as possible, tip-toeing barefoot through the undergrowth.

Half of the house was lit up. Strange. I'd expected to rouse them from sleep.

Peering carefully at the dining room windows, I noticed movement. Squinting, I willed my sight to sharpen.

Mike's lips were moving fast. He was talking to someone as he paced back and forth, falling in and out of sight. I couldn't see his companion, but I knew if I stepped to the right, I would have a better view of the dining room.

Something snapped, stopping me in my tracks. I looked around, heightening all of my senses as much as I could, but only managed to locate a stray squirrel a few yards from me.

Breathing normally again, I could not shake the feeling of something being out of place. There was something different about the neighborhood.

The cruiser was gone. Had Eric sent away the cops?

I inched over, looking back at the windows and found two others in the room with Mike. One was the elderly Mr. Allen sitting with his elbows resting on the table, the other man I did not recognize. I could only suppose him to be the infamous Eric Allen.

A fog settled over my vision, a tightness gripping my chest.

No! I thought desperately, pushing against the shadows encasing my senses. I could not black out now; I had to stay in control.

The blackness pulsed wildly as I fought it, my hands fluttering to my face.

I fell to my knees wondering why on earth this had to happen now.

My right hand gripped the knife firmly before I remembered what Hutch had said. *Pain stimulates the brain.* It was how he got me out of the unpredictable state at Damian's.

Lowering both hands to my thighs, I gritted my teeth. The blade hovered over my left palm for a long moment.

I gasped, eyes wide open as the knife sliced through my skin. Although the sight of blood gathering rapidly into the center of my palm sickened me, I smiled weakly. It had worked.

"You could almost tempt me," said a voice.

I spun so fast, I fell backward.

"Felix?"

I recognized his malicious grin. It was the same look as when he'd cornered Hutch at the mall. Even now, his shoulder-length hair was tied back. He sported a leather jacket and jeans, looking like any other twenty-some male in the city — not a murderer.

"Yours truly." He stepped closer, and I could not fathom how I hadn't sensed him.

"Randolph sent *you?*" I stood slowly to my feet, utilizing the tree behind me for support.

"I'm his best man." Felix said. He displayed his arrogance proudly, head held high. "Unlike Hutch, I do what I'm told, and I do it in a timely fashion. Well, amusing fashion. I've got a knack for letting my victims think they have a chance of making it out alive."

"Psychopath," I murmured, clutching the knife at my side.

Felix *tsked*, shaking his head. "It's all fun and games, really. I'm just one of the fortunate ones whose hobby ended up as his career."

"Your hobby is to terrorize and murder."

"It's the all-time high, baby. You should try it sometime." He winked. "But don't think me so single-minded. I do have other hobbies too."

"Like what?" I challenged.

"Like tormenting your boyfriend." Felix crossed his arms over his chest. "What I wouldn't give to see his reaction to those texts. You saw him. Did he lose it?"

"*You* sent them?" I was dumbfounded. "Why? What was in it for you?"

"Let's just say McLaren's work interfered with my personal life." Felix wasn't smiling now.

"Hutch hunts Forgotten," I said. "How can that interfere with your life?"

I was surprised when Felix did not respond immediately. Instead, he pursed his lips, eyes drifting to some distant time. "There was one Forgotten he shouldn't have hunted."

I was about to question his statement when a recent conversation with Hutch came to mind.

"A woman?" I asked boldly.

There was a split second of shock in Felix's eyes before he recovered.

"You know, you surprise me," he said, resuming his carefree attitude.

"Is that so?"

"Well, sure. Look at you. The beacon of self-control." He snickered. "I was so sure you would've broken by now. I know I did. But then again, I wasn't really trying to resist."

"What are you talking about?" I asked, though my mind had already put the pieces together by now. I bit my lip while Felix merely laughed. He'd made it obvious enough. "Does Randolph know?"

"That his only child is a Forgotten?" He chuckled again. "I'm sure he suspects it."

"You're scared of him." I'd come to this conclusion by the falter in his smile.

Felix's laugh was now forced. "Only failures are afraid of my father. People like McLaren."

"Hutch isn't afraid of him," I retorted, unsure why I felt the need to defend him.

Pearly teeth glinted against the darkness when Felix smiled. He ran his tongue thoughtfully across his incisors. "Maybe you should've paid closer attention. Then you'd understand why he became such a pill-popper."

"There won't be a next time," I spat. "I'm done. I won't be part of Randolph's cruel games anymore."

"You're right about that," Felix said. "I can't have you running off, telling everyone what you know."

His eyes flashed maliciously. I thought hard for something to say next; anything to buy me a little time.

My mind was painfully blank.

I watched Felix advance, my irresolution setting me back when he darted the last few steps. His fingers caught my shoulders.

Slamming me against the rough bark of the tree, he whispered, "I'll finish with you quickly. I have a job to get to. Is there anything you want me to tell your friends before I rip them apart?"

I stole that moment to ram the knife into his side. I pushed it until the handle prevented it from going any further.

Felix grunted, his grip tightening.

"That was... unexpected," he muttered.

My body jerked as he pitched me to the ground. Jagged stones scraped at my hands and knees, but I scrambled to my feet.

With another grunt, Felix removed the knife slowly. The blade dripped crimson. "If there's anyone you should consider being nice to, it's the one who's about to kill you," he said. "Because now I want you to scream until your voice dies first."

He just gave me an idea. Opening my mouth, I let out a piercing scream, hoping to put the neighborhood on alert. It would've done the job, too, had I been able to draw it out long enough. As it were, Felix slapped a hand over my mouth. As soon as I fell silent, he used his hand to thrust me off balance. I stumbled.

Could I sprint to the Allens without him catching me? With the knife hanging loosely in his hand, the moment I turned my back on him, I would offer him a target. And I wasn't keen on finding out how accurate his aim was.

"You killed Damian," I said with a shaky breath. "You were the Forgotten in his condo."

"You just now put that together?" Felix feigned astonishment. "Let me guess, you're still working out who set McLaren up to face more Forgotten than he could handle in the first place. Or did he even tell you why he's being punished?"

"You set the trap?" I blinked.

"And the wrong guy had to die in the process." Felix shook his head. "Such a waste. Leo was a good guy. Great work ethic."

"I take it Stix has no idea his brother died because of you."

"I'd be a fool to tell him."

"Why go to such extremes to kill Hutch?" I asked. "Why not just confront him yourself?"

"Come on," Felix grinned. "Give me some credit for my creativity."

My eyes widened. "You're afraid of him," I said. "You know he's trained and capable of taking you down. So you're finding other ways to have him killed."

"Clever," Felix granted. "But I assure you I could very easily kill him myself if I didn't have my father to answer to."

"Then you *are* scared of Randolph." I could see I was infuriating him.

"*No.*" He stepped forward.

I took a step back.

"So, which is it then?" I pressed. "Are you afraid of Hutch or Randolph?"

My goal was to keep him talking until an opportunity presented itself for my escape, but I'd managed to touch a serious nerve.

Giving me no time to sidestep his attack, I took a full blow to the face. The impact sent me to the ground, my brain doing cartwheels inside my head. Spots distorted my vision, but I managed to sit upright. Blood lined the inside of my mouth, my lips were cracked.

Felix dug his fingers into my hair and pulled me to my feet. I barely managed a gasp before I was hurled back, slamming into the trunk of a tree. The bark tore at my forehead and I collapsed.

Through the spots in my vision, I watched Felix's heavy boots thump closer. I wanted to scream, one last attempt to warn the Allens, but I could not find the energy. Felix glared down at me with hate-filled eyes. Malice radiated from his very being.

This was it? *No. I wasn't a coward.* Coward or not, I was no match against a full-fledged Forgotten. And I was weak. Tired — so tired.

I closed my eyes, heart seeking anything that might serve as a comforting last thought. *James* — he loved me and cared for me. My protective older brother.

When I tried to recall something else, I wound up thinking about Hutch and his rare smile. There was something about that vision; so precious.

My eyes flew open. Felix stood above me, but his attention was focused on the trees behind him. I knew he sensed it too. We were no longer alone.

Chapter Twenty-Four

I hadn't noticed the raindrops drumming lightly into the dirt, and it was only when I studied the trees that I felt the climbing breeze. Sprinkles of the rain feathered across my face. I could feel another storm brewing in the descending air pressure.

With another deep intake of breath through my nose, I was all too aware of Felix imitating my actions.

"I didn't think you were this stupid!" he called into the night. "Apparently I thought too highly of you. And trust me, that's saying something."

Struggling onto my elbows, my heart fluttered. I would recognize the smell of Hutch's fabric softener anywhere. He'd obviously wasted no time following me. But why, I had no idea. Perhaps he didn't want Randolph to believe he was involved with my plans of preventing Felix from getting the job done.

"You wouldn't be the first." Hutch made his appearance, stopping a few feet short of Felix. His eyes flickered toward me for a split second.

"If you came for her, you're too late," Felix said, a grin spreading across his face.

"Actually, I came to relieve you of your job," Hutch said.

"You haven't been authorized."

The uncertainty in Felix's voice rang clearly.

The wind picked up, showering a curtain of fat raindrops. Within moments, I was soaked to the bone. Electricity charged the atmosphere, and I shuddered at the first rumble of thunder.

"I'm finishing the job," Hutch went on. "Randolph wanted me to kill someone. That was my punishment, right?" He stepped closer. "He didn't think I'd be able to do it."

"And you didn't," Felix snarled.

"I'll kill Allen. Then everyone can be happy."

"What about the witnesses?" Flix asked.

"There won't be any."

Laughing outright, Felix said, "You expect me to believe you've got what it takes to slaughter every single person in that house?"

"I expect you to believe Allen will be dead before sunrise," Hutch insisted. "The rest of the family won't know of his demise until morning."

"That's your problem," Felix said, speaking slowly as though Hutch were a student and he was a critical instructor. "You never go the extra mile. You don't know my father the way I do. He wants a massacre; he wants a bloodbath. It's the only way his message will get across to others."

Hutch shook his head. "Randolph wants Allen dead for what he did. I'll take care of it." Dismissively, he added, "You may as well go home and tell him that."

My chest bloomed with respite. Hutch had listened to me — that was more than I could've hoped for. Felix still had an advantage over him, though. Hutch didn't know about his cousin's plot to kill him, or his transformation.

Straightening my posture, I opened my mouth to speak, but Felix recognized my intentions before I had time to utter a word. I barely saw his boot as he drove it into my lower abdomen. I cried out, wheezing for air.

"She has nothing to do with this," Hutch said.

"Afraid she does," Felix retorted between gritted teeth.

He lifted his foot again. I shut my eyes, tensing as I awaited the second blow, but it never came.

Felix was chuckling now, a deep, throaty sound that reminded me of Randolph.

When I peered up once more, I found Hutch with his semi-automatic trained on Felix.

"Go ahead," he chanted softly. "See what happens. I dare you."

161

Thunder rolled again. I pushed myself to my knees.

Hutch shook his head as he re-holstered the gun beneath the flap of his plaid jacket.

Felix leapt into action the moment he dropped his guard. Voice bubbling in my throat, I shouted a warning, but Hutch had already reacted, avoiding rapid swings of the knife. Backed into a tree, he grasped a sturdy branch above him. The flat of his feet clouted the center of Felix's chest with enough force to knock a man to the ground. Felix, however, retreated a few steps, smirking. Hutch watched him, perplexed.

Felix capered ahead again. He ripped at Hutch with such animosity, I winced.

My legs protested when I drug myself to my feet. I had to divert Felix's attention long enough for Hutch to collect his bearings. He hadn't come expecting to take on a Forgotten.

The rain bit into my skin as I began at a jog. I quickened my pace, muscles aflame. I could feel my strength gathering as each step grew lighter and lighter.

Arms outstretched, my shoulder rammed into Felix's ribcage, the force of the collision slamming him to the ground with me on top. From the corner of my eye, I saw the glint of the knife as it toppled into the shadows.

Rolling us a few times on the ground, Felix lashed out at my face, missing my cheek by mere millimeters. He made to strike again but was prevented from doing so when Hutch's fist slammed into his temple, causing his head to snap to the side.

"What have you done?" he demanded as Felix sprang to his feet. Hutch drew his gun again.

Felix roared in disdain, evading the bullets fired at him, the blasts muted by the silencer.

Wind gusted into my face, stealing my breath. Brushing away the wet hair glued to my cheeks, I strained to follow the on-going struggle. I staggered closer to the men until my bare toes collided into something solid, kicking the object a short distance. Foot pounding with additional discomfort, I knelt to obtain the gun, though my fingers trembled uncontrollably as I did so.

Over the pummeling rain, I could hear a muffled groan escape Hutch. Felix was straddling him on the ground near a clump of bushes. In a flurry of panic, I pulled the trigger one, two, three times, the gentle blast barely fazing me.

None of the bullets met the target. Felix was too fast. I narrowed my eyes into a squint, trying to locate him. Amid the triple gunshots, he'd taken cover between the trees, and now there was no telling where he was concealing himself.

Deep breaths failed to ease the panic rising within me. I inched closer to Hutch. Every rustle and snap sent a flood of adrenaline through my blood, making me too jittery to focus.

"Are you okay?" I asked Hutch as I drew closer. He grunted, rolling heavily to his side.

"No, he's not," came Felix's voice from behind.

I spun, aiming the barrel at his face, and pulled the trigger a fourth time. Felix counter-stepped and ripped the weapon from my fingers in a single motion. He tossed it lazily to the ground.

Loose strands of hair stuck to the sides of his face. He had a wild smirk on his lips.

He was really related to Hutch?

I'm not the monster, Hutch had once said. He was right. The monster was standing right in front of me.

"Don't you get it? I've already won."

A few feet from me, Hutch coughed another groan, his shape barely moving now. Felix gave me a toothy smile, as though reading my mind.

I hated him, and I hated his arrogant smirk. I wanted him to hurt. I wanted him to be miserable. This urge fueled enough energy for me to charge at him. When I had him cornered, Felix managed to slip away, throwing me off balance. It wasn't until I nearly fell into a briar patch that I realized it was all a game to him. He was sneering at my pathetic attempts to best him.

"You're such a child!" I yelled over the sound of his laughter. "No wonder your girlfriend is dead. You're too immature to care about anyone but yourself!" It was a low blow, but I couldn't stop the words from tumbling from my mouth. I'd been pushed far beyond the point of exasperation.

My gibe took immediate effect, though not what I'd been expecting. Felix came up from behind again, only this time he locked me in a chokehold with the crook of his elbow.

"I strongly suggest you stop talking," he said in my ear.

"Has it not crossed your mind," I grunted, struggling against his grip, "that Randolph called in that hit?"

Felix merely chuckled, but there was no humor in the sound. "He had no reason to do such a thing."

"Didn't he?" I seemed to inhale more rain than air. "You said he suspects what you've become."

"IT WASN'T HIM!" He spun me around, right fist cocked and prepared to strike. I managed to lurch out of reach just in time, my back colliding into a smaller tree.

Muffled blasts erupted from behind. Fire scorched my upper arm, just above the fold of my elbow.

For a moment, Felix stared blankly at me. His face twisted. As soon as he collapsed to the ground, I saw Hutch release the gun. The odd angling of his stance told me he was in pain.

My heart hammered uncontrollably in my chest. I rushed to Hutch's side, managing to catch him as his feet gave out from beneath him. With most of my strength drained from the recent confrontation, we both descended to the mud.

"We have to get back," he said quietly.

Blood soaked the front of his shirt, now shredded to ribbons.

"How bad is it?" I asked.

"Bad enough to need the anti-venom," he said.

I helped him back to his feet. Hutch cringed and grunted with every other step we took, even though our pace was sluggish.

"You have it in the Audi," I said as we drew nearer to the car.

Hutch shook his head. "We need to get home."

It took a great deal of effort, but we made it back to the Audi at last. After helping Hutch into the passenger seat, I hastened around to the driver's side, collecting the keys from beneath the mat.

Silence governed the streets. I drove carefully, stealing glances at Hutch numerous times throughout the journey back to the condo. He was hunched forward in the seat, breath coming in shallow pants. It was all I could do to assure myself he'd be all right — or at least as well as one could be after being slashed by a Forgotten. Shuddering at the thought, I pulled into the garage, parking the Audi.

The walk to the door was unnecessarily prolonged, mainly because Hutch refused to let me near enough to support him. When I came within arm's reach, he pushed me away, muttering something incoherent under his breath. Eventually I was submitted to following behind and praying he didn't lose his footing.

"Is there anything I can do?" I asked once inside the condo. "Can I get you anything?"

"Get me a water," he said without stopping in his tread to the bedroom.

I complied, circling the kitchen counter to the fridge. He'd stacked the bottled water into the bottom drawer the other night. Snatching one, I took measured steps to his room, moving less aptly than I wished due to injuries of my own.

I halted in the hallway. The rain sounded oddly loud, but I could not fathom why. The balcony door was locked, as I'd left it, which only led me to wonder how Hutch had gotten in. He couldn't have scaled the railing, seeing as a jump like that would've killed him.

Following the sound of pulsing rain, I entered the weight room and found glass scattered about the floor in thick shards. The broken window, I noticed, looked directly out onto the balcony.

A thump sounded in the distance, pulling me from my thoughts. Tracking back to the hallway, I continued onward into Hutch's bedroom. The door stood open, light streaming into the unmade bed from the master bath around the corner.

"I got your water," I said, not wanting to startle him. "Hutch?"

The bathroom door was ajar, revealing blood smeared ceramic tiles.

As the feeling of unease grew, I swung open the door. "Hutch!"

My knees crashed to the floor beside him, the bottle of water rolling to the base of the toilet, forgotten.

His body convulsed aggressively with cold, despite the beads of sweat spilling down his hairline.

Hutch sat with his back against the tub. He was no longer wearing his jacket, and without it, I could clearly see the damage done to his sopping shirt. My heart stuttered at the sight.

Bloodied handfuls of toilet paper littered the space beside him as if he'd attempted to clean himself up, only to realize the task to be futile.

My eyes landed on the small orange package next. It was identical to the alcohol towelette wipe he'd used at Damian's.

A tourniquet was knotted around his bicep.

"Did you use the medicine?" I asked.

Hutch shook his head, motioning to his fist still clutching the syringe. "I can't." His voice was strained, body shuddering involuntarily. He couldn't stop trembling long enough to administer the remedy himself.

Without hesitation, I reached for the syringe, but Hutch drew back with a jerk. When I shot him a questioning look, he shook his head. "It's too late."

"No, it's not," I said flatly. "Give it."

Relenting this time, Hutch didn't argue when I popped the lid off the needle and rid the syringe of air bubbles. I wondered if he could sense my apprehension as I lowered the needle to his arm.

"That wasn't so bad, was it?" I said, removing the syringe and tourniquet. I tossed them into the wastebasket by the sink, while the mess of toilet paper I flushed down the toilet.

"Just give it a few minutes," I told him. "You'll be fine."

We locked eyes and I was taken aback by the fierceness of his gaze. It didn't contain the coldness I was used to.

"You'll be fine," I repeated, voice dropping to a whisper. My fingers traced his forehead, brushing back the dampened hair. Hutch closed his eyes in response to my touch, spasms subsiding until all was still.

His head dropped to his chest.

CHAPTER TWENTY-FOUR

"Hutch," I said, my voice breaking. "Don't do this."

But he could no longer hear me. His body fell limp and he slid sideways toward the floor like a discarded puppet.

Chapter Twenty-Five

The flashback came without forewarning. I was wrenched from the bathroom, visions of a dark street cascading before me.

A car accident. Warped metal around the base of a tree. Emergency vehicles.

James sprinted from my side. He was screaming her name over and over again. Emily, Emily, Emily. Tears spilled from my eyes. Red and blue lights intruded on the darkness, flashing eccentrically. An officer held out a hand to prevent James from approaching the car, but my brother was not to be reasoned with. He nudged past the officer, yelling at the paramedics to wait before they hauled her away on the stretcher. A blanket concealed her face.

James didn't need to see her like this. I took hold of his wrist, swinging him back to me. He stumbled, clinging to me, his body shaking uncontrollably with sobs.

It was an unfortunate casualty, the officer told us. They suspected she had been texting, for she still had her phone in hand when they found her.

James held me in a rib-cracking embrace. I squeezed him back, my tears soaking into the fabric of his shirt. It was all too surreal. She had so much to look forward to—like my brother's wedding. But what was a wedding without the bride?

I opened my eyes, filing this new memory away to analyze at a later time. Matters at present were too overwhelming as they were.

The light of the bathroom didn't help my splitting headache. Steadying my breath, I found myself face down on the floor next to Hutch, curled against his form. I pushed back, propping onto my forearms as real tears streaked my face.

"Hutch." I rolled him to his back. "Please." I sniffed, choking on the words I wanted to say, but couldn't. This was partially my fault. If I hadn't run off, Hutch wouldn't have come after me, ill prepared to face Felix. But if I hadn't run off, the Allens would all be dead by now.

"Life can't be this unfair." But it was, and I knew it. My life was proof of that—Hutch's life was proof of that.

The tips of my fingers brushed his cheek. He didn't stir.

"I'm so sorry," I whispered, resisting the urge to crumble beside him.

Without him, there was no one I could trust, except perhaps Red. But how was I supposed to talk to him without Randolph finding out? Worst of all, Randolph was going to learn about what happened tonight. Would he come looking for me next?

Gaze trained on Hutch's face, I realized I didn't even care. Something was breaking inside me, far beyond anything I'd expected. As my thumb traced the curve of his bruised eyebrow—as I beheld the young man before me, I saw him differently. He wasn't the entitled jerk with a callous attitude I first thought he was. After being forced to spend the past week with him, I'd come to understand him.

"Please." More tears pushed out. "I need you."

My mind continued to reel with what was to come next. How would Randolph react to losing his nephew? Judging by what I knew of him and his despicable behavior, he'd probably be all too relieved to have Hutch off his hands. Would anyone other than Red care?

Fingers falling to Hutch's throat, a sob shuddered from deep within my chest. I was worse off now than ever before. Not only had I lost my family and my memories, but now I was losing Hutch. Not to mention I had a criminal to answer to for what happened to his son at the Allens.

"Please," I choked a third time. It was all I knew to say. The word alone embraced my feelings for him, feelings of which I wasn't fully aware until this moment of loss. After all, he'd become more to me than an acquaintance; more than an ally. Although I knew him so little, I still trusted him so much.

Foreheads touching, I closed my eyes for a moment. Beneath the smell of blood and rain, I still caught the faint scent of him. I stifled another sob, holding my breath. Despair bled from my soul. He was unresponsive, countenance relaxed as if asleep. I'd never seen him like this. When he passed out drunk in my room at Randolph's, he bore a drawn expression as if prepared for battle in his sleep. Now he was peaceful.

I squeezed my eyes shut, breath held inside myself. Then I heard it, faint though it was.

Eyes wide open, I repositioned my fingers on his throat.

A pulse.

Drawing a ragged breath, my lips stretched into an uncertain smile. He was alive. Unwell, but not yet dead. I had to trust the anti-venom would pull through, but until then, I could not leave him caked in mud and blood on the bathroom floor.

Not knowing the first thing about dressing wounds, I fished Hutch's phone from his pocket, praying the rain hadn't gotten to it. When the internet pulled up, I allowed a sigh of relief, tapping hastily on the keypad.

Thank goodness for Google.

I read through the steps three times before I scavenged for equipment, not that much was required. When I'd collected the scissors and clean wash rags, I returned to the floor next to Hutch.

"Hang in there," I murmured, knowing he couldn't hear me. "Let's hope you don't need stitches. I doubt I was any good at Home Ec."

Using the scissors, I removed Hutch's shirt, tossing it into the tub. My gaze returned to his solid build, hearting sinking. Thin lines of old scars dispersed his skin, similar to the fresh cuts centering his torso. Scar tissue circled the brawn of his shoulders, embellishing his chest and abdomen with lines that reminded me of casual strokes of a paintbrush.

Tearing my eyes from the old scars, I began my work of clearing the crimson stains from around the wounds. The bleeding had subsided, scars not appearing deep enough to require stitches, thank goodness. With another damp wash rag, I cleaned the mud from the cuts and bruises located on his face and hands.

I took my time, putting off what came next. A small part of me was hoping Hutch would awaken, even if he only remained conscious long enough to stagger to bed. Seeing as I could not leave him in the bathroom, I still had no desire to drag him across the floor and into the bedroom. At this point my muscles felt too inadequate to perform such a task.

"Now would be a good time as any to wake up." I held his hand in my lap, fingers knitted as I fought the mounting loneliness of the condo.

Hutch, of course, did not respond to my words, nor did he make any inclination that informed he was alive. But I knew he was, and I had faith in his recovery.

With no reason to put the task off any longer, I climbed to my feet. My fingers I laced across his chest in my attempt to haul him out of the bathroom, throwing my sore rib cage into a flaming furnace.

"You're heavier than you look," I grunted, legs trembling. I didn't stop to rest until I managed to pull him to the bed.

After stripping the comforter from the mattress, I turned back to Hutch's slapdash form on the carpet. My body pleaded I rested, but I gritted my teeth and bent down to lift him to the bed anyway.

Many grunts later, I successfully rolled us onto the bed without breaking any limbs in the process—his or mine. I shifted to my back, exhaustion wearing on my bones. But there was still no time for rest.

I removed the Timberlands from his feet, followed by sodden socks, dropping them to the floor beside the bed. Once a pillow was secured beneath his head, I crawled from the comfort of the bed and headed for the bathroom in the hall. I had myself to take care of now.

***

I was filth-free, and so was Hutch's bathroom. Finally. I threw the last of the wash rags into the tub. Those could be dealt with later. For the time being, I needed something for my head that hadn't stopped throbbing since the flashback.

Pushing aside the Epsom salt, I determined there was no Tylenol beneath the bathroom sink. I then moved to the mirror, but after sifting through the medicine cabinet, it was evident there was no Tylenol there either. Instead

171

I found a handful of orange pill bottles. I glimpsed at the names, but they might as well have been Chinese for all the good it did. I couldn't pronounce half of them.

Meddlesome curiosity overruled my better judgement. I collected the bottles, convinced some research using Hutch's phone would shed light on the purpose of the medication.

My heart froze as soon as I reached for the phone. Five missed calls all from someone listed as BR.

Who was calling at this hour? And why couldn't Hutch have entered names into his contact list instead of initials?

Paranoia kicked in. Dumping the pill bottles onto the mattress, I darted down the hall to make sure the security system had been activated. Randolph wouldn't have discovered what happened so soon, would he? He shouldn't be awake for another few hours—unless he was waiting for Felix to update him on the progress of his work at the Allens'.

Wrapping my hands around my middle, I returned to the bedroom, taking in the starkness of it. The walls were bare of pictures. A lumpy pile of clothes occupied the striped armchair in one corner. A wide-screen TV was perched on an oak dresser on one side of the room, a matching nightstand balancing a lamp next to the bed. There was but one window near the closet door to the left. Darkness pushed on the glass from the outside, barely marking the start of a new day.

Slinking to the bed, I curled up, arms clinging to my knees. I kept envisioning the worst-case scenario possible: Randolph sending his thugs to the condo to—what? Kill us? That didn't seem likely. Even a brute like Randolph would have sense enough to question us. Right?

In hopes of distracting myself, I grabbed the nearest pill bottle and searched it on the internet. I then repeated the process with the other four bottles, growing more and more tired as the minutes ticked by.

Two pills were the same, one being the generic version of the other. Sleeping pills. And by the looks of the refill date, Hutch hadn't been taking them as prescribed.

The other pills were used to treat a variety of cases, anxiety and depression among them.

Stifling a yawn, I strained my ears. Hutch's pulse was thumping—stronger now? Perhaps it was just my imagination. I wanted him to get well bad enough, I'd started hearing things.

The navy-blue shirt I'd snatched from his dresser fit perfectly around my knees as I coiled onto my side. The mental dam I'd built to block my ascending fears was on the brink of combusting. I felt it in the tremble of every muscle, every aching joint.

By some miracle, I fell asleep. Considering the amount of stress I was under, I hadn't thought it possible.

My empty stomach woke me sometime later. Eyes refusing to open, I rolled stiffly, reaching to check on Hutch. Hunger clawed its way up my insides, and I willed my eyelids open into slits.

The scene dawned on me slowly. It was too early for my brain to function properly, but eventually it sunk in. The other side of the bed was vacant. I was alone in the dark room.

Chapter Twenty-Six

Dim light peeked through the drapes of the single window. The door was shut, trapping the darkness within the bedroom—not how I'd left it.

I hissed at the sear of pain in my arm as I sat up, pushing the comforter off my chest. Somehow it had managed to return to the bed from the floor. I shivered, chill air engulfing me.

Padding to the door, I opened it. Murmurs of the television grew louder, while a monotone hum-drum of noise trailed from the kitchen.

Laundry.

Flapping of wings prickled my insides. I never would've expected the smell of coffee to bring so much joy. With the agility of a cat, I tip-toed down the hall, stopping to peek around the corner.

Coffee mug in hand, Hutch was just about to seat himself on the sofa when he looked up, face shadowed by the snapback on his head. A gray hoodie concealed his fresh wounds of the night before.

For a long moment, he watched me as I stood half-hidden behind the wall. His expression was unreadable, eyes as if penetrating the sacred barrier of my thoughts. I didn't like it.

"You're alive." I groaned inwardly. Thanks, Captain Obvious. "I mean. I'm glad you're not—you know…" The sultry taste in my mouth prevented me from finishing the sentence.

Hutch raised a hand, removing the gray hood from his head. Not once did he break eye contact. The flapping on my insides increased. I stepped back half a foot, suddenly aware of his T-shirt reaching the middle of my thighs.

"You're bleeding." He motioned to my arm. I glanced down. Sure enough, blood seeped into the sleeve, smearing along my skin.

"Oh." I pried the sticky material from the wound. It was where one of Hutch's bullets had grazed my arm. "I'm sorry."

My breath got lost on its way down to my lungs. Hutch had closed the distance between us, taking my elbow into his hand to better examine my arm.

"Why are you sorry?" he murmured, fingers gently prodding around the mangled flesh.

I gulped. Why was I sorry? "I messed up your shirt. I probably got blood on your sheets."

Hutch presented me with a crooked smile—something I wanted to see more often.

"There are a few tricks to removing bloodstains." He released my elbow.

I inspected my arm to hide my flush. "Why didn't it heal? The others have scabbed over."

"It's too deep," he said. "Abstinence of blood will inhibit your ability to recover."

Drat. There was no getting out of stitches.

"Give me a minute and I'll take care of it," he added.

I was prepared to turn down his offer, but Hutch had already left my side, disappearing into his bedroom. Weighing my options, I found it wisest I got dressed before entangling myself in anything else.

In the bathroom, I stuffed my legs into a pair of jeans and pulled a soft pink top over my head, easing the sleeve carefully around the tear in my skin.

Hutch was waiting for me by the dining table when I returned, the contents of a medical kit strewn across the glass top. He was sipping from his mug, gaze held by the flickering television.

"So." I sidled closer to the table, stomach clenching at the needle and tweezers soaking in a bowl of disinfectant. "What do I do?"

"You could sit down." Snarky, but not spiteful. His tone was almost teasing.

I sat, examining the other items on the table while Hutch washed his hands.

Cotton balls, gauze, thread, more disinfectant. Thank goodness I wasn't required to perform stitches on Hutch last night.

"Put your elbow on the table," he instructed, sitting in front of me. Our knees bumped as he did so.

Hutch examined the wound once more, reaching for the disinfectant. A whimper escaped my lips as soon as the liquid touched the gash. Hutch paused for half a second as if hesitating.

"What?" I asked, glancing away from the sizzling wound.

"I'm just not accustomed to working with people of your stature." He gathered the needle and thread.

"My stature?"

"You're significantly smaller than Randolph's guys."

I couldn't help but laugh. "I didn't realize you had your own private practice."

Shrugging, he explained, "Before I moved here, I helped a few of the guys at the mansion. I learned by helping Samuel when he couldn't patch himself up."

I clenched my teeth, stomach roiling as I saw Hutch draw the thread in my peripheral. Just as I marveled on the absence of pain, an unexpected pinch pressured the sore skin.

"Try to relax," Hutch said, the visor of his snapback obscuring his face.

Searching for a means to distract myself, I asked, "How did you get to the Allens' house last night?"

"Uber."

"Uber?" I asked in disbelief. I couldn't quite picture Hutch rating his driver before he found Felix and me. Pushing the thought aside, I noticed his cell phone on the kitchen counter. "You had a few missed calls last night."

"I know." He drew the thread again. "I haven't made time to return Red's calls."

So that was what BR stood for. "What do you think he was calling about?"

"I won't know until I call."

Pinch, wince.

"You don't think Randolph knows about last night?" I squirmed in my seat.

"By now, I'm sure Felix has already given his twisted version of what happened."

"He's not dead?" I gaped at the blank panels of his hat.

Hutch shook his head. "If Forgotten were that easy to kill, anyone could do it." He shifted closer. "Felix underwent shock, but his condition would've restored him by now."

My chest tightened. "What about the Allens?" Did Felix finish the job?

"I know as much as you do," Hutch said. "I'll find out more when I talk to Red."

"It was him all along," I said. "The texts, the disappearances. The murders. Felix killed Damian, and he's trying to kill you, too."

"I guessed as much." He dug a penknife from his pocket and cut the excess thread. "After what happened last night, at least. I couldn't tell you why he has it out for me all of a sudden."

"Because you killed someone important to him," I said. "The case Randolph handed you, involving a female Forgotten. You told me it was kept under wraps. Probably because he didn't want Felix hearing about it. Randolph knows he's a Forgotten. I'm almost positive. That's why he wanted this Forgotten out of the picture—she was responsible for his son's transformation."

I repeated what I'd learned of Felix's failed scheme and how Leo's death was his fault, not Hutch's.

It was only when I finished talking that I realized Hutch was no longer tormenting me with the needle. He sat back in the chair, hands tucked away in the pockets of his hoodie. Teeth clenched, he deliberated this new information. "Looks like I'll need to make another trip to Franklin."

"We need to get this sorted out before things escalate," I agreed.

Hutch straightened, shaking his head. "You're not coming. Especially after what happened the last time you paid a visit to Randolph's mansion."

Opening my mouth to argue, I thought better of myself and shut it. He had a point. I only went the first time, because of the job Hutch and I shared. Now it was done, and I was no longer a part of his uncle's business. I did not need to walk into unnecessary danger when I had enough surrounding me as it was.

Gaze sinking to the neat stitches, I chortled. "That's a lot better than what I would've done. Think homemade ragdoll."

"That's because I actually paid attention in Home Ec," Hutch said, scooping up the roll of gauze.

I froze suddenly. Surely his words were mere coincidence.

There was a sideways grin tugging at the corner of his lips as he wrapped my arm. "I did tell you the properties of Forgotten venom."

"You told me it's fatal." My tone sounded more accusing than I meant it to.

"Ultimately," Hutch nodded. "First it paralyzes the victim. One at a time, each organ shuts down until the body fails to function as a whole. It could take hours, of course, but it gives the Forgotten time to consume the victim's blood while they are still alive."

"When you say paralyzed..." I said slowly, dreading what came next.

"Disabled, but not comatose."

"Okay."

Kill me now.

Last night flashed before my eyes: my pitiless sobs, my uncertain hands and the graceless manner I used to get him to bed. All of which he'd experienced. Wide. Awake.

My face was burning. Hutch saw it, I knew, because his eyes were alight with mirth.

Mortified, I skipped to my feet. "Thanks." I gestured mechanically toward my arm as Hutch pushed from his seat. He was a mountain before me, broad and towering. I stood planted before him, willing myself to look up from the drawstring of his hoodie.

He wasn't smirking now. His gaze was profound; jaw tightened. I inhaled, but it was as though air was being vacuumed from my chest.

Hutch outlined the scar on my forehead with his thumb, his fingers enshrouded beneath the tresses of my hair. I felt his hammering pulse against my scalp. "You were right about saving the Allens," he said quietly. "I shouldn't have pushed you to such measures. I'm afraid working for Randolph has cost me my humanity over the years."

"Not all of it." I tried to smile. Every fiber of my being pulled closer to him; I wanted him to know just how glad I was for his recovery—that I hadn't lost him. But I could not yield to my mixed emotions. Being humiliated once was bad enough.

"I'm famished," I lied.

Spinning away, I allowed my feet to carry me to the kitchen. Sure, I was hungry—up until a few moments ago. At present my gut was complete with an army of fluttering butterflies.

After bumbling about the kitchen for longer than necessary, I settled down on the couch with a bowl of cereal. Hutch had cleared the dining table and retreated to his room with his cell phone. I was all too happy to be alone. I sank into the cushions and let the mindless chatter of the television melt my brain.

The empty bowl clanked onto the coffee table when I finished eating. My eyes descended to the worn photograph deposited on the edge. I groaned, running my hands through my hair. It was the picture of Hutch and his mother.

Slipping it between my fingers, I was suddenly taken aback by the young Hutch. There was a resemblance now, as opposed to when I'd first located the photograph at Randolph's. The similarity was in the way his smile brightened his eyes from their dusky, reddish-brown hues.

I chewed my lip.

If memory served, I'd stuffed the photograph beneath my pillow so Hutch wouldn't discover it. I knew he'd get the wrong idea if he found it in my possession. Heaven knew what he thought now.

Why *did* I still have it?

I left the sofa and made for the bar mantle. The photograph I stood leaning against the wall—where picture frames were meant to decorate the panel.

It was silly of me to bring the photograph in the first place. Hutch probably had it buried in his desk drawer at Randolph's for a reason.

But I had to hold on to it. I hadn't known Hutch very well and needed to cling to the hope that some little piece of that boy still existed.

Now I knew he did.

Chapter Twenty-Seven

The morning was overcast, filtering the atmosphere of the condo to a grayscale. The pattering of rain on stone drifted in from the balcony, only making the overall mood gloomier.

I crouched above the broken glass in the weight room, shivering in response to the cool breeze sweeping through the window. With the temperature dropping overnight, the air was left cold and damp. I tugged the lace cardigan closer around me.

A towel sprawled on the floor collected the larger shards of glass. Despite my hope of using work to distract myself, rampant thoughts dissected the possibilities of Felix's actions. Dread crept up my spine like a venomous spider. I couldn't shake the fear that my efforts to save the Allens had been futile. After everything that happened last night, did Felix finish what he went there to do?

As soon as the majority of the glass was gathered on the towel, I allowed myself a moment of apprehension. Elbows on my knees and fingertips massaging my forehead, I pushed heavy locks above my hairline.

I couldn't handle this level of stress. No wonder Hutch had a handful of prescriptions lining the shelf of his medicine cabinet. Working for Randolph, his life revolved around this sort of tension.

My second finger grazed the mark on my forehead, a reminder of last night's battle. The sensation called forth the ghost of Hutch's touch, his fingers buried within my hair. I dropped my hands to my thighs, spurning any emotion the thought could inspire.

The bedroom door opened at the other end of the hall. Hutch hadn't stepped foot from his room since he'd retreated an hour or so earlier.

"I talked to Red," he said quietly. He was standing in the doorway of the weight room, one hand gripping the frame. "The Allens are fine."

"What happened?" I stood, dusting my jeans.

Hutch glared at the mess on the floor, his jaw pulsing. Something was wrong. I could tell by the change in his disposition. He was now guarded, the good-natured man I'd witnessed earlier gone—concealed behind the cold façade with which I was all too familiar.

"When Felix recovered, the house was swarming with the heat." He picked at a flake of paint.

"The what?"

"Cops."

I gawped. "How?"

"The two officers on rotation last night were found dead in the trunk of their cruiser."

I drew a ragged breath.

"The Allens are gone," he said. "Off the grid again."

"Randolph can't be too thrilled about that." Was that what was bothering him? I doubted it.

Hutch dropped his arm to his side. "You don't have to worry about this." He motioned to the bits of glass embedded into the carpet.

"There's not much else to occupy my time." I tilted my head, wishing there was some way I could know what was pestering him, besides the obvious.

I had a theory. "Did you learn anything about your parents?"

Hutch's startled gaze met mine. In the shadow of his visor, his eyes were rimmed with exhaustion.

"You've been listening."

"No." Not this time, at least. "Felix's text."

We both fell silent for a moment, as if recalling the first message sent Thanksgiving Day. *Wanna know what happened to ur parents? Try murdered.*

Hutch's jaw pulsed again. He exhaled, shoving his hands into his pockets. "Red uncovered some details that hadn't been released to anyone."

"How did he manage that?" I asked.

With a brief glance, I could tell he was considering whether he should reveal this information. Typical.

"Our contact at the precinct," he said.

I nodded, deciding it was a sufficient explanation. "I take it your mother didn't...," how to say this nicely? "OD."

"My mother didn't use," he said firmly. "But my attempts to prove otherwise were worthless. And Randolph wouldn't help my case."

"Do you think he was involved?" I asked, horrified at the concept. Yet there was something in his tone that implied his suspicions.

When Hutch neglected to respond, I wrung my hands behind my back. "What are you going to do?"

I knew what he was going to say, but that didn't mean I had to like it.

"I'm going to confront him." He shrugged, a gesture I recognized as deceptive. He'd offered the same shrug at the gas station the night we met. Only now I believed him when he'd claimed to have no intention of letting me die at the hands of a petty thief.

Challenging Randolph was no small task. Hutch's indifference did not fool me. His hurt and anger were clear as day. Armed with these emotions, he was leaving to face the core of his hatred. Although I knew good could not possibly come of this confrontation, I understood it was something he needed to do.

Brimming with concern, I acted on impulse, looping my arms around his torso. Hutch didn't make any attempt to pull away, even if his hesitance was evident. His palms found my shoulders, their warmth saturating my arms through the cardigan.

"Please be careful," I heard myself whisper.

Why was my heart breaking for him when I had my own problems to face? Why did I wish to go with him, to be there for him? Of course, I couldn't go. We both knew it. This was something he had to do alone.

With a deep breath, Hutch relaxed. The tip of my nose grazed the line of his neck, the gentle scent of soap lingering on his skin.

We were quiet: our heartbeats pirouetting to a similar rhythm. I squeezed my eyes shut. With Hutch gone, loneliness threatened to smother me with the same force as last night when I believed him to be on the brink of death.

"I know you have to do this," I said, "but please don't forget about me."

Faltering, Hutch stiffened. I opened my eyes, peeking at his expression. Sepia irises searched my jade ones.

"I couldn't," Hutch murmured. His sincerity quickened the animated dance of my heart. There was a softness about his eyes; one that illustrated a depth I never noticed.

It was the second time today—the second time in less than two hours I was convinced he was prepared to kiss me.

I stumbled, narrowly missing the collection of glass on the towel.

Wrong. I was unmistakably wrong. Hutch hunted others like me. I had no legitimate reason to believe he felt anything but pity; that is, if he felt anything other than revulsion.

In an attempt to ward off my sudden awkwardness, I asked, "When will you be back?"

Hutch dug his hands back into his pockets, seeming bewildered to my actions. "I can't be sure. It depends on how things play out." He paused, contemplating what he was about to say next. "I'll leave you my cell. If anything happens, if you need to reach me, contact Red. I won't be far from him."

"'If anything happens'?" I repeated. "Like what?"

He shook his head. "Just…if you need me." Turning away, I watched him pause in the doorway, his back to me.

"You wanted to know how someone can be exposed to the threat of transforming," he said, glancing back. "It happens when the blood of a Forgotten fuses with the blood of the victim."

At first, I couldn't fathom why he chose this moment to enlighten me. As I watched him leave the room, it suddenly hit me: he didn't know if he was coming back.

***

Hutch was gone before the end of the hour. He left a handful of cash for takeout if necessary, along with his phone, sealed with the promise to check in later.

I finished cleaning the weight room and taped a garbage bag over the window to keep out the wind. It was a temporary solution, not at all attractive. But Hutch would have it fixed as soon as he returned. Because he would return.

The mere thought of him reminded me of his absence. As much as I hoped everything worked out in Franklin, an ominous feeling pulsated in my gut. How would Randolph react to his accusations? By the amount of cash he left behind, I could tell he'd been considering the worst-case scenario. If it did come to that and Randolph tried to come for me, there was easily enough money for me to catch a flight across the country and reside at a hotel for about a week.

Not that I had any intentions of doing so.

I suddenly felt sick. Stuffing bloody sheets into the washer, my thoughts patronized me. I should've gone with him. My safety was trivial compared to what Hutch faced. Randolph had dozens of men to do his bidding. What if he called an order to silence his nephew?

A vision of Hutch taking on the handful of troublemakers at the gas station assured me he could take care of himself. Besides, would Randolph really try to assassinate him?

By dusk, there was not a speck of dust visible in the condo. Having run out of rooms to clean, I slumped at the table in the dining room, glaring at the black screen of the phone. Why hadn't he called yet?

The growing trepidation was getting harder to ignore. I needed to stay busy. I needed to...

I scooped up the phone. It was time to worry about myself right now.

As my thumbs typed *missing persons near me* into the search bar, my insides did an anxious jig. I doubted Hutch would be bothered by my snooping now. The job was done. There were no more secrets to keep.

Navigating to a promising website, I held my breath. There were a number of images regarding missing individuals. I scrolled down the page until I found what I was looking for.

My chest heaved. I covered my mouth with one hand, clutching the phone with the other. Tears gathered, but I blinked them away.

James stared back at me, his hair combed to the side, dressed in a suit and tie. It was his graduation picture. Below was the caption: *James Wyer, 24, Kingston Springs*.

Kingston Springs? The name drew up blank.

What happened to you? I longed to reach out and touch my brother's face as the memories of my emotions for him sharpened.

Tears suddenly spilled down my cheeks as reality hit with a virulent blow: they'd never found him, either. We were both lost.

Reining my emotions—or at least trying to—I wiped my nose on the sleeve of my cardigan and scrolled to the next picture.

My face beamed back, a semi-sincere smile; a yearbook photo. I scrolled to the caption, freezing for an extended moment.

Aprilynne 'Rily' Wyer, 18, Kingston Springs.

There must be a mistake.

I whispered the name repeatedly, but it was alien on my tongue.

Worrying my lower lip, my mind raced. This was wrong. It wasn't me. Hutch had spoken my name when we met.

What else had he lied about?

The truth settled, escorting with it a queasiness in the pit of my stomach. I'd be a fool to commit my loyalty to someone working with crooks. I was a *fool*.

The screen transitioned, phone vibrating savagely in my grip. Melinda's name appeared, the telephone icon bouncing merrily below.

My stomach bungee jumped to the floor. Why was she trying to get in touch? They were supposed to be in hiding. Witness protection or something—heck if I knew.

Taking a chance, I swiped upward.

"Hayden?" Melinda's delicate voice filtered through the line.

Aprilynne, actually. "Yeah, hi." I didn't sound okay. I cleared my throat. "How are you?"

CHAPTER TWENTY-SEVEN

Melinda scoffed. "Physically or emotionally?"

"I don't know. Both."

Her sigh gusted through the earpiece. "Alive and confused."

"What's wrong?" I asked.

"I wish I knew." She paused. "Mike told you about Dad showing up?"

"Yeah, last night." I nodded, even though I knew she couldn't see me. Holy Ritz crackers, was it just last night I saw Mike at the party?

"Yeah, well, everything's spiraling out of control."

"How so?" I asked, feigning ignorance. Of course I knew what was going on. I was part of it.

"I don't even know," she groaned. "Dad's not telling us anything. Something happened this morning, but no one's talking. We were told to gather our things and leave the house."

"Oh." I struggled for words. "Is there... anything I can do?" Why was she even calling to tell me this?

Melinda laughed, though she sounded on the verge of hysteria. Poor girl. If something didn't give, a mental breakdown loomed in her near future. "No. There's nothing you can do. But thanks." She sighed a second time.

I smiled despite myself. She had no idea how fortunate they were to be alive right now. If Felix had gotten to them first...

I pushed the thought aside. No need to go there. I drummed the table in a Hutch-like manner.

"Oh, right," Melinda gave an awkward laugh. "I was calling to see if you were free tonight."

My fingers halted mid-drum.

"Why?" I asked, dragging out the question.

"We're going to BrickTop's at eight. I wanted to see if you could join. I was *hoping* you would join."

My eyebrows did a sprint to my hairline. Were they seriously exposing themselves this soon after what happened last night? Had it not occurred to Eric the danger he and his family were in?

"Hayden?"

"Yeah, sorry." What was I supposed to tell her? Associating with them would be a precarious move, but then again, Randolph had no idea of their location. For all he knew, they could be on the other side of the world.

Hutch would advise I declined the offer.

I pursed my lips, chest flickering with flames of anger and betrayal.

"Sure," I said. Eight o'clock at BrickTop's."

Chapter Twenty- Eight

Doubt spilled from my mind into my chest on the drive to the restaurant. I sat quietly in the backseat of the Uber driver's car, wondering if what I was doing was considered reckless. My brain screamed I was a fool, but my heart was still infuriated by Hutch's lack of faith in me. What I was trying to prove by meeting the Allens, I did not know. Yet I simply could not stand the thought of being alone in the condo for another wretched minute.

Droplets of rain trickled down the length of the window, my breath fogging the glass. I was glad for the radio. The driver did not appear enthused to strike up a conversation, and I didn't care to socialize. Somewhere between the condo and the restaurant we'd made a silent agreement to allow the seasonal music to drown the silence.

He was getting a decent rating from me.

My destination rolled into view. I inhaled, tightening the ties of my coat around my middle. As I managed to thank the driver and shut the passenger door behind me, someone called my name across the parking lot.

Melinda led a party of three. Mike followed behind, along with the stranger I'd seen through their dining room window last night.

Eric Allen, up close and personal.

I resisted the desire to glare at him. Did he not realize the danger in which he put his family?

Mustering a smile, I approached them. "Where's Max? And Mr. and Mrs. Allen?"

"Max was tired," Mike said, his eyes lowered to the pavement.

"And Dad was eager to meet you," said Melinda, gesturing to the middle-aged man with them.

Eric stepped forward, offering a hand as he introduced himself.

"I heard good things about you and your brother," he said. "James, is it?"

I nodded, unable to vocalize the untruth of Hutch being my brother.

"You should've brought him along," Melinda said, herding us to the door. An oversized wreath bearing ribbons and twinkle lights hung before the glass.

Thankfully I was not expected to respond as a hostess led us to a corner booth, promising the arrival of our waitress.

Mistletoe decked the wall lamp in our booth. Now that Thanksgiving was all said and done, it was apparent everyone was cutting loose on the Christmas decorations. Poinsettias and garland met my gaze with every turn I made.

Eric took a seat across from me, his regard making me feel as though I were placed on a pedestal. Mike sat next to him, still avoiding eye contact. And then there was Melinda, her long hair spilling around her face. She gave me a small smile, but there was something so very wrong with this scene.

As soon as I removed my coat, the left pocket began to vibrate. The waitress swooped by to leave us each a glass of water and take our drink orders. By the time I managed to retrieve Hutch's phone from the pocket, I saw a missed call from *BR*.

That would've been Red's number. Hutch had taken his sweet time to check in.

"Is everything all right?" Eric asked and I realized everyone at the table was watching me glower at the cell phone.

I nodded again, blushing this time. Grabbing a menu, I stuck my nose behind it, hoping someone would change the subject.

"Melly tells me you're from around here."

I peered over the top of my menu. Eric's cerulean gaze held mine. I wasn't dense enough to miss the fact that the man had his qualms about me. Just like the elderly Mr. Allen, Eric wasn't quick to trust.

Mike shot a nervous glance in my direction, only fueling my suspicions. Clearing my throat, "Yes."

"The sushi looks good," Mike displayed his menu for us to see, as if we didn't have our own.

"Do you go to school around here?" Eric asked, ignoring his son.

"I'm homeschooled, actually." I applauded myself for the quick response.

"Any particular reason?" he questioned further. "I was under the impression only hermits and simple-minded students were the ones who required homeschooling."

"Dad." Melinda shot him a warning glance. "Please."

"That's how it was in my day," he muttered, scanning the page with the entrées. "I didn't realize it was a personal question."

The cell phone started to vibrate again, creating a grinding noise on the tabletop. I snatched it up, and swiped to decline the call.

"Any plans for college?" Eric tried again.

"I'm thinking about deferring a year." I dropped the phone into my lap.

"What do your parents think about you deferring?"

Riding the tail of Hutch's fib, I said, "It's just my dad, and he's supportive of my decision."

Eric's expression turned thoughtful. I could see the resemblance between him and Mike, the way a small V appeared between their eyebrows when deep in thought. "What happened to your mother?"

"I agree, Mike," Melinda said, "sushi sounds good. What do you think, Hayden?"

I started, unable to decipher the uneasy atmosphere at the table. "Sure."

"Here's an interesting fact," Melinda propped her elbows on the table, inclining her head toward me. "It turns out Dad knows your father from work."

I nearly choked on my water, but no one paid me any attention.

"I wouldn't say I know him," Eric said. "But Caleb and I have exchanged words before."

When Eric looked up at me, my heart sank into my stomach.

He knew.

Of course he would know. He would've done his own research on me and Hutch, otherwise known as James.

The waitress came by and took our orders. When the phone rang a third time, I politely excused myself from the table, navigating my way to the restrooms.

I wasn't interested in Hutch's excuses for lying to me about my true identity. I had no intentions of answering the phone to talk to him. I just needed an excuse to get away from the table.

Declining the call, yet again, my gaze drifted to the wide mirror above the sinks. I stared at my reflection, cursing myself for walking into Eric's ploy. Why else would he have wanted to meet me? He knew I wasn't who I claimed to be, and he made it clear. So what was his plan? Kidnap me, demanding to know who I worked for?

Shuddering, I inhaled deeply. I had to take an early leave from this little dinner party. But how? Eric would see through any lie I came up with. And I could hardly make a speedy escape if I had to wait on a ride.

Contemplating this, a knock sounded on the door.

Instinctively, I peered around at the stalls, confirming I was the only individual in the ladies' room. Just when I thought it was the maintenance guy knocking, Mike's voice pushed through the barrier.

"Hayden?" He hesitated. "Are you still in there?"

Taken aback by his need to check on me, I pulled open the door and stepped out.

"I was barely two minutes." I forced a smile, crossing my arms. The Spanish style dress was lovely with its lace and off-shoulder sleeves, but it hadn't been the wisest choice, considering the season.

"I know." He was finally looking at me, concern drawing the same thoughtful expression as his father's. "I just needed a minute to talk to you. Alone."

"What about?"

He scratched the back of his head. "My dad. If he comes off as... a little odd, it's because he cares about his family. Don't get me wrong," he added in a hurry before I could get a word out. "He feels indebted to you for saving

192

Mel. You have to understand, it's in his nature to question good deeds of others."

"You make him sound like a sceptic."

"He's seen a lot in his day." Mike's scrutiny begged me to understand. And I did; more than he knew. Eric's line of work left him to live with a guilty conscience. Of course he would be cynical.

"It's fine." I lifted my hand to his shoulder, hoping to reassure him. "Really. I get it."

Mike's grim expression broke into a relieved smile. He removed my hand from his shoulder, squeezing it gently. "You're amazing."

Last night's party flashed across my mind, the center of everyone's attention, while my fingers curled around the hair on the back of Mike's neck. Our breath mingled, bodies close.

I pulled from Mike's grasp, heat creeping into my face. "We should head back," I said.

He opened his mouth then closed it. It was evident I was not the only one recalling the kiss that transpired between us.

With a nod of his head, Mike and I returned to the others, our food following shortly thereafter.

The conversation at the table strayed from Eric's curiosity of me as Mike and Melinda shared humorous anecdotes of their childhood. Although I was convinced Eric was sure to resume his interrogation, I found him quietly entertained by his two oldest children. A smile quirked the corners of his mouth, and he studied Mike and Melinda with a tenderness that disappeared the moment he caught me watching him.

When the bill came, I was prevented from paying for my meal. Eric muttered something about returning the favor while Mike and Melinda brushed off my insistence, assuring me it was no trouble. With no desire to argue further, I settled for leaving the waitress a generous tip.

"We should do this again sometime," Melinda said as we followed her out the door. Rain spilled from the heavens in buckets now.

"Do you have a ride?" Eric asked, removing the Velcro clasp of his umbrella.

I held up my phone with confidence. "I'll get Uber."

"Don't be ridiculous," Mike said. "We'll drop you off. You shouldn't have to pay for a ride."

"I'm not worried about it," I told him, already pulling up the app.

"It's getting pretty late," Melinda joined in. "With all the bad stuff they talk about on the news, there's really no reason for us to leave you here to wait for your ride to show up."

"Come on, we'll take you home." Mike draped an arm around my shoulder. "Right, Dad?"

"Of course." Eric sounded genuine, but I didn't believe he'd suddenly grown to trust me in such little time. Had this been his plan all along? Force me into his custody on the backs of his good-willed children?

Looking from Mike to Melinda, I wagered Eric wouldn't do anything incriminating in front of them. Right?

Despite the added risk to the situation, I agreed to let them take me back to the condo. All the while, I wondered if Eric's sole reason for meeting me tonight was to intimidate me. He obviously knew I'd been lying, but he did not know the extent of the lie. He did not know with whom I was involved. This suggested the shared meal tonight would not be the last time I crossed paths with the man.

Relief filled me as the car pulled up to the building. I thanked the Allens for dinner, and left them to sprint across the lot through the rain.

On the way up to Hutch's floor, I shivered, hair clumped in wet knots. A warm bath sounded soothing. I punched in the code, swinging open the door to complete darkness. Kicking the door shut behind me, I tapped the screen of Hutch's phone. There was a message I hadn't noticed from *BR*.

Where r u?

Wouldn't you like to know, I sneered, flipping on the lights.

"Nice to see you again, doll."

I sensed him before he spoke. Stix reclined on the sofa, one ankle resting casually on his opposing knee.

Spinning on the spot, I saw Red step forth from behind the door. His face was dark, livid.

"What's going on?" I directed my question to the heftier man, ignoring

CHAPTER TWENTY-EIGHT

Stix's haughty laugh.

"You're coming with us," Red replied.

From the corner of my eye, I saw Stix push to his feet. A brace swathed his left wrist.

"Why?"

"Save your questions for later," Stix said, approaching me.

I didn't look away from Red. I didn't understand why he was angry. Where was he trying to take me? Did Hutch know about this? Would he let this happen?

My stomach knotted at the thought. I'd been so foolish to believe he would go out of his way to take me home. It was all an act. He didn't trust me, and he didn't trust my ability to harness my bloodlust. Instead, he was willing to hand me off to Randolph's chumps.

Rage escalated within me. Red must've comprehended my change in demeanor, for he stepped forward, hands outstretched in a calming manner.

Snarling I launched at him, pushing with the full force of my body until he stumbled backward. Stix wasn't an immediate threat, being feet away from where I stood. I darted for the door, and managed to make it to the corridor. I could disappear. Just keep running until I was far away from this place. I didn't need Hutch to get me home.

A gentle *pop* reached my ears about the time something sharp pricked me between the shoulder blades. I lost my footing on the stairs, smashing my shoulder on the way down. When I hit the platform below, I groaned. Pain thumped, a chill numbness spiraling slowly around my spine, as though gripped by an icy fist. My fingers reached for the aching spot on my back so I could remove the dart, but it fell almost immediately from my grasp as my fingers grew too clumsy to hold on to it. My head whirled. The paralyzing ache was enough to tell me I was doomed if I failed to inject the anti-venom into my veins.

Chapter Twenty-Nine

By the time my feet made it back to the top of the stairs, Stix cornered me.

"I thought that might change your mind." His breath was hot in my face, smelling of stale tobacco. He waved his tranquilizer gun condescendingly.

I pushed at him, my strength wilting by the minute. Behind him, Red took brisk steps toward us. "Stix, you blundering idiot," he said, snatching the gun from the other man's grasp. "This will kill her."

"Isn't that the point?" Stix snarled.

"No, it's not." Red gripped my shoulder, steering me away from his partner.

My legs buckled, fingers groping his blazer. "The remedy. It's inside." Shivers peeled from my core.

Red assisted me inside to the master bath where Hutch's medical kit was stored. Only now it was missing.

Moaning in distress, I dropped to my knees, digging all items from beneath the sink. Epsom salt exploded across the floor when it hit the tile.

"He took it with him," I whispered. Sweat dampened my scalp, and I pushed my hair from my face, unable to give in to defeat.

I couldn't die like this.

Strong hands lifted me from the floor. "Then there's no time to waste." Red shuffled me out of the condo.

Hutch's usual parking spot was occupied by a glossy Infinity. After seating me behind the driver's seat, Red removed his blazer, tucking it around my trembling form. His black eyes met mine for a moment, offering a silent apology for the dramatic turn of events. I could do nothing but set my jaw to keep my teeth from chattering.

As soon as we were on the road, I leaned my head back on the headrest. Red crushed all of Stix's attempts to excuse his actions. With a few taps on his phone, he pressed it to his ear.

"Get McLaren on," he barked to the person on the line.

"You're about to piss Randolph off," Stix growled from the passenger's side.

"Not after the stunt you just pulled," Red retorted, then said into the phone, "Then tell him we have a Frank Sinatra. ETA is twenty-two hundred hours."

Realization set in. Hutch wasn't the one trying to contact me at the restaurant. This whole time, it had been Red. They were waiting for me at the condo, having not anticipated I wouldn't be there. What was so important I had to be carted off to Randolph's?

I wanted to demand an answer, but I had suddenly grown too unfocused and too tired to think straight. I could feel my body failing in its battle against the venom. Ice crept beneath my skin, draining my muscles of their life force. It was all I could do to remain in an upright position, let alone keep from shifting with the twists and turns of the road. Eventually, I let myself slide into a reclined position on the seat. Burrowing as far as I could beneath Red's blazer, I gritted my teeth against the convulsions.

The ice slowly encased my chest. My body ceased its violent shivers. I blinked once, twice, staring at the dashboard's pale glow from between the seats of my captors.

Then I blinked no more.

***

My shoes were gone. I couldn't remember when or where I'd lost them. The flats most likely slipped off during one of my cartwheels down the stairs.

Cigarette smoke circled the interior of the car, choking me. Stix's cracked window drew in gusts of cool air, turning my bare toes to icicles.

Easy breathing became a demanding task. Death by smoke suffocation was plausible, and I could do nothing about it. I couldn't open my mouth, or even twitch my jaw. It was as though my body forgot how to function all together. All it was capable of was basic instinct in order to survive, leaving me utterly vulnerable. I was a prisoner within myself.

I could've sighed with relief when Red pulled to a stop and the engine died. I was eager to withdraw from my place in the backseat, what with the seat belt buckle digging into my side.

The front doors opened, followed by movement.

"Bring him inside." It was Hutch's voice that reached me. Distant, but my heart fluttered all the same.

I was glad to hear him, because he had the anti-venom. Nothing more.

"Hutch." Red's voice was stern.

Seconds ticked by. The passenger door near my head opened, and Hutch's familiar scent fanned around me.

"What happened?" He was quiet, tone matching Red's.

"Ask *him*," came Red's response.

Hands traveled beneath my middle, releasing the tongue of the seatbelt from its buckle. The pain in my side eased somewhat.

"Help me get her," said Hutch, already drawing me from the backseat.

A second pair of hands supported my lower end, eventually cradling me into Hutch's arms. My head balanced on his shoulder, forehead drinking in the warmth of his skin. His arms were like steel embracing me, solid and secure.

Moving swiftly, Hutch took me into the mansion, lowering me on a cushioned surface. By the feel of it, I was lying on a sofa of some sort.

The ties of my coat were loosened, buttons parted from the button holes. I recognized the impression of Hutch's calloused hands as he freed one of my arms from the sleeve.

Weight thudded at the end of the sofa.

"What did you do?" Hutch's baritone was sharp enough to fracture bone.

"My job," Stix said nonchalantly, shifting near my feet.

"Your job required you to drive to my home and stick her with venom?"

I flinched inwardly at the rubber tourniquet he secured around my bicep.

"Actually," Red intervened, "we were instructed to bring her here."

The needle pricked my inner elbow. "Why?"

"I don't have to explain anything, son."

Hutch stiffened at the sound of Randolph's voice. He finished his work, pressing a band-aid to my arm.

"I already told you," he said darkly. "This is none of her business."

"On the contrary," Randolph said, "you made it her business when you brought her here last weekend. I can't turn a blind eye to her knowledge of the business. Nor can I underestimate her abilities. You said so yourself, she can prove valuable once your task was completed." He paused. "Red. See to it our guest gets settled in her room. And Stix." Hesitation filled the moment of silence. "Remind me not to employ you if I need the subject alive, next time. Otherwise, well done."

Hutch swore loudly, bringing the atmosphere to a standstill.

"Something you want to add?" Randolph said. I could hear his mocking smile as he spoke. "If so, we'll talk about it tomorrow. I have to call recess to our meeting. There are more pressing matters I need to address."

"You're digging yourself a hole," Hutch said.

Randolph chuckled. "You've become arrogant with age. But I'll have you know, my greatest successes involved digging myself into holes. You've got nothing to worry about, as long as you have a way out."

Despite Stix's sneers, the room fell silent at Randolph's departure. Rage hung thick in the air, rustled by the movement around me. My nerves raced the moment a hand fell to my wrist. I could sense Hutch crouched beside me. He did not have the softest touch when he tucked my hair behind my ear, but his thumb left a burning trail on my skin as he brushed my cheek.

"I'll fix this," he said, voice low so only I could hear him.

In a moment, his touch was gone, replaced by Red's unmistakable scent of aged cigars. The man lifted me into his arms, my coat falling from my other shoulder. A chill ran the course of my insides.

When he lowered me onto a new surface, I found it was less comfortable than the previous. Springs screeched, my unmoving body resting on a lumpy mattress—if it could be called a mattress. It felt more like a sack of thatch.

Red didn't linger. With his silent encouragement of 'hang in there', he was gone, leaving me in the dark.

I was wide awake for what felt like hours. Dull thuds and knocks sounded from surrounding rooms, but otherwise, I was entirely on my own.

The ice-cold fingers of the venom continued to seize my spinal cord. Waves of anxiety washed over me. What if my chest dropped and my lungs failed to take another breath? I would die here, all alone in the dark.

Don't panic, I repeated to myself numerous times, but there was no silencing the voice of doubt. My breathing slowed. I choked for mere seconds, tension growing in the forefront of my mind. The pressure grew with frenzy.

Dark trees and a pale moon flickered before my eyelids. I couldn't breathe. Pain struck me with an overwhelming force, my consciousness melting into the woods of my memory.

The full moon hung high above me. My chest tightened; air slipping from my lungs. Without my inhaler, I was going to suffocate.

Pushing from the ground, I called out to James. He could not confront our pursuers alone. Forgotten or not, it was two to one.

"James!" I gasped, my hand clutching my chest. My feet fumbled over vines and roots. A pair of hands caught me before I fell headfirst into the nearest bush.

"Careful now, birdie." The young man before me displayed a set of even teeth. His smile was charming—or would have been, had he not threatened to kill my brother. A line of blood trailed from his nose, dripping from his chin. At least James put up a good fight.

"David," I wheezed. "Please."

"Please, what?" He smirked. "You want more? The dress wasn't a grand enough gesture?"

My chest was crumbling in a fiery pit of agony. I gazed at him beseechingly, my voice lost. My knees gave out and I fell to the ground.

"Your brother did this to himself, birdie." David's hands cupped my face. "But you... you never asked to suffer. Not in this life." His palms traveled down my arms, lifting my left wrist to his shoulder. Shadows of trees surrounded me as I thrashed

about on the ground. I couldn't breathe. My chest was painfully constricted, but my focus was on the man leaning over me.

"Please," I gasped. "I can't—I can't..."

"I can help you," he cooed.

I winced, gulping for air. His thumb nail sank into the soft skin of my wrist, drawing blood. Flashing me a wicked grin, he inclined his head, pressing his lips to the wound.

With my focus fading, I did not notice his absence until I opened my eyes. Groggily, I sat up.

"YOU KILLED HER!" James bellowed, swinging a fist at his fellow Forgotten. "YOU LIED TO ME!" He kicked David in the chest. "I BECAME THIS BECAUSE OF HER!"

"You became this to save your sister," David growled, climbing to his feet. He managed to block James' next blow. "But you're right." My brother was shoved to the ground. David straddled him. "We lied about your Emily. Just like we lied about how you could save your sister by joining us. Because in the end, she will be one of us, too."

James roared. The two pivoted on the ground, fighting for the upper hand.

Air returned to my lungs just as flames licked at my veins from where David's lips had met the tear in my skin.

Someone groaned, but it was impossible to tell if it was James or David.

Grabbing the nearest stick from the ground, I rushed at David, prepared to ram it into his back.

Someone smashed into me from the side. Their arms circled my waist to keep me from falling.

"Kelley."

"Has no one taught you to play fair?" he smirked. His appearance was much different from David's, although he wasn't lacking in arrogance.

A fist collided with the side of his face. Kelley released me in shock, spinning to face James. My brother's face was beyond recognition. Beneath the streaks of blood I knew could not be his own, his jade eyes were filled with animosity.

"Rily, go home."

"What?" I said in disbelief.

James' gaze never left Kelley, who continued to smirk in return. "Leave."

"She's not leaving," Kelley taunted. "David may have won the deal between us, but since he's unable to claim his prize, thanks to you, it should go to the runner up. Otherwise known as myself."

Barely waiting for Kelley to finish speaking, James soared into attack, but his opponent reacted swiftly. Kelley reeled to the side, bringing his knee into James' groin.

"Go, Rily," he grumbled, descending to his knees. "Let me take care of this."

"Or stay here." Kelley took a fistful of my dress, hauling me to his side. I nudged him hard in the ribcage, but my weak attempts to escape his grip were useless. His nose traced the line of my jaw to my ear, inhaling noisily. "The innocent ones are always the most satisfying. Just like Emily."

The following sound that left James would forever haunt me. It was the mangled cry of a wounded man, set on revenge. He launched at Kelley again, causing the Forgotten to push me to the ground.

"GO, NOW!" James demanded, and this time I did not argue.

This time I ran.

Chapter Thirty

Cold water splashed my face, surging up my nose and into my lungs. Rolling to my side, I sputtered. Coughs racked my body.

"She lives."

I shuddered at the voice. "So does he, apparently."

Felix chuckled. "Legends never die."

I would've scoffed, had I not been choking.

"Have you come here to finish what you failed to do the other night?" I asked.

"Not quite," he grinned. "I say we call a truce. We'll have plenty of time to work out our differences later."

Peering around the room, I found it was a small rectangular hole in the wall. The only piece of furniture was the screeching cot beneath me. The once white walls appeared to be stained by water damage, and there wasn't a single window. My only source of light came from the bare lightbulb descending from the low ceiling.

"Why bother me now?" I shivered, comprehending the cold for the first time. I lifted what I thought to be a blanket from my lap, only to find it was a gray hoodie.

"Randolph wants to see you."

"'Randolph'? You call your own father by his name?" I pushed my arms through the sleeves, vaguely aware of the new wrappings secured around my stitches.

"Given the situation." He took two steps to the door. "You can walk, or I can carry you, but you should know, walking will be less painful."

The evil pleasure written in his expression didn't scare me. If anything, his attempts at intimidation were a joke. He wasn't going to hurt me if Randolph told him not to.

My knees buckled weakly the moment I stood, but my strength returned slowly as we walked through the corridor beyond my prison. Once we ascended from basement level, we followed the winding corridor, branching off to the kitchen. The elderly lady I'd met on my last visit was there, stirring a large pot of something that made my mouth water. She didn't cast us a passing glance as we made for the exit at the far side of the kitchen.

Eventually, we came to a room with great windows lining the walls. The world beyond appeared cold and gray. The sky was gloomy, threatening more rain.

In the center of the sunroom was a table large enough to seat eight. Yet, only two seats were occupied: one by Randolph, the other by a portly man with a balding scalp.

Felix nudged me to the chair across from the stranger before disappearing from the room. I assumed the man to be Randolph's bookkeeper by the way they discussed the figures and charts on the papers scattered before them. Nothing they said made sense to me, so I studied the room instead.

A shelf to my left held various crystal ornaments which would catch the rays of sun on a cloudless day. Next to it on the wall hung a stainless steel platter designed into a clock. Silver vines with glistening leaves twined around the face. It wasn't something I could picture Randolph picking out himself; perhaps it was his late wife who'd decorated the room.

Considering the time was accurate, I'd slept nearly thirteen hours. My last flashback had left a dull throbbing in my head. I lifted my hand to massage a spot on the back of my neck, but remembering what I'd seen in the flashback, my shoulders drooped.

It had been me. I abandoned James, not the other way around. The vision of him, face bloodied and eyes wild, haunted my thoughts.

"I trust you rested well."

Looking up from the table, I found Randolph watching me, fingers forming a steeple on the table. The bookkeeper shuffled the papers and files into order, scrawling notes onto margins. He was prepared to get up, when Randolph stopped him. "I may need you to stay for this."

I tugged Hutch's hoodie tighter around my form.

"What do you want?" I asked.

"Right to the point with this one." Randolph chuckled as his employee settled back down in his seat. "I want to know how my nephew has been treating you this past week."

"What do you care?" I snapped, my gaze jumping to the other man. His presence made me uncomfortable, but to be fair, he didn't look like he enjoyed being there, either. Sweat glistened on his forehead, forcing him to dab at it with a handkerchief.

"I am responsible for the individuals I employ," said Randolph. "If my employees aren't happy, I risk losing them. And that would be bad for business."

"I'm not your employee," I said.

"Not officially. But Hutch dragged you into this mess when he shouldn't have." He sipped his coffee. "I hate to think of everything he's put you through."

"And what about all *you've* put me through?" I said.

He set the cup down. "Red and Stix took it too far. They were only supposed to escort you here. Not harm you."

"Why bring me here in the first place?" I glared at him. "I was fine where I was."

"Like I said, Hutch had no right to involve you in this business—"

"So, you want me dead," I interrupted, the words streaming out before I had the mind to stop them.

"Excuse me?" Randolph appeared baffled, but I wasn't buying it.

"I know too much," I said. "You said so yourself last night. You can't have me waltzing around town with that kind of knowledge. I'm a loose end you plan on tying up."

"McLaren did a number on you," Randolph said. "He's the one who sees you as a liability. He tried to convince me of your usefulness last weekend.

Dead or alive."

"What?" Stunned, I dropped my guard.

"He's been pushing the business of venom extraction for years now." Randolph shrugged. "He claims you'll make a decent subject for experimentation."

"You're lying." I glowered at him. I didn't hold enough venom to be extracted; Hutch said so himself.

Unless he lied about that, too.

"I don't want the boy to fool you. He's excellent at his job."

My fists curled. "Why do you care what happens to me?"

Randolph pushed back at the table, heaving a sigh. "I've been in this business long enough to know potential when I see it."

"Potential?" I shook my head in disbelief.

"I've taken a look into your records. You live in a house standing on its last legs. Your brother's gone missing, probably running with the wrong crowd. Your mother has been arrested multiple times for DUIs and public intoxication. You, yourself, have seen the inside of a holding cell since your graduation in the spring. Looks like the apple doesn't fall far from the tree. You're following in your mother's footsteps and you're barely old enough to vote." He scratched his rugged chin. "Is there really anything waiting for you at home?"

I scowled, not gracing his question with an answer, not that Randolph minded.

He went on. "You're out of options at home, but if you still want to return, I will make sure that happens. However," he exchanged a significant glance with the other man, "I would like to offer you a place here."

I blinked, unable to comprehend his offer.

"Food, clothes, a nice place to stay," he went on, gesturing around the room. "We can even make sure certain needs are met regarding your appetite."

I shot to my feet, the chair raking across the floor behind me. Anger pulsed through me. It was insulting, him trying to tempt me with thoughts I fought on a daily basis.

The bookkeeper flinched at my sudden movements. Randolph on the other hand, continued to look upon me with a patience that suggested he'd seen his share of outbursts.

"Let me get this straight." I gritted my teeth. "Instead of killing me to be sure I don't talk, you're trying to keep me close. Is that it?"

Randolph shook his head. "I'm offering you a job. A well-paying, respectable job, and a place to stay."

"Out of the goodness of your heart," I said. "You're willing to hire an inexperienced teenager, fresh from high school and hope for the best?"

"I never said I wouldn't benefit from it," Randolph shrugged. "Sit down so we can discuss this."

I weighed my options. Dividing my attention between the two men, I returned slowly to my seat.

"What's in it for you?" I asked.

Randolph chuckled. "There's been a lot of business lately. Changes have been made, and I find myself struggling to keep up with appointments."

"You want a secretary," I said. "Why not advertise on job sites. Or Craigslist?"

"The nature of this work is not necessarily considered legal," the man spoke up for the first time, sounding as nervous as he looked. "It would be easier to hire someone who is qualified and already aware of the premises of the job."

"You don't know that I'm qualified," I said.

"I'd say you've already surpassed the expectations I had from the start," said Randolph. "And at least here you would be safe. Not even my nephew could lay a hand on you under my watch."

I opened my mouth to speak but was interrupted before I could properly form my next question.

"Randolph."

The three of us turned in the direction of Hutch's voice. He was with the elderly maid from the kitchen. Her expression was strained as she carried a tray of food in her hands. Behind them was Red, his beige cowboy hat shielding his eyes.

Despite myself, a sense of relief washed over me, waning almost instantly when Hutch neglected to meet my gaze.

"Speak of the devil," said Randolph.

Although Hutch's snapback concealed his hair, I noticed a trail of sweat dampening his sideburns. His shirt was soaked, breath short as though he'd just run ten miles."What are you doing?" he demanded.

"I'm in the middle of a meeting." Randolph beckoned the hesitant maid with the food. "I told you we would talk later."

"You push our meeting to make small talk with an adolescent girl?" Hutch threw a hand in my direction, still refusing to look at me.

Wow. That wasn't ageist or sexist at all.

"There's no reason to be uncivil," Randolph said, shaking out a napkin and draping it over one knee. "I'm sure my new secretary will be able to pencil you in for a meeting today." He winked at me, curling my stomach like sour milk.

Hutch noticed the gesture and dropped his gaze to me for the first time. His eyes wandered to his hoodie pulled tight around my middle. I eased my grip on the material, forcing my anxiety to retreat. With little success.

"How about we talk now?" He paced around the table, hand jumping to the bookkeeper's neck. He pressed an oblong object into the man's skin. "Otherwise we can see how deep this OTF will penetrate your puppet's neck."

Hutch's victim began to sweat more profusely. He stammered something incoherent as he watched his employer stir his food.

Randolph's lips twisted into a smile. He lifted the spoon to his mouth and paused. "Red, take our guest back to her room."

Red moved closer to the table, tugging me from the chair. I wanted to resist but thought better of it. The last thing I needed was to risk witnessing a man die before my eyes. I wasn't totally convinced Hutch wouldn't kill to hurt the man he so despised. There was a hard look in his eyes as he stared at his uncle. His lips pursed, jaw ticking.

"Come on," Red murmured, and I complied.

"Where did we leave off yesterday?" I heard Randolph say as we exited the sunroom. The rest of the conversation faded as we proceeded through the winding corridors, back to the tiny room at the bottom of the stairs.

Chapter Thirty-One

The moment I stepped back into the room, I paused, eyes landing on the bottled water and paper bag resting between the lumps of the mattress.

"I was bringing you lunch when I noticed you weren't here," Red explained. He stood in the doorway, fingers gripping the handle.

"And you made the mistake of thinking Hutch would care?" I uncapped the bottle. The water livened something within me. I was already feeling halfway better.

"Easy there," said Red. "There's no telling how many bathroom breaks they'll give you over the next few days."

My heart sank. Was I really to spend my next days in this prison? Maybe not if I took Randolph up on his offer.

As if reading my mind, Red asked, "What did he want with you?"

Curling my legs beneath me on the cot, I tore into the bag and pulled out a sandwich. My stomach rumbled with delight.

Despite my lack of response, Red didn't stir. He waited, watching me closely as I sank my teeth into the first bite.

"He offered me a job," I finally said, deciding it was okay to trust him.

Red continued to say nothing, giving me the opportunity to tell him everything said in the sunroom. When I finished recounting the conversation, he studied me. "I reckon you know better than to trust a word the man said."

"Well, Hutch didn't do a great job convincing me he's on my side, either." I ripped another bite from the sandwich, the dill pickle calling my taste buds to a playful dance. "His opinion of me is lower than I thought."

Aware of Red's scrutiny as I finished the sandwich, I crumpled the wrapper, tossing it back into the bag. "What?"

"Do you comprehend the danger you're in by being here?"

I shrugged. "I never asked to be here. In case you forgot, you're the one who kidnapped me."

"I volunteered to partner with Stix last night, because the man can't be trusted," Red told me. "No one here can be trusted."

"Are you saying Randolph doesn't really plan on hiring me?" I asked in mock surprise, placing a hand on my chest for effect. "Why ever would he care to talk to me then?"

Red, who obviously did not catch my sarcasm, said, "Hutch is convinced he's trying to gauge how close the two of you are."

Forcing a laugh, I opened the bag of chips accompanying the sandwich. "You realize we met a week ago. How close can we be?"

Red shrugged this time. "You're the only lady-friend the kid's ever had."

"We're not friends," I said quickly. "I don't even know what we are."

"Might as well ask him next time you see him," Red muttered. "I haven't seen him this concerned in years."

A fluttering sensation bloomed in my chest, but I chose to ignore it. "If Hutch decides I'm worth the visit, then I will ask him."

There was a moment of silence. I could tell Red was considering my words.

"You won't see him here," he said at last.

I swallowed a mouthful of chips. "Because he's too busy."

Red shook his head. "Because the last time he was here, he couldn't handle it."

Clarity settled over me and I bit my lip, suddenly regretting my attitude. "This is the hole."

The stained walls, the unstable cot. This was where Randolph dumped his nephew when he was angry. It was in this room Hutch was punished; beaten and left to himself.

Recalling the image of five-year-old Hutch splintered my heart. He had no mother, no father. Nor did his aunt live long enough to see his graduation. He pushed people away, having faced enough pain in his twenty-one years. Was self-preservation his excuse, then?

"He stayed long enough to remove your stitches," said Red, pulling me from my thoughts. "I had to get him outside afterwards, otherwise he would've experienced a full-blown panic attack."

"When?" I asked, forcing my voice to remain steady.

"This morning."

My arms coiled in my lap. I stared at my hands, guilt-ridden. After all I'd learned of Randolph, I'd been willing to give the criminal the benefit of the doubt, even if for a few minutes. True, I hadn't known Hutch for very long, but I'd seen sides of him in the past week I was sure no one else did.

Clearing my throat, I asked, "Has he learned anything more about his parents?"

"Randolph's not foolish enough to talk about it." Red scuffed the vinyl floor. "The evidence I found made it clear. Keith McLaren was followed one night and driven off the road. I would assume because he threatened to turn Randolph in for his corrupted business. It wasn't hard for Ellis, his wife, to piece together his true cause of death. She told her sister about it. It looks like when Erin confronted Randolph, he put a hit out on Ellis to make sure she told no one else. He covered his tracks to make it look like suicide—had the whole thing swept under the rug."

I covered my eyes with the heels of my hands. How could someone be so evil? I sat with that man just a few moments ago. I stared him in the face while he mimicked concern for my well-being.

"We suspect Erin knew what really happened to her sister," Red went on. "Or at least she guessed as much. The simple apology in her note could've been written for Ellis."

"How could she do it?" I said in disbelief. "How could she leave her nephew—her son even—in the care of a monster?"

"I met Boss Man's wife a few times before the tragedy took place," he said. "She was never quite all there. In hindsight I'd say she was driven mad with guilt. And as for Felix," he ducked into the hallway for a brief moment to be sure no one would overhear us, "from what I hear, that kid's never been disciplined a day in his life. Especially not after his mother lost her mind."

"Hutch told you about… what he did to himself?" I asked, clenching my fist.

"About becoming a Forgotten?" When I nodded, Red chuckled. The sound was bitter. "Not that he needed to. We all guessed it. But Felix is Boss Man's golden boy. He can do no wrong in his father's eyes."

"Have they always been rivals? Hutch and Felix?"

"Since the day McLaren moved in. At least that's what I gather."

"But why?"

Checking his watch, Red said, "Some bullies never grow up." He motioned to the water bottle in my hand. "Drink sparingly. I'll try to make it back later with more food."

"Wait," I said hurriedly. Red turned to face me, hand on the door. "When Hutch called me Hayden last weekend, you laughed. You said I couldn't be Hayden Barnes."

Red adjusted his hat nervously.

"I know he lied about my name," I added, hoping it would convince him to tell me the truth.

Shifting his weight from one foot to the other, Red said, "You've seen the scars on his neck." When I nodded, Red went on, "Courtesy of Hayden Barnes, the first female Forgotten he ever encountered."

***

Minutes bled into hours as loneliness breached my sanity. I managed to busy myself with dreams of escaping the mansion, as well as conversations with Red. He brought food, always the same sandwich and chips. While I ate, I asked him about his family. I wanted to know more about his wife and daughter. Although he was hesitant at first, by the second day of my hostage situation, he was more willing to open up. He never did stay long, but his company meant the world to me.

A few times a day, two of Randolph's henchmen escorted me to the bathroom around the corner from the hole. It was a half bath, dark and filthy, but I knew better than to complain. I didn't need to have my bathroom privileges revoked.

It was the dawn of the third day when I could no longer put off the pressing thoughts of my past. I'd ignored my memories long enough and they'd begun to fester. Having not slept since my first night, exhaustion dampened my attempts to remain positive. Even my faith in Hutch was weakening.

Randolph wasn't entirely wrong about there being nothing for me back at home. After all, I'd ditched my friends and endangered my brother's life. All for what I perceived to be the unreachable: camaraderie with the young men whom everyone in the neighborhood avoided.

I knew why I pursued them. It was the desire for something more in life; it was the power these men held that appealed to me. They did what they wanted, suffering no repercussions for their actions, all because people feared them.

And because of me, James had transformed—or started to. I was the one responsible for the corruption of his soul. And I'd left him behind, along with everyone else.

Taking after my father was what I did best.

All the more reason to go back and break the cycle, I thought longingly, considering I ever had the chance to return to set things right.

A tear slid to the bridge of my nose. I pulled the hoodie further over my damp hair, huddling tighter on my side for warmth. On my last bathroom excursion I'd attempted to wash my hair in the sink. True, the bar of soap didn't work quite as well as shampoo, but it did the job.

Desolate words spoke to me in the dark. Even if I did make it home, there was nothing left to make right. I'd burned all my bridges, and now I was left buried beneath the ashes. All I could do now was mourn. Mourn for my lost life, and mourn for my brother. If he was still alive, he would've come for me by now. But his absence told me what I needed to know. It was the truth I'd been ignoring since my last flashback.

Tears continued to spill from my eyes and I allowed myself a moment to weep, my breath coming in sharp gasps.

Losing track of time, my sobs eventually died down, though my insides still felt like mush. I wiped my face on the sleeve of the hoodie before reaching for what little water I had left. It was as if crying had left me dehydrated.

A tapping sound came from the door. With all the thumps I'd heard all day, I chose not to react. Instead, I curled back up on my side, pulling the hem of my dress over my knees.

The tapping continued, this time accompanied by whispers.

"I don't have to go to the bathroom," I called, voice cracking. I just wanted everyone to leave me alone. Except for Red. He was always welcome.

At the sound of the lock turning, I sat up. Hadn't they heard me?

The door swung open, emitting only more darkness.

"Hayden."

My stomach clenched painfully.

"It's Aprilynne," I said. "You should be one to know."

I didn't mean to sound so harsh. Hutch's being there was nothing short of a miracle. Yet, after days of hearing nothing from him, I couldn't help but feel rough around the edges.

"You're upset," he said. "I get it. I'll explain everything, but we don't have much time."

"Upset?" I shook my head, though I doubted he could see in the dark. "Hutch, I'm *confused*. I can't decide what's true and what's a lie anymore."

"I told you I would fix this," he said curtly. My sight was sharp enough to see his form advance. "I wasn't lying about that."

Was he serious? "Randolph's not going to let you walk out of here with me by your side," I told him. "He'll find me. He'll find *you*."

Hutch was silent for a moment, leaving me to believe he finally realized just how hopeless my situation really was.

"I know," he finally said. "That's why I'm going to let Allen burn his business to the ground."

Chapter Thirty-Two

With a click of the pull chain, light flooded into the room. I closed my eyes, temporarily blinded.

"Allen?" I rubbed my eyes with my fists. "What does he have to do with this?"

"He's been trying to collar Randolph for his illegal activities for some time now," Hutch said.

When my eyes adjusted, I met his solid gaze. His hat was pulled low over his forehead, a steel blue hoodie, not unlike the one I wore, stretched across his shoulders.

"I don't get it," I said. "He's an undercover cop?"

"Something like that." There was a slight incline to Hutch's head, otherwise his stance remained taunt, arms rigid at his sides. "He's an agent for Cornerstone Alliance. His team has been following Randolph, gathering evidence for his arrest."

"I thought Cornerstone Alliance was a law firm."

"It is, among other things."

I showed no sign of understanding, leading Hutch to add, "They do a lot more than argue justice in the courthouse."

Muscles aching to move, to *do* something, I stood from the cot and stretched. Hutch noticed the socks sagging around my ankles and cocked an eyebrow at the sight. Anyone could decipher I was not the true owner, being that they were much too large for me.

"Red," I said simply. "How do you know this about Eric?"

216

"Allen's been in touch with the Chief of Police," he explained. "He's the one who requested watch over his family's residence since the explosion. When the officers were found dead the other day, word of his undercover work circled the precinct."

"And Randolph's contact heard and passed along the information," I said, piecing the rest together. "But Eric has already dealt with Randolph before. Why not bust him then?"

"Randolph sold his traphouses, clearing all evidence at the time."

My big toe traced small lines across the floor as I contemplated this. "What evidence does Eric have now? How is he supposed to corner him?"

"Other than storing contraband in the next room, he can easily rack up charges for abduction," he said. "All Allen needed was someone to tell him where to find him."

I stared at Hutch, taken aback. "You?" I whispered.

He nodded.

"But why?" I asked. "Why would you do it? Why now?"

"He's done enough damage," he said without a second thought. "He's taken enough lives, and told his share of lies."

I snorted in agreement. "He tried to feed me some baloney explanation about why I'm here."

Hutch sighed, his expression mirroring the one from the sunroom.

"Maybe you could tell me why I am being held against my will," I said quietly.

Hutch faltered a moment, the hardness of his features slackening. "Randolph thinks he has a hold on me."

I flexed my toes, working them for warmth as I waited for him to continue.

"When he refused to acknowledge my accusations, I told him I wanted out. And then you showed up a few hours later."

"He thinks keeping me here will prevent you from leaving?"

"He thinks by sparing you, he can keep me from leaving."

So, my fate rested in Hutch's career choices. Great.

"All he wants is to keep his mules busy," he went on. "He doesn't care what it takes to get it done."

"I'm not dead yet," I pointed out. "I take it that means you agreed to stay."

"I told him I needed time to consider it."

A small laugh burst from my chest. "That settles it then."

Just beneath his visor, I saw Hutch's eyebrows draw close together. "Settles what?"

For a moment I cursed myself for speaking so bluntly, but then decided it didn't matter. How much worse could my situation get, anyway?

Steeling myself, I said, "Red told me your uncle wanted to know just how important I am to you. That was his real reason for talking to me the other day." I chortled, the sound anything but gleeful. "I still can't believe he fooled himself into thinking I meant anything to you."

Hutch said nothing, not that I expected him to respond.

"So, when is this thing happening?" I asked, shoving my hands into the pockets of the hoodie. "When will Eric and his guys raid the mansion?"

Lifting his wrist, Hutch dropped his eyes to his watch. It seemed like the most he'd moved in some time now. "They'll be here at dawn. That gives us a few hours."

I started, not expecting it to happen so soon. "Is there anything I need to do?"

His gaze returned to mine. "Just wait for me."

The fact that we were standing in a tiny room together, bodies close enough to feel the other's radiating heat, did not elude me. Hutch's warmth pulled at me, filling the icy chasm located in the very depths of my chest. This comfort, however, I did not deserve.

"That shouldn't be difficult." I began turning my back to him, but the unexpected touch of his hand on my elbow stopped me. Studying the rough skin of his knuckles clutching my arm, I waited with bated breath for him to say something.

A quiet tremble reached me where his hold connected us. It was a solemn reminder that he'd willingly returned to the room where his darkest memories lived. Hutch faced his anxiety just to talk to me, when he could've sent Red.

Maybe I did mean something to him after all?

Upon seeing the strain in his expression, my heart filled with compassion. I moved back to him, barely aware of my hand reaching for the visor of his hat. Hutch kept his eyes locked on mine, as though I were a life raft, meant to reel him back to safety.

Removing the snapback felt oddly like I was exposing him, but he did nothing to stop me.

"I will wait for you," I murmured. "At dawn."

Resolution shattered the stoic mask. There was barely space between us, but Hutch closed the gap anyway. Excitement bubbled in my pulse at the realization that I wanted him to kiss me. This time I wouldn't try to avoid him.

Despite his solid frame, Hutch's eyes were soft.

I haven't seen him this concerned in years. Red's voice echoed in my head, just as Hutch brushed my cheek with the pad of his thumb. His eyes drank in my features, sending my heart over the edge. With a gentle pressure at the nape of my neck, he tilted my head back until our lips were aligned. I didn't breathe. This moment was fragile; a vigilant doe marked in the scope of a hunter. A single startling movement could end the familiarity of Hutch's embrace.

Being this close and at ease with another was something I wasn't used to. After losing my memories, the world had felt cold and alien for so long. But not now; not in this moment.

His actions were experimental. From beneath my lashes I watched him incline his head a fraction, the tip of his nose brushing mine. Then his lips caressed the corner of my mouth before moving slowly down.

I bit back a giggle at the unsureness of his kiss, but Hutch's confidence quickly grew and I was soon crushed against him, our lips moving in sync with a hunger that complimented the other. A wildfire of emotions erupted through me. I'd denied them long enough. My arms encircled his neck.

At some point, I'd dropped his hat, only coming to realize this when we parted. Once I seemed to catch my breath, I stepped back, kneeling to retrieve it.

"You should really get some rest." Hutch said this, accepting the snapback

I offered. There was a slight tremble in his voice and a new fire in his countenance. "Otherwise you'll wind up looking like me."

One corner of his mouth quirked, stilling my heart. I grinned senselessly in reply.

"It won't be much longer," he promised, pressing my fingers. I pressed back. "Red will keep an eye on you until I return."

"I can't just slip out now?" I said, half-joking. "What's a few hours?"

A painful expression flitted across his face. "I'd get you out now, if I could. But Randolph's made enough changes around here, there isn't a single hallway left unmonitored."

"We can't risk losing the element of surprise." I nodded glumly. "Randolph would expect something if I suddenly disappeared." I hated that it was so, but my only way out was by stifling my desperation a little while longer.

The door cracked open.

"You best get going," Red said quietly, peering into the room. "Brock's been giving me the stink eye."

With one more look at Hutch, I shooed him out of the room. I stared for a long moment at the locked door after he left, digesting everything that had just happened.

Pretending Hutch was simply an acquaintance was now impossible, especially when I still felt the impression of his lips against mine.

My gaze dropped to the OTF he'd pressed into my hand before leaving. Unable to suppress another grin, I resumed my place on the cot. What the heck was I supposed to do until dawn?

⁎

An explosion of noise jarred me from sleep. I blinked several times until the fog in my mind lifted. Staring at the cobwebs on the ceiling, I registered bellowing voices and thuds coming from the other side of the wall. Had it begun already?

My feet hit the ground in an instant, and I darted for the door.

"Red!" I called, trying the handle, only to find it still locked.

220

In the absence of a response, I released a puff of air. I turned to plop back down onto the cot when the scent of blood hit me with a crushing force.

Choking the smell from my lungs, I spun back to the door in time to see a deep red puddle inching into the room. It claimed the vinyl flooring a little at a time, entering through the crack beneath the door.

"Red!" I called again, this time with more urgency. Darkness threatened to take over. My fist pounded the door, pounding away the demon that fought its way to the surface. Pushing my fears aside, I focused solely on a reply from Red on the other side. "Red! What's going on?"

The lock clicked. I stood back, allowing the door to swing open, only to be met by a nightmare.

Stix smirked at me, standing above Red's body. The blood pooled around his boots, but he made no indication of this bothering him.

"That's what happens to traitors." He cocked his gun.

"What are you talking about?" I bluffed, my heart holding on to the hope Red was merely injured. But I knew better. The man wasn't breathing. That much I could tell.

"You think Randolph doesn't know what goes on under his own nose?" Stix laughed, covering the sound of the sob that escaped me. "Oh, yes, he knows all about the little ambush McLaren planned. Boss Man's craftier than you give him credit for."

My eyes jumped to the stairs in the hall.

"He ain't coming," Stix told me as though reading my thoughts. "Randolph gave us strict orders to execute the traitors."

"And he considers me a traitor, too?" I challenged, masking my distress. He wasn't going to relish the sight of my fear.

"You're unnecessary baggage," Stix said. "We don't need something else to worry about on the road. Besides, if I don't kill you, one of the others here will."

Thumps continued to rattle the neighboring wall, and I finally understood. "Randolph's fleeing."

"McLaren left us no option when he snitched," Stix growled.

I looked past him at the stairs again.

"He's *dead.*" Stix lifted his arm, pointing the gun at my face. "So you can stop looking for him."

"No, he's not," I said, my voice quivering. That was impossible. Hutch could overcome two armed men jumping him in his sleep. Randolph couldn't get rid of him that easily.

Tears sprang to my eyes as I realized these were the same thoughts I'd had regarding Red. Yet one bullet was enough to stop his heart—the gunshot that had awoken me.

If what Stix said was true, I truly had nothing left now; no family and no friends.

Taking a deep breath, I inhaled the smell of blood, my senses screaming at me to release all control to the monster within.

Why fight it now?

The moment the question surfaced my mind, darkness engulfed me, suffocating. I lost sight of my surroundings; I lost sight of Stix. The last thing I registered was the ear-piercing explosion of the gun.

Chapter Thirty-Three

Resistance waged war inside my skull. My arms ached with strain. I wanted to shut out the pain; I wanted to black out and let the monster take over.

No. A flicker of anger sparked deep within my core.

What is there to fight for? I argued. *Why resist the inevitable?*

Something tightened around my chest, nearly crushing my ribcage. My arms swept past me, slamming the door before drawing it open once more.

I don't give up, my voice raged quietly, amplifying with every swing of the door. *I can't give up.*

Suddenly, the scene flashed before my blank eyes. Sounds rushed through my ear canal, striking my eardrums with a deafening volume. I roared as my hands slammed the door on Stix a final time in his attempt to drag me out of the room. Battered, he sank to the ground, releasing me at last.

I didn't wait. Taking a shaky breath, I stepped back for momentum, jumping over the puddle of blood. Voices at the top of the stairs distracted me. My ankle rolled upon landing, and I let out a yelp as I collapsed to the ground. A gangly man exited the neighboring room with an assault rifle strapped around his front. To inspect the noise, I was sure. Where was he when Stix tried to empty his clip on me?

Having failed to avoid the growing puddle of blood, I wagered my appearance was somewhat disturbing. With one side of the hoodie splashed crimson and my hair wild enough to nest chicks, I used the alarming sight to my advantage.

Baring my teeth at the man, I rose slowly to my feet. An involuntary hiss left my lips when my twisted ankle threatened to give out on me, but my opponent took it as a warning sign. He backed away, his gun trained on me. When I took a step forward to relieve the pain in my foot, he turned and darted down the hall.

Obviously Randolph had shared my condition with his men. Considering he had two armed thugs escort me to the bathroom each time, I guessed he was unsure how dangerous I was, which served to my benefit. No one wished to risk death at the hand of a Forgotten.

Limping after the man, I trusted there was another way out of the basement. Taking the initial stairs up was out of the question. There were too many of Randolph's guys lingering at the top.

There had to be a back door.

My breath came in sharp rasps as I proceeded down the hall. All was quiet, save for the shouts coming from upstairs. Footsteps hammered the floor above. I pressed on, glimpsing around to ensure I was alone.

Where was everyone?

After trying a few doors, only to discover they were locked, I turned another corner. A dimly lit stairwell came into view, but I had no time to rejoice.

All at once, noise erupted from every direction. Stix's voice was nearly drowned by the powerful shockwaves of rapid gunfire.

Fingers groping the railing, I pulled myself up each step. I was circling to the next set of steps when Stix caught up with me, yanking my hair back. He uttered a handful of disgraceful monikers just before he back-handed me. My head snapped to the side, pain blurred my vision. Tottering forward on hands and knees, I made it to the corner of the stairwell. Stix blocked my escape, his expression illustrating his hatred with the curl of his lips and narrowing of his eyes.

A part of me knew I should feel threatened, but anger and disgust overruled all emotions. Leaning against the wall, I stood, scowling at Stix the entire time. My lack of fear annoyed him. He raised his fist, giving me just enough time to prepare myself for the blow.

The skin of my cheek tore upon impact. Gritting my teeth, I came back with a counterattack, jabbing my fingers directly into his throat.

Stix fell away, having not expected my retaliation. He wrapped his fingers around his neck, coughing violently. While he was distracted, I limped around him, but he reached out, taking a fistful of my hoodie. We did an awkward dance along the railing until I managed to get a hold of his face. I buried my nails into his skin, dragging them down his eyelid and cheekbone. He screamed, releasing his hold on me. With the weight of my body, I shouldered him hard. His arms windmilled in an attempt to keep his balance. A grappling hand reached for me, but I rolled away and watched him topple down the stairs.

The echoes of more gunfire filled the stairwell. Before I could reach the handle of the door on the upper landing, it burst open, throwing me back a few steps. I winced.

A beefy man stormed through, nearly plowing me to the ground. I immediately recognized him as one of my routine escorts to the bathroom. Eyes landing on me, he lifted his gun.

Gunshots fired, rooting me to the spot. It took a moment before I realized my opponent had fallen to the ground instead of me. I lifted my eyes, shocked to find Eric Allen, clad in a navy uniform of combat gear. His eyes flashed angrily.

"Thank you," I said, hoping he didn't do the same to me.

Battle cries rang out from behind. Eric swung around, aiming his weapon with a proficiency I did not expect him to possess. He relaxed, looking back. "Follow me."

I gaped at him. "You expect me to run through a hailstorm of bullets?"

"I've got guys covering for us, but not for long." He beckoned me forward, but I was unable to move. "You have to trust me."

But I couldn't. All I knew of him had been a lie. I didn't know the man. I didn't know if he meant well for me. Why would he?

"We don't have time for this." Eric clasped a hand around my wrist, towing me out of the stairwell.

We hurried along the wall, crouching behind bits of furniture. My head spun, ears ringing at the ear-splitting gun blasts. I lost track of the different rooms we entered, concentrating solely on shadowing Eric's movements, even though my swelling ankle made the task more difficult than necessary.

Sliding behind a man sporting the same gear as Eric, we entered a dark room, the outer walls lined with windows.

I was back in the sunroom.

Glass crunched under Eric's heavy boots. The room appeared to have been ravaged and abandoned. The shelf lay on its side, all crystal ornaments shattered across the floor. I stepped carefully between the shards.

The sounds of war quieted somewhat. I dared myself to breathe normally for once, glad for the moment absent of chaos. The sky outside was dark still, the light of the room behind us reflecting our silhouettes across the windows.

"Where are we going?" I whispered, inching around the fallen shelf after Eric.

"I'm getting you—" one of the windows exploded, cutting him off. Something heavy thumped to the ground on the other side of the room, a green light flashing rapidly.

Eric gripped my arm, yanking me behind the shelf. My knees slammed onto the tiles the same moment the entire room quaked with a deafening blast. We were soon immersed in a smothering wave of heat, flames raising high above us, singing hair. The rest of the windows burst as a result, adding to the clamor. I shielded my head with my hands, my knuckles sliced by the shower of glass.

"Stay down!" Eric yelled, his voice muffled by the ringing in my ears, but I felt him lean over me and sensed the violent pulse of his rifle as he defended us from oncoming assailants.

Flames engulfed the area, blocking our exits at the other end of the room. We either had to retreat or run straight outside into the hands of our attackers.

I was prepared to give in when half a dozen of Eric's comrades stormed into the room behind us. With the addition of men, it didn't take long to clear the opening to the stone patio outside.

As soon as the men searched the area and signaled the coast was clear, Eric nudged me onward.

I tiptoed around the glass, careful not to catch any in my socks. Red's socks.

My gut wrenched at the thought of Red still lying lifeless in the basement. Tears stung my eyes, and I blinked them back. I couldn't think about him right now.

The pre-dawn air chilled my bare legs, raising a shiver up to the rest of my body as my mind wandered to thoughts regarding Hutch.

He's dead. An invisible dagger pierced my chest as I recalled Stix's words. *Randolph gave us strict orders to execute the traitors.*

"We've got vehicles waiting a quarter of a mile out," Eric told me. My ears were still ringing, leaving me to read his lips. I enviously remarked his earplugs.

With the others keeping watch on our surroundings, Eric helped me limp along the patio, past the pool.

"GET DOWN!"

I didn't know who yelled it, but I didn't stop to find out. Flinging my body flat on the ground, a heavy object crashed to the stone with such force, it bounded once before sliding into the pool.

Curiously, I climbed to my knees just enough to peer into the water to see what had threatened to fracture my skull.

The pool lights illuminated a semi-automatic at the bottom. Perplexed at who would pitch their weapon at me, I tugged out of Eric's grip, straightening my posture. Gunfire flashed in the several places from within the house, but there didn't appear to be any immediate danger.

The ringing in my ears faded, my hearing slowly returning. Glass shattered from above. My gaze rose to the balcony. A familiar form collided into the railing, his face contorted in anger. His expression changed, however, the moment our eyes met.

"Hutch," I breathed, withdrawing the OTF from the pocket of the hoodie. I'd entirely forgotten about it.

Glancing behind him, Hutch ducked, disappearing as his opponent swung with impressive agility.

Felix.

"You have to get to safety." Eric offered his gloved hand, but I pushed him away. He tried to help me as I climbed to my feet, but I shrugged him off again.

"All right. Let's go." Eric signaled to the others.

I limped forward with them, staring at the knife in my hand. Then my gaze drifted to the pool.

It was Hutch's gun. He wasn't armed.

Taking a deep breath, I mentally prepared myself for the pain before spinning away from the others and darting back into the mansion.

Eric called after me, but I couldn't make out his words over the ruckus inside the house. I didn't have much time before my ankle gave out on me entirely.

Glass stabbed at my feet and I cried out, but did not stop in my sprint.

I managed to locate a spiral staircase, but was thrown into a state of shock when a hand ripped at the hoodie from behind. By clutching the handrail, I succeeded in remaining on my feet.

There was no time to be held up. Lifting my arms, I ducked out of the hoodie, continuing my way upstairs.

Tears of pain streamed down my face, my feet leaving bloody footprints behind me. The agony nearly caused me to miss the balcony. Skidding to a halt, I backpedaled.

The balcony didn't match the rest of the mansion. It appeared outdated with its rusty patio furniture piled carelessly to one side. Even the awning was ancient with its faded colors and questionable ropes.

An idea formed.

At the far side of the balcony, Hutch was dodging Felix's punches. He didn't have time for a counterattack, and it was a wonder he was able to keep up with Felix's combination of attacks in the first place.

For a moment, I thought he noticed me by the door, but then Felix's knee came up, catching him off guard. He took a blow to the stomach, followed by one to the head.

CHAPTER THIRTY-THREE

"HEY!" I yelled, deploying the OTF.

Felix spun around to face me.

"I figured you out!" I said.

"Oh, yeah?" Felix tucked loose strands of hair behind his ear.

"Yeah." I swallowed my breathlessness. "You were right. You're not afraid of Hutch. You're jealous."

A laugh rolled out of Felix. "Jealous? That's the best you could come up with?"

I looked at Hutch. He was still on the ground, recuperating from the hit to the head.

"Your mother gave him all her attention," I said. "And you hated him for it."

"That's your best guess?" Felix chuckled, strolling leisurely toward me.

"Yes." I gulped, willing myself to wait a moment longer until he came closer. "And I don't blame her. I would be ashamed of having a son like you, too."

The laughter died from his face the moment I spoke the words. He snarled at me, skipping forward.

Utilizing the OTF, I sliced the rope of the awning. It rolled open, right for Felix's head. He ducked, just as I had expected him to, but it earned me time enough to make it to Hutch's side. With blood caked to my socks, I slid at the last second, unable to stop. The knife fell from my hand when I hit the railing, my momentum causing me to tumble over the edge. My reflexes saved me, hands clinging to whatever would hold my weight.

"Hayden!" Hutch extended an arm for me.

"Get the knife," I grunted. Through the wrought iron design of the railing, I saw Felix advancing, his expression murder.

Hutch moved, engaging in another altercation with Felix.

I couldn't watch the fight, being distracted by my own struggle. My feet dangled above the stone patio. If I fell, the chances of surviving were slim, part-Forgotten or not.

My arms were about to give out on me, yet I tried to pull myself up anyway. Fingers slick with sweat and blood, my one hand lost grip, setting me back.

I slid further down, gasping and gritting my teeth.

I wasn't strong enough. I'd expelled all my energy already.

Holding my breath, I looked behind me to see if Eric was below, but him and the others had disappeared by now. There was only the shattered glass and the swimming pool.

The pool.

It wasn't directly below me, but if I pushed off in the right direction, I could land safely in the water. Or else miss and smash my brains across the patio.

What choice did I have?

Having slid too far down the railing to see how Hutch was holding up, I knew my best chance of helping him was by staying alive. The rest was up to him.

I said a silent prayer, sucked in a breath and lifted my knees. With the remaining energy in my possession, I kicked off the side of the balcony.

Then I was airborne.

Chapter Thirty-Four

I was running out of time.

My eyes flicked to the counter where the kitchen timer shaped as a pig tick-tick-ticked *away.*

Five more minutes and I hadn't even begun adding shadows to the bowl. The table was mere lines on the paper, barely distinguishable.

Teeth chewing my inner cheek, I contemplated giving in. But how could I? This opportunity meant everything to me.

"There's got to be a way to do this!" I groaned.

"Do what?" James slinked into the kitchen, his gaming headphones hung around his neck.

"The only way I can get into this class is if I draw a decent picture within the span of an hour," I said, slamming my sketchpad onto the table.

As if to taunt me, the piggy timer peeled its signal of my time being up. James reached for one of the apples in the bowl, sinking his teeth into it with a crunch.

"Excuse me, I was drawing that," I snapped.

"Excuse me, hasn't anyone told you that drawing a bowl of fruit is cliché?" he responded.

"Well what would you suggest?" I ripped the picture from the notebook, crumbling it into a ball and hurling it at the wastebasket. It missed, hitting the wall and bouncing to the center of the room.

"You're working on a portfolio, aren't you?" James said after a moment of contemplation. "Try this."

He moved to the sink, removing the potted plant from the window sill. The poor thing had been dead for as long as I could remember.

Next, he rummaged through one of the drawers, withdrawing a carving knife. He stabbed it into the soil.

"There." His smile was lined with juice from the apple.

"You're not serious."

"Dead serious." He motioned to it with his free hand. "Who else would come up with this?"

"Only a sociopath," I sighed.

"Precisely." He retrieved the piggy timer, spinning the head to the hour mark. "Show them you're different. And while you're at it..."

He set the timer next to the potted plant.

"I can't draw that," I protested. "The face turns with every minute."

Casting me a mischievous grin, James took another bite of the apple. "Then I suggest you pick up your pace."

***

Was I crying or choking? I was too tired to discern the two. Perhaps I was shivering. My hair, my clothes, my skin were dripping with water.

"She's okay!" someone yelled.

Dazed, I didn't fight the hands that lifted me from the ground.

"Get her out of here." That was undeniably Eric's voice.

The world began to shake beneath me. Whoever held me was moving swiftly away from all the noise.

"Hutch?" My eyes stung, I guessed from the water. "Where's Hutch?"

No response.

"Is he okay?" I demanded, holding on to the mite of strength I had left. The man carrying me kept his eyes ahead of us. "Say something!"

"He's with the others."

"Then he's okay?"

Try as I might, I could not get him to answer me. I hoped his lack of knowledge was the sole reason he refused to respond.

The sun was climbing over the hilltops by the time I was seated in a van. I kept my eyes closed, accepting the blanket drawn over me. A medic stopped by to tend to the cuts on my feet and my swollen ankle. He checked for signs of a concussion, but otherwise seemed content enough to hurry away upon someone else's beckoning.

Between the lost moments of my conscious slipping, I couldn't tell how long I sat in the van, curled beneath the blanket. It felt like hours. When the door slammed shut, my eyes flew open.

The engine ignited beneath me and I straightened.

"We can't leave," I said to the two men sitting in the front. "I'm not going anywhere without Hutch."

"He's with the next group," the driver said.

"We can't leave without him!"

"Ma'am, we're following protocol," said the second guy. He continued to speak his nonsense, but I'd already tuned him out.

A few vehicles away was a line of Randolph's men, all handcuffed and guided, single file, to the back of a van similar to the one in which I sat.

Hutch was at the end of the line, hands secured behind his back. Eric's team shoved him into the van after the others.

I gripped the handle of the door just as the van started rolling. The door wouldn't budge.

"What are they doing?" I cried, yanking the handle frantically. "You can't arrest him! He's the one who got you here!"

Locking him in a cramped space with the others who all knew he'd betrayed them was a cruel joke. Was this how Eric repaid the people who helped him?

"Let me OUT!" I yelled.

"Ma'am, settle down," guy number two said. "He agreed to this. You'll get to talk to him, but we need to get back to base."

"Back to base? Where's base?" I wanted to know. I settled reluctantly back into my seat as the vehicle began to accelerate.

"It's about a forty-minute drive," the driver said.

I crossed my arms over the blanket, swallowing the threats that sprang to my lips over Hutch's well-being. If something happened to him before we arrived at our destination, Eric would sorely regret his actions.

***

"We aren't doing anything, but playing Ring Around the Rosie," I said heatedly. "I've told you what I remember."

"And we value the information you have provided," Eric said, looking at his partner for agreement. "But if there is anything else that may help us locate the Forgotten you associated with before you were subjected to the transformation, it would benefit our search."

"You still haven't explained the importance of this interrogation," I argued. "I've answered everything I can, so do I get to ask a few questions now?"

Eric's partner—Nelson—tapped something into his tablet, saying, "Perhaps we can give her the scope of what it is we do. After all, she would understand better than most."

The significant glance that passed between them told me there was unspoken history.

Running a hand along the length of his face, Eric finally said, "We specialize in tracking down Forgotten."

"Like Hutch." There was an apprehensive pinch in my brain as I said this.

"Our services exceed Mr. McLaren's job description," Nelson provided, tucking away the tablet. "Where he merely followed orders to eliminate them, we investigate. We strive to raise awareness of Forgotten to civilians."

I crossed my legs, leaning in on the couch. When I imagined an interrogation, it didn't play out in the breakroom of a corporate building with state-of-the-art appliances. A prison cell seemed more appropriate for someone like me.

"If we find someone like you, who resists the transformation, we do everything in our power to reverse it," Nelson said.

"What's your success rate?" I asked.

"There aren't any," said Eric. "Most weren't strong enough to control themselves."

My stomach plummeted.

"You have to understand," Nelson said, "we don't come across many who have put off the transformation for as long as you have."

"You said 'most' weren't able to control themselves," I said slowly. "What about the rest?"

"They became too overwhelmed by their circumstance." Nelson frowned.

"They took their own lives," Eric explained. His expression was just as grim as Nelson's.

"By what you've told us regarding the Forgotten you and your brother associated with," Nelson said, purposefully changing the subject, "there is a better chance we will be able to track them down. We will look into the matter and be sure they do not return to endanger you or your family."

"Why did I have to pee in a cup?" I asked. I needed to distance my thoughts from my family as well as my fate. My hand brushed my elbow where a nurse had drawn blood a mere hour ago. "What's with all the tests?"

"We are screening you for contamination," Eric said. He sat back in the armchair, loosening the top button of his shirt. "Before we can allow you to return home, we need to be sure you won't prove dangerous to others."

I stared blankly at the men. "You're letting me go home?" Just like that?

"We are still waiting for the results," Nelson said. "Another hour or so and we should see how prominently you've been affected."

"There hasn't been a case where we could send the patient home," Eric said bluntly. I caught the dark look Nelson shot him, leading Eric to add, "But your case may prove different from others. If what you said is true and you haven't had blood except for the one time—"

"It was a squirrel," I said sharply.

"—then your odds are very decent." Eric cleared his throat, picking something off his pants.

Okay, there was definitely something they weren't telling me. Why not just come out and say it: I'm doomed.

Great, I was back to thinking about my future.

"Where's Hutch?" I asked.

"Mr. McLaren is undergoing questioning, just as you," said Eric. "He has been seen by our doctors on staff and treated for minor cuts and bruises.

We have been very fortunate to have him on board with us."

Eric's last words were forced, his insincerity reinforced by his tight smile.

"What about my brother?" I asked. "Has he made any appearances at all that you're aware of?"

"According to police records, his whereabouts are still unknown," Nelson said. "But we will institute a search for him, utilizing our best PIs and other resources."

I sighed, relieved I could at least trust them with this much. It was certainly more than I could do alone.

"Do you have any more questions?" Eric asked, and I caught a hint of scorn in his tone.

"Not right now." I shot him a wary glance. "But I will let you know the moment I do."

"Very well." Both men stood.

"If I get to go home today, I want Hutch to take me," I told them.

"He is currently assisting us and will not have time for a three-hour round trip to make you happy." Eric's annoyance was growing. Nelson shot him a warning expression. I saw the silent conversation between them, raising my own suspicions. Whatever was going on, I could probably get Hutch to talk to me. If I got to see him.

"I will wait until he has time, then." To illustrate my patience, I snuggled deeper into the blanket I'd carried with me from the van.

Eric stalked out of the break room without another word, leaving Nelson to linger behind long enough to say, "Help yourself to whatever you find in the fridge. You may also turn on the television while you wait. If you need anything, Callahan and Gibson are in the hall. You can talk to them."

"You've got guards outside the door?" I scoffed.

"Safety precaution."

With that, he was gone, leaving me alone with my thoughts. It bugged me that I was in a comfortable room, lounging around until they figured out what to do with me.

Was that it? They were keeping me comfortable until they decided to eliminate me, like they did other Forgotten? Keeping me in a jail cell would only make me want to escape, whereas enjoying a little bit of luxury kept me ignorant like a turkey led to the chopping block.

It was noon before anyone else entered the break room, bringing a rustling with them.

Nelson and Eric returned, accompanied by the last person I expected to see.

"Mike." I sat up on the couch.

"I hear you've had a long night," he grinned. It was odd to see his easy smile in the midst of my turmoil.

My eyes darted between him and his father. "You know about all this?"

"He knows enough," said Eric.

"Dad explained himself the other night when he showed up," Mike said.

So that was what they were talking about the night he paced the dining room floor with his father and grandfather present.

"What are you doing here?" I asked.

"We sent a team to retrieve your belongings from McLaren's home," Nelson informed me, lifting the shopping bags in his hands, all of which I recognized. "Your results came back, passing with flying colors. We've never seen such admirable charts for someone who has been through everything you have."

He was too peppy. I didn't like it. They all knew something I didn't, but no one was talking.

"As soon as you get cleaned up, Mike will take you home," Eric said. I could tell he wasn't onboard with this arrangement by the shadow over his eyes. So why did he agree to it? Surely he would be afraid I would strike at his son like a hungry viper.

"Just a few things, first," Nelson began, but I cut him off.

"No."

The discomfort hanging in the air around us could be cut with a knife, but I was going to see Hutch one way or the other.

"We brought your request to McLaren, and he agreed to have someone else drive you," Eric said pointedly. "He doesn't have time to respond to your every beck and call."

There was another apprehensive pinch in my brain.

"I told you I would wait for him," I retorted. "I'm not going anywhere. End of discussion."

While fire blazed in Eric's eyes, Nelson appeared to find my behavior amusing. Mike, on the other hand, was uncomfortable.

"We will see about that," Eric grunted, storming out.

Nelson dropped the bags into one of the armchairs. "Mike will show you to the facilities when you are ready."

When we were left alone, my gaze locked on Mike.

"I'm sorry," I said before I had time to chicken out. "For everything."

"What are you talking about?" Mike said. "You saved my family. Dad's just being a major turd."

"I lied to you—to all of you."

Mike shrugged. "Maybe. But we're alive. And by the sound of it, the alternative would've been far worse than being lied to. I think it's safe to say you're forgiven."

A smile grew on my lips, chest filling with gratitude. Mike was an amazing guy. A part of me wished I felt the same way about him as he felt about me. He had so much to offer.

"Any girl would be lucky to have you," I said.

He grinned again, but it didn't reach his eyes this time. "I take it James and Hayden were aliases. You're not really related, are you?"

I shook my head, glancing at the ground. I couldn't bear the hurt in his eyes now that he knew my display of affection for him had also been a lie.

"But he's important to you, isn't he?" he asked.

Biting my lip, I nodded. I didn't want to elaborate, because that would only make things worse.

I still cared for Mike. He and his family had grown quite dear to me—well, except for Eric. That guy had real issues he needed to hash out.

Mike cleared his throat. "I wanted to warn you that night at the restaurant, but I didn't know who would overhear us."

"Overhear us?" I repeated, puzzled.

"Dad had a few guys tag along to monitor things and make sure… no one got hurt."

238

CHAPTER THIRTY-FOUR

"So you know about me."

"That, and about his career." He ran a hand through his hair. I could tell he was still trying to accept what he'd learned.

"I thought Dad was jerking me around at first," he said. "But then he showed me this place."

"Does Melinda know?"

Mike shook his head. "No one else knows. Except Pops."

I didn't know why this brought me comfort, but I nodded, grateful for his honesty.

After gathering clothes, I followed Mike down the hall to the washroom. I took my time, enjoying the warm water as it cleaned my wounds and released the tension in my muscles. For the most part, I was healing. My ankle still ached, but my scars were looking better already, including the one on my cheek from when Stix had hit me in the stairwell.

It felt pleasing to pull on a fresh pair of jeans as opposed to the dress I'd been wearing for the last few days. With a maroon sweater over my head and sneakers on my feet, I began to feel more civilized.

No one waited for me outside, which I found strange. I made my way back to the break room, hearing a hum of voices as I approached. Five men circled the table in the kitchen area, some sitting, some standing, but everyone had a Styrofoam cup of coffee.

I ignored the others, my attention jumping to the person nearest me. The nylon bag of toiletries in my hand dropped to the floor. I hurried to Hutch, slamming into him, my hands groping the fabric of his shirt.

The pinch in my brain returned. I remembered my last flashback and the desperation I had encountered while drawing.

I was running out of time.

A hush fell over the room. Hutch's posture remained stiff, and I was convinced he wasn't going to return the hug. But then his arms locked around me and his lips brushed along my ear, taking in the scent of me. There was so much I wanted to say, only not with a bunch of older guys gawking at us.

"The sooner we get this done, the better," Eric said, ending the moment.

I pulled away, finding Hutch's sepia gaze. There was sadness in his eyes, and I knew he'd heard about Red.

He's with his wife and daughter now.

We weren't given time to talk. Herded into an elevator and outside into the overcast afternoon, Hutch and I were stopped at a sedan idling in the parking lot.

"The GPS will direct you to your destination," Nelson told us, then he turned to me and said, "Hutch will explain some things you'll want to know on the way. Should you need anything at all," he handed me his card.

I liked Nelson. He was the only one who appeared genuine, taking the time to wish me well, while the others went on their way. I shook his hand before turning to the car.

When finally seated, I turned to view Hutch more critically. He was wearing the same clothes, his shirt torn at the collar. His right forearm was wrapped in gauze, a butterfly bandage extending above one eyebrow. Other than that, all I found were bruises, though nothing serious.

"What happened?" I wanted to know.

Hutch did not respond immediately. He drove more cautiously than usual, following the instructions of the GPS's female voice.

"What happened is Randolph and his business are no more," he said at last.

"They have him in custody?"

Hutch shook his head to this. "They found him dead in the study."

"What? How?" I was shocked.

"It's too early to be sure," he said. "They are performing an autopsy, but it appears to be the work of a Forgotten."

"There was a Forgotten in the house?" The moment I asked this, I realized the absurdity of my question. Duh. "Felix... killed his own father?"

"Felix hasn't been himself in a long time," said Hutch. "But like I said, it's too early to be sure. Allen has a team collecting evidence."

"You killed him, though, didn't you? You killed Felix?" I asked.

To this I received no response. The answer was obvious enough, I did not press him.

How had things gotten so out of hand? I wasn't sure if I should feel bad for Hutch, seeing as whatever family he had left was dead.

Everything was a mess.

"Why were you arrested?" I settled on this question, seeing as it seemed the safest move. I didn't want to poke the bear too deeply while still nursing raw wounds. "Those guys could've ganged up on you. Eric didn't think about that?" I was angry, but Hutch's expression remained unreadable. I wanted to shake some emotion back into him. He was capable of feeling, I knew. Every last shred of proof was confirmed when he kissed me.

"It was easier to keep tabs on everyone through the chaos." Hutch's words snapped me back to reality.

I didn't believe him. I wasn't the naive girl everyone clearly thought me to be. There was more to all this, and no one wanted to spill the beans. Not even Mike. "Are you going back after you take me home?"

"I have to, don't I?" He merged onto the busy interstate, his driving still more cautious than usual. He kept to the speed limit for once. "Allen is building a case. He needs all the information he can get, and since I'm the only one talking…" He didn't need to finish his sentence. We both knew he was a great asset to Eric and his crew.

"They didn't ask me anything about your uncle," I said, running my hands down my thighs. "I mean, maybe I had something to say about him."

Hutch scoffed. "Like what?"

I looked at him, slightly offended. "I was involved, too."

"You should count yourself lucky they aren't involving you more than necessary," Hutch said. "They're getting you home. Isn't that what you wanted?"

"Yeah, but," I paused. "It doesn't make sense. Why are they letting me go?"

"Maybe they think you don't need to add more complications to your life. You should be glad. After all, you're a hero. You saved the Allens. Twice. And you saved me."

Heat rose to my cheeks. I looked away, studying the world beyond the passenger window.

I didn't feel like a hero. My memories told me I was anything but. Perhaps Hutch was right, though. This could be my chance to start over. Perhaps it was a blessing I'd lost my memories. Otherwise I'd be haunted by all my wrongs. How many people were given the opportunity at a clean slate?

We merged again, following signs for Memphis. When Hutch shifted lanes, I noticed in the side mirror a white sedan shifting lanes also.

"We're being followed," I said, not taking my eyes off the reflection of the car.

"I know."

"That doesn't worry you?" I glanced at Hutch, alarmed by his ease.

"It's Callahan and Gibson."

"Why are they following us?"

"They will be installing some equipment into your home," Hutch said.

"What equipment?" My voice was heated again. I just knew there had to be more to the terms and conditions of going home.

"It's to make sure you and your mother can live safely. Until everything settles back to normal, they will be keeping an eye on you."

My jaw dropped. "That's invading my privacy!"

"These guys are strict on safety," said Hutch. "Callahan and Gibson have been instructed to inform your mother of your condition. They need her consent for the equipment installation. For that she needs to make an informed decision of whether she feels safe to have you home."

"Well, that can't be good for me," I mumbled.

I watched the sedan the rest of the journey. My thoughts were all over the place. The urge to talk to Hutch about our shared moment in the hole was pressing, but I couldn't bring myself to it. A timer ticked away in the back of my mind, like the kitchen timer at home.

Home. I could hardly believe I was going back. But for how long?

There were three cars in the driveway. Two were outdated models, while the third was clearly a brand-spanking new vehicle. Its barbie pink coat startled me. Who the heck would want to draw such attention to themselves?

Hutch parked on the side of the road, Callahan and Gibson doing the same behind us. My nerves raced. I didn't like not knowing what to expect. Would my mother be happy to see me or would she send me away when she learned the truth? Was she even sober? Who else was here?

To my surprise, Hutch placed his hand over mine. I looked up to find him watching me, his expression finally showing a hint of softness.

My heart thundered in my chest.

"Come on," he said.

I made to collect my bags from the back seat, but he beat me to it. Refusing to let me carry them, he gestured I moved on toward the house.

If Randolph was right about one thing, this home was certainly standing on its last legs. The siding was long overdue for pressure-washing, paint on the porch peeled in several places. The bottom step had been replaced by a block of concrete.

Taking a deep breath, I approached the porch. Before I could make it to the top, the door swung open, revealing a pretty girl, her hair the color of honey wheat. We stared at one another for a long moment. I tried and failed to place her in my memories.

The girl shrieked, jumping at me, her arms dragging me into a bone-crushing embrace.

"Jo, that's—" Scottie stepped out next, his eyes landing on me before they found Hutch.

"Mrs. Wyer, Rily's home!" the girl named Jo shouted, nearly shredding my eardrum.

"Who are you?" Scottie asked, sizing up Hutch by his bruises.

"No one to you," Hutch said. His tone matched Scottie's sharpness.

A third person stepped out the door and I recognized my mother immediately. She looked like me: dark hair, jade eyes. Only she was older. She held a hand over her mouth as tears streamed down her cheeks.

"They called and told me you were coming home," she said. "But I couldn't believe it."

I didn't know what to say to that. All I could do was stare at the woman I resembled; the woman who ran her children away from home.

My mother pulled me into a hug, sobbing on my shoulder. I knew forgiving her was the right thing to do, but I couldn't. Not yet. The most I could settle with was patting her shoulder, awkward as it was.

"We're so glad you're home!" Jo said, a little too enthusiastically.

Scottie continued to glare at Hutch.

I heard the bags drop to the ground and looked around to see Hutch retreating.

"Wait," I said, disentangling myself from my mother's arms.

Hutch didn't stop. I caught up with him halfway to the car. "You don't have to leave this second."

"I can't stay," he said. "You're home now. I have things to do."

"Are we just going to pretend, then?" I blurted out. "You want us to pretend we don't care about each other? That nothing happened?"

He looked me straight in the eyes, and I knew what he was about to say. "Nothing happened."

The words shattered something within me. The timer in my mind shrieked. It was over. He was leaving and there was nothing I could say to stop him.

"I don't believe you." I wouldn't. There was something there, he just didn't want to acknowledge it.

Where his words were normally followed by a hard expression, I now saw a trace of meekness in his eyes. There was pain there; loneliness.

"It's okay to be scared," I said quietly. He wasn't about to get rid of me so easily.

Callahan and Gibson chose this moment to exit their vehicle. They thumped the doors shut after them, making their way toward us.

Hutch shook his head, turning back to the road.

This time I didn't stop him. I just stood and watched him drive away.

Then I let Callahan and Gibson walk me inside.

Epilogue

His head thumped painfully. Every time he blinked, his eyelids felt like doors swinging on unoiled hinges. It was nearly three in the morning, which explained his agitation.

Heaving a sigh, Hutch shifted another box to the growing pile. The kitchen was finally packed, along with the living room and most of the bedroom. Amid his strategies on how to proceed, the faint buzz of his phone caught his attention.

Where had he left it? The only person expected to call at such an ungodly hour was Callahan. If Hutch didn't answer, the man would be at his front door, snooping around for an excuse to get him in trouble.

This is your only chance to get your life on track, Allen had told him before they last parted. *You do anything to raise suspicion, and we'll have you locked up with the others.*

The Android was tucked between two boxes on the couch. Before Callahan had the chance to hang up, Hutch snatched the phone, pressing it to his ear.

"I'm here," he said, voice cracking from lack of use.

"Did I wake you?"

The female voice on the other end of the line startled him. He glanced at the screen. An unfamiliar number glowed at him.

All air dissipated from his lungs when he realized who he was talking to. "No."

"I'm sorry," she said. "I shouldn't have called, I—"

"Rily." When he spoke her name, it somehow felt inappropriate. But it was her real name. "Did something happen?"

Fear seized his heart for a moment at her hesitation.

"Everyone's fine," she said at last. "I'm just overwhelmed. Will the dreams ever stop?"

She sounded worn down, as though she carried the weight of the world on her shoulders. It was something Hutch could relate to. He'd spent the majority of his life wracked with an anxiety he could not overcome, the pressure of it leaving him breathless when triggered.

"I don't know," he said truthfully. He wished he could offer comfort of some sort, but his knowledge of Forgotten did not stretch to what became of those who resisted the transformation.

Rily breathed into the phone.

"I don't know what to do," she said quietly.

Call Gibson, Hutch thought. That was what the man was there for. He wasn't staked out at her house for nothing.

Jaw clenched tight, there was no controlling the pang of guilt in Hutch's chest. He was glad she'd called him. For the first time in two weeks his world was less glum.

"Do you need me to swing by?" he asked before he could stop himself.

Rily fell silent for a long time, and he regretted his words spoken in haste.

"Could you?" Her response came as a surprise, lighting up something within him; something he didn't realize had gone dark.

Without faltering, he said, "I'm on my way."

The address she'd provided was to a home located in Franklin. Jo's home. Apparently, Rily had been staying with her friend since her brother's funeral. Finding what was left of James was one of the few things that had reached Hutch through the grapevine of Cornerstone Alliance. Anything else he had to put together himself, with scraps of information provided by different agents.

Gibson was parked in front of the house, engine off. Hutch would recognize his car anywhere, seeing as he'd spent enough time dealing with Allen's crew. They were all the same black SUVs, chrome rims.

He pulled up behind the man's vehicle, wondering if he should stop by and explain himself. He didn't need Gibson ratting him out for doing something out of the ordinary.

The passenger door opened unexpectedly, erasing all previous thoughts from Hutch's mind. Rily hopped in next to him, bringing with her the warm scent of vanilla.

"Go, go," she hissed, slamming the door after her.

Hutch did as he was told, thumping the gear back into drive and pulling around Gibson's car.

"You're not fond of Gibson?" he asked.

"There's nothing wrong with him," Rily said. "But I didn't want to hang around long enough for him to wake up."

The corners of Hutch's mouth quirked. She'd had enough of her babysitter just about as much as he was sick of Callahan hanging around him.

"Where to?" he asked.

"Anywhere, but here."

Stealing a sideways glimpse at the petite brunette beside him, wrapped in an olive green jacket and thin cotton pants splashed with colors of pink, orange and yellow, Hutch felt another uncharacteristic pang in his chest. She was watching him, studying him, but he pretended not to notice.

"How's life?" she asked.

"It's been different," he said simply. That much was true. He was leaving his condo, changing jobs and toeing a thin line as far as Allen was concerned. There was no reason to complain about what discomforts this new life entailed, now that Randolph was no longer in the picture. Words would change nothing.

"Different as in better, or worse?" she asked.

He shrugged. "Depends on my mood."

"Well, knowing you, I'd say I caught you in a good mood." Rily's voice was light. It was a pleasant change from all the stiff agents he'd encountered lately.

Glancing at her a second time, he found her lips curved into a smile. It was then he noticed the absence of his anxiety. The ball of distress residing within him had lifted, like the end of a drawn-out storm. He was calm.

Hutch returned his attention back to the road where it was easier to focus. There was only one place he knew he could take them in the dead of night.

"I thought they were going to throw you in jail." Rily's comment caught him off guard.

"They had every right to," he said, forcing a bout of apathy into his tone. Rily didn't need to know how close he'd cut it. He was guilty of trying to kill Allen's daughter, after all. If that wasn't enough to warrant his arrest, he didn't know what was.

"I'm glad they didn't." She tucked her palms between her thighs for warmth. "It would've been such a waste of potential."

"I'm sure they would agree. That's why they are trying to recruit me," Hutch said, pecking the dashboard to warm the passenger seat. "Once my probationary period is over, they will decide what to do with me."

"What do you mean?" Rily sounded perplexed. "You can't go to prison when you led them to Randolph's front doorstep."

"Allen feels differently about it." He was the only one fighting to keep him off the team.

The concerned look on Rily's face tugged at Hutch. Her eyebrows were knitted, creating a crease on her forehead and her bottom lip was puckered ever so slightly. He was suddenly reminded of the softness of her lips on his. He shook the thought from his mind. Life was challenging enough without a woman involved.

"Will you get in trouble for coming to see me?" she asked.

"I don't know," Hutch said. The truth was, he could very well get in trouble. Callahan didn't know where he was. Gibson didn't know where *she* was. There would be hell to pay in the morning. But as it were, he didn't care. Getting into trouble for the little bit of relief he experienced with Rily was well worth it.

When Hutch turned into a dark street, Rily shot him a questioning look. The road looped aggressively, the headlights of the Audi lighting up the residents on the outskirts of the circle.

Shutting off the engine on the side of the road, Hutch took a moment before meeting her gaze.

"Where are we?" Rily leaned over the console to get a better look out of the driver-side window, her warm scent swirling around him.

"Come on." Hutch slid out of the vehicle and waited for her to meet him.

Together they climbed the hill in the loop's center, the sound of crunching fescue breaking the silence.

Rily gave a satisfying gasp the moment they reached the top. Hutch bit back a grin. From Love Circle, the city lights looked like a sea of stars reflecting the night sky above.

"Where are we?" she asked again.

Hutch shook his head. "I don't know the name," he lied.

"Starry Hill," she mumbled. "That's what I'm going to call it."

His grin spread wider as he watched her continue to gaze in awe at the view. His hand itched to touch her. More memories of their moment together in the hole flooded his mind.

Everything about her was soft and gentle. The way she felt against him, her hands in his hair.

He never dwelled on memories. He never had anything good to remember. Not until he met her.

Hutch cleared his throat. "How've you been holding up?"

"What?" Rily tore her eyes from the lights.

"I heard about your brother," he said. "I'm really sorry."

He watched her expression turn from wonder to sorrow. He hated bringing it up, mostly because he'd lied to her about James when he honestly had no clue where he was. But as one who'd experienced loss, he knew he would want someone to acknowledge his pain instead of feigning ignorance.

"I'm coping." She flashed him a weak smile. He understood the pained look in her eyes all too well.

"That's all you can do right now," he said.

"Gibson told me they found the perpetrators," she said. "That's what he called them. *Perpetrators*. As if I didn't know what they really are." She curled a lock of hair around her forefinger. "Two were already dead when they were found. One they were able to detain, but there is still one at large."

"They'll find him," Hutch assured her. "These guys know what they're doing."

She nodded, though the gesture seemed forced.

"Did you mean it?" Rily said without warning. She faced him, eyes boring holes into his soul. "When you said nothing happened between us. Do you really feel that way?"

Hutch shifted his weight uncomfortably, hands leaving the safety of his jacket pockets and hanging loosely at his side.

Rily went on, "I've been home for a while now, and even though my mom and my friends understand my situation, I feel like there is a lag in connection between us. But when I stopped hating you, I actually felt like what we had was real. Not the kiss, in particular." She paused. "I guess I hoped we could at least be friends."

Watching Rily struggle to find her words only stirred more unfamiliar feelings within Hutch.

He couldn't do it. He couldn't lie and tell her what she needed to hear.

"I don't want to be your friend," he said. "I'm sorry. It wouldn't work."

The weight of Rily's stare was discomforting. She was trying to figure him out, and Hutch wasn't sure he wanted her to.

"Then why did you come for me tonight?" she asked. There was no hint of anger in her voice, just curiosity. A part of Hutch wished she would be angry, because it would be easier to take her home and leave her there if she started throwing a tantrum.

"You drove forty minutes because I had nightmares. Are you sure you don't want to be pen pals, at least?" Rily grinned at her own joke.

"No." The word came out sounding harsher than he meant it to. He ground his teeth. "You're overthinking everything."

"I don't think so." She stepped closer, bridging the gap between them. "I think I was right. You're scared. But you know what I've learned? You don't have to be the strong one all the time."

She searched his face.

"I don't want to be your friend," Hutch said again, weaker this time. "I can't."

He couldn't be friends with someone who plagued his thoughts day in and day out. He couldn't be friends with someone for whom he cared so deeply. He would always want more than what a friendship could offer.

A knowing look crossed her face and she smiled.

"Yes, you can." Her chill fingers took hold of his hand. "I still need you. And I think you could use my help, too."

She wasn't wrong, but at the same time she wasn't right. If Rily knew the secrets he kept from her, she would feel utterly betrayed. She would turn her back on him forever.

Hutch didn't have the guts to speak up. He didn't have the strength she possessed. After all, Rily was stronger than she realized.

He squeezed her hand, knowing full well she could not really save him, for he was too far gone. Yet he couldn't turn her away a second time, so he gave in, returning her smile.

About the Author

J.M. Cavender is a hopeless romantic, obsessed with autumn, foxes and books, books, books. Having spent her childhood overseas, she is happy to finally settle down in Tennessee with her husband and two dogs (no foxes, unfortunately).

MORE FROM CITY LIMITS PUBLISHING

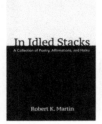

Six years of writings sat unfinished until COVID-19 gave Robert Martin the time needed to finish the job. *In Idled Stacks: A Collection of Poetry* provides a glimpse into the life and mind of the author. Featuring poetry about the Coronavirus pandemic, racial civil unrest, relationships, life's storms, and more, In Idled Stacks is an emotional and fascinating look into the life of the everyman.

Dances with Words, a collection of over 500 haiku speaks to the pathos, pain, and passion of this journey we call life. Random thoughts, rants, raves, reminiscences, prayers of praise, et al – framed in poetic bite-size bits – 17 syllables at a time. Built around song titles and lyrics, the writer weaves themes that touch the deepest part of us. Love, God's love, forgiveness, tears, sadness, healing and loss – et al. My prayer is that my passion and pathos – my loves and losses can speak to you, wherever you are – whatever your story.

Poems of Political Protest: An Anthology is a collection of poems by various authors who are attempting to make their own waves in their community and in the global community. They're the words of the hurting, the fighting, and the driving force behind real and impactful change. All we have, all we own freely and clearly, are our words. May this collection bring about action.

Portraits of the Pen: A Collection of Short Stories features over two dozen short stories that paint glorious portraits of the characters within. From stories of life lessons to romance, suspense to fantasy, be taken away to many worlds where rich characters tell stories of the every man, and every woman. Watch time pass and romance blossom in The Beach House. Journey to Chalcey in the thriller Foundling. Learn a valuable life lesson in Paxton's Socks. Each piece has been hand picked and features layered stories that invoke strong senses and paint detailed pictures in the minds of the readers.

An emotionally scarred woman in 2019 gets the chance to go back in time to stop a terrible tragedy. But there's a catch: she must overcome her insecurities and learn to trust people — and herself — in order to save dozens of innocent lives. Brenda Lyne lives just outside Minneapolis, Minnesota with her two kids and two cats. *Charlie's Mirror* is her first novel, and she believes it is never too late to follow your dreams.